THE
THERAPIST

BOOKS BY NICOLE TROPE

THE THERAPIST

NICOLE TROPE

bookouture

Published by Bookouture in 2025

An imprint of Storyfire Ltd.
Carmelite House
50 Victoria Embankment
London EC4Y 0DZ

www.bookouture.com

The authorised representative in the EEA is Hachette Ireland
8 Castlecourt Centre
Dublin 15 D15 XTP3
Ireland
(email: info@hbgi.ie)

ISBN: 978-1-80550-040-7
eBook ISBN: 978-1-80550-039-1

For D.M.I and J

PROLOGUE

NOW – WEDNESDAY NIGHT

The scream can't be coming from my mouth but it has to be. I recognise my own voice.

As I crouch on the ground, rocking while the blaring sirens get closer and closer, I feel some part of me step back.

Get a grip, I hear the better version of me say. *Pull yourself together. You're a therapist. Act like one.*

But that part is not as strong as the part that is hearing the sirens, smelling the heavy smell of blood in the cold air, staring down at the body on the ground. That part cannot control what is going on here.

I was supposed to help. That's what I do. In my consulting room, patients come to me with their worries, their fears and their secrets and I do my best to guide them to a better place. I hold their secrets close to me, keeping them even when they distress me because that's my job. I try to make things better.

But I have made things worse, so much worse, and now there is a body and the screaming and the sirens. I have not managed to hold on to someone's secret. Instead, I have lost control of the truth and now I am here.

And then there is shouting from someone else.

'Put down the gun!' a man yells. 'Put it down, put it down now.'

I lift my gaze from the body to follow the sound of his voice, see his face screwed up in anger and something else... fear?

He is afraid of me. 'Put it down!' he yells again and I look down at my hand. I am holding a gun. That's what he's afraid of. He is holding a gun too.

But my gun is different to the gun he is holding because his comes with a uniform and authority.

I have no authority here. I shouldn't be here.

I was trying to help; I want to explain but he doesn't care about anything except the gun in my hand.

He takes a step closer to me and shines a torch in my face. 'Put it down, put the gun down.'

I lift the hand holding the gun, finally managing to get the words out.

'I didn't mean for it to happen,' I tell him. 'I was only trying to help,' I wail as I hope that he believes me. I really need him to believe my side of the story. I need him to believe me.

ONE

Lana

As I close the door on Natalia, my last client for the day, I take a deep breath, hoping that it will help the headache but it doesn't.

I know better than to overload my day with appointments and yet I had been unable to refuse anyone for today. I took off two weeks for the July school holidays and now that my son, Iggy, is back at school, I have to get through the backlog of patients who have waited for me to return, which I'm really thankful for. It's taken me some time to build up my practice and I know that every client who comes through the door is another opportunity for me to help someone, another person who has put their trust in me.

I've only been back for two days and the glorious holiday in Bali, where Iggy and I revelled in the warmth and the sunshine at the beautiful resort I booked for us, is a memory that I will always treasure. The pictures of the bright blue sky and the sparkling waters of the infinity pool have filled up my phone for me to look through and enjoy on dark, damp days.

Winter in Australia is not supposed to be terribly cold, and for the most part it's manageable during the day, temperatures only dropping to freezing at nighttime. But this winter, the rain is so persistent that I know it's contributing to the low-level sadness all my patients seemed to have walked through the door with. My office has a large window that looks out onto a park across the road and it usually allows a lot of light into the space, but today I've had to have the bright overhead lights on all day, dispelling the shadows, both literal and metaphorical. I'm sure that's contributing to my headache.

I feel guilty for leaving my patients and indulging in a holiday with my son but I needed to recharge the batteries, to take some time for myself. Something I am always advising my patients to do.

When people are struggling, poor weather like this rain can contribute to feelings of melancholy. Even now, it drums against the window as below, drains on the street fill up and overflow. Getting home in the traffic will be a nightmare for everyone. Peak-hour drivers tend to be more aggressive when it rains but I'm still holding on to my holiday glow so I will use it to extend patience to everyone else on the road.

The rain wasn't the only reason I made the decision to treat my son and myself to a holiday. I might have qualifications and the ability to steer other people through any emotional difficulties they may have, but sometimes, it's a different story for my own life.

My ex-husband, Oliver, remarried six months ago. His new wife is only a few years younger than me but she is a fitness instructor and a great cook and she has a persistently cheerful view of the world. When we were slogging through our own months of therapy as we tried to save our marriage – before Oliver made it truly unsalvageable – Oliver often pointed to my tendency to over-analyse everything, to dismantle his thoughts for him until he found himself questioning his own ideas, as one of my worst traits. 'Why can't we ever simply sit on the sofa and watch a movie without it turning into an intellectual exercise or a discussion about my faults as a human being?' he said. That was in addition to all the other things he said. 'Why can't you take a compliment without wondering why I've said it?' 'Why can't you let it go when I look at another woman, it's just a look, it's what men do.' 'Why can't you control your jealousy?'

If I never hear that phrase again, I'll be fine.

Becky, Oliver's new wife, is exactly what he wanted. Her perfect body and glowing skin are complemented by thick auburn hair and ice-blue eyes. And Iggy loves her. 'She makes the best brownies and she likes to build Lego cities with me,' he informed me after he got to know her. 'Daddy says she makes him feel peaceful. What does that mean?'

'Just that he likes her,' I replied. I never gave Oliver any peace, is what he meant.

But I've been like that most of my life, always watching, always waiting for the other shoe to drop, for something to go wrong. I can't blame my parents, they're lovely. My anxieties started at school when I realised that not only would I not be adored by everyone but that I was one of those kids who are, for one reason or another, actively disliked. I rubbed people the wrong way without even understanding how I was doing it. As I grew older, that knowledge shaped me, making me shy, wary, worried all the time.

'Try to have fun,' my mother would say when I was a teenager and I was invited to a party – something that seldom happened. In self-defence perhaps, I've developed into an introvert and that's something I have accepted. Being around people sometimes wears me out, which is why I find long days of patients so exhausting, but at the same time, I am compelled to help people and this is the best way I know how. I have seen what can happen to a person who has no one to talk to, who feels they can't reach out for help or that the help they've reached out for is not there when they need it most.

And even though I can't abide small talk and meaningless chit-chat, the things people are hiding from the world have always fascinated me. Who are they behind their masks? Perhaps I did my degree for the same reason many psychologists do: I wanted to heal myself. I think I was actively searching for who I was behind my own mask, for the reasons that people didn't like me. What did they see? Who was the person I was showing to the world, and was she very different to the real me? Growing older has helped, as has becoming a mother, but I am scarred by my formative years and I know that.

My mother used to tell me that the teenage years are the best years of your life: 'Lots of freedom and no real responsibility,' she would say with a laugh. From the things she told me about her life, I know that her teenage years were very different to mine. She attended parties, dated, experimented with fashion and played every sport she could. I stayed in the shadows, hid in the library, hoped that if I was noticed, it wasn't by someone who wanted to make me the focus of their entertainment for the day. I was bullied from my first year of primary school, but high school was where it reached an insufferable level that I nevertheless suffered through until the very end. 'You can move schools,' my mother offered many times over the years, but I knew that I would be taking myself with me to any new school. There was something about me, about my looks and behaviour, that made me a target. I hoped that university would be different because there would be not hundreds but thousands of different people and perhaps finding like-minded souls to connect with would be easier. And it was. Life changed and moved on but I can never forget those years.

I suppose few people are unscathed by their childhoods.

Becky has never been bullied. I know that without even asking her the question. I'm sure she was one of the popular girls at school, surrounded by friends and always invited to every party. And now she is Oliver's new wife.

At least I am no longer in love with Oliver. When we finally admitted to each other that our marriage could not be saved – partly thanks to him, it must be said – my ex-husband and I agreed that we would do everything in our power to make the transition easier for Iggy, who was only three at the time. And we have stuck to that, remaining friendly and letting Iggy know that we still like each other. That's taken some work on my part but Iggy is a combination of me and his father, inheriting my olive skin, a darker version of my brown hair, and Oliver's green eyes and smile. When I look at him, I see Oliver, and so I could never hate Oliver because of how much I love Iggy, but I still hold a lot of anger towards my ex-husband. His marriage to Becky, to beautiful Becky who is so at ease in her skin, affected me more than I would have liked. Oliver hated how jealous I was of other women and I hated how much attention Oliver paid to other women. But that's not what bothers me the most about his new marriage. It's how much Iggy likes her. No one likes to be replaced, especially in their son's affections, and Iggy does seem to adore Becky. She is sweet and kind and always finds time to play with him, something that a single working mother has in short supply.

Don't be ridiculous, I chide myself. *You're his mother, he loves you more than anything. Be happy he gets along with her and that means Oliver spends as much time as possible with him.*

Being grateful came so easily in the Balinese sunshine after a sumptuous buffet breakfast of exotic fruit and pancakes. On a day when the rain has splattered against my office window for the last five hours, it's difficult to remind myself that I have lots to appreciate, but I am trying. Oliver is in Europe, where it's summer, with Becky, who dresses in tiny skirts and tight tops. They are doing the grand tour that he and I were going to do for our tenth anniversary. The anniversary we never got to.

Back to work. Stop all this ruminating, I instruct myself.

Iggy is in after-school care until 5 p.m. so I have half an hour before I have to leave to get him, even factoring in the extra time I'm going to need because of the weather. I sit down behind my desk, grabbing a couple of Panadol from one of the drawers and taking them with some water. If I can get some notes done now, I won't have to work after Iggy goes to bed.

As I wait for the Panadol to work, I read through the notes I have taken on Natalia. She's a young woman who is a devoted nurse but she is struggling with being unable to leave the job at work. I know how hard it is to do that so I feel I have some understanding of her concerns.

The headache is receding so I power up my computer, but as I go to start entering my notes, there is a knock at the door. 'Come in,' I call, knowing that it can only be Ben. There's no one else in the office right now because Kirsty, our receptionist, asked to leave early today for a doctor's appointment. She doesn't seem unwell but perhaps it's only a check-up.

'Hey,' says Ben, opening the door, 'do you have a minute?' His smooth English accent never fails to make me smile.

'I'm leaving soon to get Iggy,' I reply, and I try, really hard, not to be worried that my black hair is lying limply on my shoulders, that the dark shadows underneath my brown eyes will be more obvious now that my make-up has worn off at the end of the day and that I am wearing my most stretchy pants after eating whatever I wanted on holiday with Iggy. I feel like an unprofessional disaster.

Ben looks immaculate, as usual. His brown hair is a mess of perfect curls and there is a light stubble across his chin. He studies me with pale grey eyes behind neat, rimless glasses and I shift in my desk chair, uncomfortable with the way he is looking at me. He is only two years younger than me at thirty-four but he looks a decade younger than me at least. He's never been married and he has no children. He never talks about a girl-friend but I'm sure he's rarely alone. I have seen Kirsty's eyes light up when he walks into the office and I am a little worried about what may happen between the two of them.

Kirsty is twenty-six, around the same age as my patient Natalia, but she has an entirely different attitude to her life. She is pretty, with dark hair and hazel eyes, and frequently has flowers on her desk from young men, always a different one from what I can gather. She mentions Jack or Sven or Oscar for a few weeks and then the name changes. She believes she deserves to have as much fun as possible with her life, and so despite having a business degree, she's spent years travelling the world and is happy to be our receptionist until she wants the pressure of a job in her industry. I admire her attitude although I never could have done that myself. All I ever wanted was my Master's of Clinical Psychology so I could start my own practice. I feel like I've worked non-stop since I entered university, only taking a six-month break when I had Iggy. Anytime I relax, guilt taps me on the shoulder, especially now that I'm a single mother. I'm thirty-six and starting to feel really conscious of the passing of time.

I shake off my thoughts and focus back on Ben.

'It's always hard the first day back at work.' He smiles and I flush slightly, realising that I do indeed look as tired as I think I look.

'Well, nice vacations have to be paid for,' I say with a smile.

Ben and I share office space and both contribute to Kirsty's salary but we are essentially separate entities, despite both practising under the banner of my clinic name: Calm Minds. I leased the office space first and then advertised for another therapist to take the other office to help with the rent. I've had three different therapists rent the office over the last eight years and Ben is the first man. He's been here for six months.

We've developed a tentative friendship, which I'm glad of. He's an attractive man, very attractive, and it's admittedly hard for me not to notice that or to worry about how I look when I see him. It's drilled into every woman, I think. But luckily there are zero feelings there other than friendship and professional trust.

'What's up?' I ask.

Ben comes into the office and sits down on the navy-blue sofa my patients use, stretching his long arm over the back. 'I have a favour to ask.'

I close down my computer. 'What can I help you with?'

'There's a patient...' He hesitates.

A therapist never discusses their patients, except with their own therapist, which we are all required to have. My therapist is the woman who mentored me through my two registrar years, SueEllen Granger. She's ten years older than me and one of the wisest people I know. I see her once every six weeks or so, even if I don't feel I need to. She puts things into perspective for me, both in my life and with my patients. Ben has only referred to his therapist as Nancy and I don't want to push him into telling me exactly who she is, but I think she's in the UK, where Ben lived for the last thirty years, after his family left Australia for the UK when he was four.

The truth is that Ben and I do sometimes discuss our patients if we want an immediate input.

'Go on,' I encourage him.

'I think she's attracted to me.'

I laugh. 'Well, that wouldn't be the first time, Ben.' It's called transference, and it's when a client redirects their feelings about someone in their life onto the therapist. I've had a couple of male patients tell me they're in love with me over the years, which I know better than to find flattering. It's because we listen, we sympathise, we do everything they are hoping for from a person in their life they are having difficulty with. A therapist's job is to help the patient understand that their feelings towards their therapist are not real and to use the situation to delve deeper into their patient's life to see if they can identify why the feelings are occurring. A last resort, if the situation cannot be managed, is to end the relationship by referring the patient to another therapist.

'I know,' he rubs his jaw, 'and we've discussed it and she seems to understand but the truth is...'

'Is?'

'I'm actually attracted to her as well, not that I've told her that at all, but I can see that this could go the wrong way. I've never been in a situation where I was attracted to the client as well.'

'That is difficult,' I say, even as I feel an unwelcome streak of jealousy run through me. I wish I could control it but I can't so now I accept it. I was never beautiful or even pretty and I have always been aware, in every relationship I've been in, of other women around me. Still, I look very different to how I did in high school. So different that once, Iggy giggled and pointed at an old picture of me at my mother's house, asking, 'Who is that weird girl?'

'It's me,' I told him, staring at the picture of myself standing on-stage, holding up my award for the highest grade for English in my final year of school. I wanted to cry for the awkward teenager still wearing braces at seventeen. My fellow students were more concerned with the formal school dance but I hadn't been invited and had told my mother, 'I don't want to go anyway.'

My buck teeth have been fixed, my mousey brown hair dyed jet black, and I've lost a lot of weight. Though I let myself go in Bali and will now need to be vigilant to get back to the goal weight I spent years working towards.

I've changed but the insecurity remains. I suppose that's what allows me to connect so well with my patients. I understand their worries and their fears because I am as human as they are, as complex as they are, and I know that everyone is fighting their own battles every day, including me.

I take a sip of the water on my desk, bringing my focus back to what Ben needs.

'You should probably refer her somewhere else,' I say.

'I know but...'

'What is it, Ben?' I ask, curious. He's not usually this hesitant.

'She's in a bad relationship with her husband, like it's really bad, and I don't want to send her off to see someone else because it's taken her months to open up to me, to tell me what's really going on, and I'm afraid if she has to go somewhere else, she won't get the help she needs.'

'Are you telling me that you want to keep seeing her? If that's the case, why come and tell me about it? You know I'm going to tell you it's a bad idea.'

Ben sighs. 'Yeah... I mean, I know that already but I just... needed some help talking it through.'

'I get that. It's hard when you start to question yourself.'

'Exactly,' he says.

I understand Ben wanting a discussion about this decision on this patient but I think there is more that he wants to say.

He stares down at the beige speckled carpet in my office. 'I don't want to send this woman out into the world with no help. I want her to be able to trust someone immediately.'

I sit back in my desk chair and fold my arms. I need to leave in a few minutes to get Iggy. 'What are you saying, Ben?'

'Can you take her on? If you say yes, I can explain that I have... I don't know, I'll figure it out but at least I wouldn't have to feel guilty about not seeing her anymore.'

I take a deep breath, rub my head where the headache still lingers. 'No, Ben, no... I can't do that. I already have a full patient list and I really can't, especially when you've told me what you've told me. It will cloud everything.'

'Please, I would really appreciate it.'

I shake my head, standing up and grabbing my bag. 'I know,

but it's not a good idea. Look, I'm sorry to rush out but I need to get Iggy. I can think about some names, about the best possible person for you to refer her to, but I can't take her on for you, Ben. I know too much already and I don't think it would be good for me or for her, and if you happen to see her here, waiting for me, it wouldn't be good for you either.'

'Okay, okay.' He sighs and repeats, 'okay,' as he stands up. 'I'll see you tomorrow.'

'I'm sorry, Ben. I'm not trying to upset you here...'

'I know, I know. That's why I asked you. You have a level of integrity I really respect, Lana, and I knew you would make the right decision.'

When Angela, the last therapist who rented the space, told me she was taking a year off to care for her baby as I had suspected she would, I spoke to three other therapists, all women, before Ben came in.

I worry about why I offered the space to him over any of the women. We all have the same basic qualifications but Ben spent years practising in the UK so perhaps I thought he would bring a different perspective. *Or perhaps you really liked his smile.* I hate having to question myself. My ability to maintain control over everything is a source of pride. Even through my divorce, I remained calm, unruffled, able to communicate logically with my lawyer and negotiate with Oliver, despite what he had done.

'It's just that...' Ben shoves his hands in his pockets, walks around the room looking at the few benign objects I have on display like the wooden bowl filled with dry, lightly scented rose petals and the glass vase filled with multicoloured marbles – objects that add some colour but cannot upset or offend anyone.

'Just that?'

'I'm really worried about her.' I feel like there is more to this than Ben is telling me, some other reason why he doesn't want to tell this woman to find another therapist, but I don't really have the time to go into it with him now.

A rumble of thunder makes me turn towards the window and I silently curse the rain, knowing that I am wasting valuable driving time. 'I understand,' I tell Ben, 'but I don't think it would be the right thing to do.'

He nods his acceptance and smiles. 'Thanks for listening anyway,' he says as he leaves and goes back into his office.

I make my way down the back six flights of stairs of our building so I can get some incidental exercise in, and as I climb into my car in the parking garage, I think about the client Ben says he's attracted to.

I wonder what she looks like. I'm sure she's really pretty, beautiful even.

Quickly dismissing the thought, I put her out of my mind because I can't treat her. It would obviously be a very bad idea.

TWO

Sandy

No one ever told me that ageing would be the worst experience
of my life.

Every morning, I get out of bed and go to the bathroom
mirror, stand close and study my face, searching for signs of
decay. With microscopic intensity, I examine my skin for wrinkles and marks and my body for sagging parts. I am fighting time
and gravity and I hate it, but that's not what I hate most about
getting older.

Today I can see that the line between my eyes is a little
deeper, a little more visible. No doubt courtesy of last night's
drunken argument with him. I see the two of us, me with my
wine, him with his beer, shouting and spitting our hate for each
other. Leaning forward, I use my fingers to stretch the skin.
Would a facelift help? Botox? Fillers? All of that is so expensive.

But the loss of physical beauty is not the worst thing. The
worst thing about ageing is the loss of hope and expectation and
choices. At sixteen I was glorious with peachy skin and a firm

body. I was the girl who turned heads wherever I went. Boys danced to my tune and they were so entertaining to play with, to use and discard, to destroy when I could.

The world was my oyster. I was going to do everything, go everywhere. I was going to leave my small life behind and conquer the world. I saw the rest of my life as a bigger version of school, where my looks opened every door and always got me what I wanted.

But then I was seventeen and eighteen and nineteen and I realised that conquering the world is not as easy as it seems because beautiful girls are everywhere.

I had to take a mundane job so that I could live. Money is boring but so very necessary. But even at nineteen and twenty, even at twenty-five, I still had hope for a grand life. I was waiting, biding my time until the hand of fate gave me everything I wanted.

And then I fell into infatuation. I won't say it was 'love' because I don't do that. I can't do that. But I was drawn to his physical beauty and so I let my guard down a little. That was stupid. And then I got pregnant and I let him convince me that it was a good thing. And now I am here with two children and 'the husband'. We are two beautiful people who have made each other ugly by staying locked together in a toxic marriage dance.

When I'm not in an argument with him, I feel trapped and bored as I watch the wrinkles write themselves onto my face. When I am in an argument with him, I am filled with fury and venom and I hate myself as much as I hate him.

Is it any wonder that I need to entertain myself, that I find ways to keep myself amused? What other choice do I have as I stagnate in this small house, tied to a family I have no interest in?

I watch the man I married as he ties himself in knots to keep me happy and then lashes out when he sees that he's failed. It makes me smile to see him out of control. I like it.

And until a few months ago, that was at least keeping me going. But then it wasn't enough. I needed someone outside of my life, a stranger, someone who would listen to whatever I said, someone who would give me all his attention. I crave attention, focused and pure. It feeds me like water feeds a plant. I know myself in a way that few people ever do. I know who I am and what I need.

I found the perfect person. A therapist. Who better to listen to me, to tell me that I am perfect and the world around me is damaged, the people around me a disappointment? I walked into his office with my prepared story and my mask in place.

'Sandy, Sandy!' I hear him, the husband, my husband, my burden, calling me, and I groan, leaving the mirror to go downstairs.

'Can you take over here? I have to get to work. Stop crying, Felix, just stop,' he screams, and my stomach turns at the chaos in the kitchen. My seven-year-old son's nose is running and he is only half dressed.

'Mr Teddy is coming to school today,' my daughter tells us, attempting to stuff the large purple toy into her backpack.

'No, he's not,' I reply. She's a real little madam, this five-year-old child of mine. I can see my own personality every time she opens her mouth and I have to resist the urge to tell her, 'There can only be one little girl, only one.'

'Mr Teddy is coming to school today,' repeats Lila, a look of pure determination in her green eyes.

'For God's sake,' he mutters.

And then he stands and grabs the teddy away from Lila. I wait and watch, interested to see how this goes for him. I know he would like to wake up to a quiet kitchen with two angelic children sitting at the table, eating their breakfasts. He would like me to be more involved, more present. But you can't have everything. He has me and he should be ecstatic every day.

He takes the teddy to put it back in Lila's room as the child begins to wail.

'Great, just great,' I shout, watching his shoulders tense. He makes things worse and then he tries to blame me for the chaos. If he would accept that mornings are loud and messy, this would all be easier, but he keeps trying to fix things. I hate the mornings as well and try to leave him to deal with them as much as possible.

'Shut it,' he says, looming over me, and I feel my heart race. I can't push him too far. He's too big, too strong, and he could really hurt me. I know that. And I also know that if he did hurt me, he would find a way to make it my fault, because everything is my fault. Maybe it is? That's part of the toxic dance: the lying. He lies; I lie – but who lies more?

Yesterday I spent the afternoon making burgers, applying myself to the domestic task with as much enthusiasm as I could muster, which was not very much at all.

'Why are we eating this?' he said when he sat down at the kitchen table, after the children had finally been sent off for their television time and things were blessedly quiet.

'That's what you wanted,' I replied. 'You asked me to make burgers. When we spoke on the phone – you called me from work.'

'Bullshit,' he snapped, 'you said we were having pasta.' Such anger over a meal choice and so obvious that it had nothing to do with the food at all.

I knew he was searching for something to get angry over the moment he walked through the door with hunched shoulders and his square jaw more tensed than usual. But it was such a weird thing to get upset over that I laughed and then I had to keep quiet because I could see how irate he was. I did make up the phone call about burgers to upset him. I do that sometimes.

But last week he made up a story about my agreeing to take the car in for a service, and I never would have agreed to such a thing, unless I was drunk, in which case he shouldn't have asked me until he knew I was sober and concentrating. Maybe I like upsetting him but maybe he likes upsetting me too. He has his side of the story and I have mine. Maybe the truth is somewhere in the middle but maybe there's no truth at all. 'Just eat it,' I said and he did, even as he drank one beer after another, knowing that I would comment on that, knowing it would lead to a fight.

'You're an alcoholic,' I yelled at him last night.

'That's rich coming from you,' he sneered, pointing to my full wine glass. Alcohol dulls the senses and I need mine to be as dulled as possible to survive this life.

'Shut it,' he repeats now as I hold my breath in the messy kitchen. I drop my gaze as he waves a fist at me, the teddy in his other hand making him seem ludicrous.

He moves away from me and violently stuffs the teddy down into the backpack. It's not even 8 a.m. and I can see that he wishes the day was over and he was back in bed already. Lila stops crying abruptly in the way that she can and she sits down on the floor, patting the teddy stuffed down in her bag, her thumb going into her mouth.

She looks like me – not as pretty of course but that may change over the years. She has golden-brown hair and a heart-shaped face and the same green eyes. Felix is like him, blond with blue eyes and a square jaw. He looks exactly like his father and I can't abide the child's crying or maybe I just can't abide him, the little boy who trapped me here, whose first breath meant the end of my life as I wanted it to be.

'You're such a gorgeous family,' strangers will tell us at the park when we are all together, and I must admit that I get a kick out of that. We are gorgeous. Picture-perfect in every way.

But scrape the surface only a little and there are things no one wants to see.

I wish I wanted to be here, and maybe if he and I could find a way to be better as people, it would be fine. After a glass or two or three of wine, I always feel hopeful that the two of us can change and life can turn into the fairy tale it was supposed to be. But then I sober up and he's yelling or lying about something and that hope feels misplaced.

'I need to get out of here,' he says, picking up his briefcase as he heads into work, where he will sit behind a desk and try to convince people to buy the shitty mattresses his company makes. He's failing. I know he's failing. There are rumblings about the business closing down, something to think about for me. I don't work. Caring for these children and this house and holding on to what beauty I can is enough work for me. With each passing year, more exercise, more complicated skin routines and more effort are required to look the way I used to look, and I am losing that battle.

Turning away from the children, I pour myself a cup of coffee and take a sip. How much would a facelift cost? Exactly how much?

I hear the sound of the garage door closing and I know he's gone.

Slamming my cup down on the counter, I yell, 'Get dressed and into the car, both of you.' And they listen. They always listen when he's not here. Despite how big he is, how scary he can be, they adore him, want to be with him, push his boundaries, knowing that he will give in on bedtime and television time and exactly how many treats are allowed. I'm not like that.

I need to get them to school, get them out of my hair, and then I will make myself beautiful. I will perfect my mask so that I can go in today and see my therapist. I will sit on his sofa and let him look at me as I speak. This thought cheers me, even without the help of a glass of wine.

I do a quick clean-up of the kitchen, stopping in front of a cupboard to look at the large blue cookie jar I have stored on a high shelf. I feel a little shiver run through me at what I have in there and at what it means for my future.

Because I can feel it getting closer now. I can feel the day is coming when I show the world exactly what my dear husband is really like, exactly who he is. And what a day that will be.

THREE

Lana

I show Elizabeth and her husband, Jack, out of my office and close the door on them gratefully.

They were my fifth session of the day. A married couple trying to regroup after Elizabeth had an affair.

Now I have an hour to eat a late lunch and get ready for my last patients of the day. I always like to start my break with a ten-minute meditation and stretch.

I lie on the floor of my office with my legs up against the wall and close my eyes, breathing deeply and relaxing my shoulders.

Sometimes my sessions with couples hit a little too close to home and I cannot help but remember the end of my own marriage. Oliver and I were in therapy and we were, ostensibly, fighting to save our marriage, slogging through the he said/she said of it all, exhausted but still trying. And then I noticed a sudden withdrawal from Oliver, a stepping back from the drama of our failing union. He was almost disinterested in our therapy sessions and I believed I knew what that meant.

It was not the first time a man had cheated on me. I knew the signs.

My boyfriend before Oliver had cheated as well and it made me distrustful of men in general. When we began dating, Oliver was aghast at the idea of cheating on someone, telling me, 'It's morally wrong.' But he seemed happy enough to push his morals aside as our marriage foundered. People say a lot of things at the beginning of a relationship, make a lot of promises and mean them then.

Oliver and I met at university, where he was studying architecture and I was studying psychology, our paths crossing at the bar and our glazed eyes meeting at the toga party. I had, by then, discovered that alcohol loosened me up, made me forget my ever-present insecurities. It was after I had lost the weight and dyed my hair and I felt as good as I had ever felt about myself, helped along by three glasses of Roman punch, which tasted like cough syrup but went straight to my head.

We clicked, and the next day, we still had stuff to say to each other. He told me I was beautiful and clever and he made me feel like I was. I was attracted to his green eyes and his passion for his work. We dated, lived together and then slipped into marriage easily; both sets of parents were delighted. We should have known each other better after being together for some time but we hadn't anticipated what a baby would do to our marriage.

Things began to go wrong when we had Iggy – I was stuck at home while he was growing his practice and meeting glamorous clients with millions to spend on houses. And for some reason, even after I went back to work, we couldn't rescue it.

When I felt Oliver disengaging from our therapy sessions, I should have gone to him with my suspicions. That would have been the mature thing to do, the thing that I, as a therapist, would have advised a patient to do. But I was hurting and unable to apply logic right then. So, I found a private detective named William Owens online. I called him and explained my dilemma over the phone and paid the fee. And a few days later, I had my evidence. I never even met up with William. It was that fast, that easy to catch my husband out. Oliver wasn't really trying to hide anything.

When I confronted him with evidence of his affair, William's damning pictures in my hand, he was mortified and I was... relieved. He and the woman, a twenty-three-year-old named Ariel with long blonde mermaid hair, were still texting each other when I found out about them, even though he had no real interest in seeing her again. She was pretty, obviously, younger than I was and slim as a willow, everything Oliver always told me he had no interest in.

Whatever was between them ended as soon as we decided on divorce. She was the proverbial straw that finally broke the camel's back.

'It made me see that there is life beyond this,' he told me apologetically. 'I'm sorry, Lana, but I think we're done.'

I wanted to be angry, to accuse him of killing whatever was left between us, but I saw the affair for what it was: a desperate attempt to find a way out. Oliver is not one for confrontation. He would probably have never revealed the affair to me if I hadn't caught him. But he was right. We were done.

We spent our next few therapy appointments figuring out how to parent Iggy and how to do divorce better than we had done marriage. Oliver was effusive in his apologies and he gave in on a lot during mediation, letting me have Iggy for every Christmas Day and the apartment where we lived at the time and asking for nothing even though he had contributed to the mortgage for years. I was indebted to William for his work.

Oliver was only single for six months before he met Becky, and now, they're married and she is my son's stepmother. Every time I look at her, I feel like I am doing womanhood wrong.

The couple I have just seen did not need a private detective.

Elizabeth confessed and I do believe that eventually, they will be able to move past the affair as a couple. And maybe they will look back on all of this one day and believe it has brought them closer. Sadly, most affairs end a marriage, like it did with mine. They are usually the final nail in a coffin that has already been built out of resentment and disdain.

Knowing I need to let go of all thoughts about my last patients and my ex-husband, I imagine myself on a beach, hear the crashing of waves against the golden sand I am walking on.

And then I hear yelling.

Alarmed, I drop my legs and stand up, opening my office door. Ben is standing in front of reception with a woman who is shrieking, 'You can't do this, you can't do this.'

Ben raises and lowers his arms. 'Sandy, listen to me, listen to me, I understand how hard this is. Let's go back into my office and talk...'

'I don't want to talk in your office, Ben. I don't want to have you tell me how to feel about this. You're abandoning me when I need you the most.' She rubs at her cheek, getting rid of tears, and then she sniffs loudly. 'You're an arsehole, a complete arsehole.' Her voice is loud in the small office space.

'I understand your anger,' says Ben firmly and I know he's trying to de-escalate the situation but he's not having much luck.

'Don't use that therapist bullshit on me,' she shrieks and then she steps towards him and shoves him so that he steps back, his hands going up again. 'You can't just decide this, you can't,' she spits.

I step forward, glad that Kirsty must have gone to get coffee so she's not watching this. 'Hey, hey,' I say softly, alerting them both to my presence. They stop speaking and turn to look at me. The shouting woman is petite, pretty with porcelain skin, deep green eyes and fine highlighted brown hair that tumbles over her shoulders in perfect waves. I feel my breath catch as I stare at her.

The most noticeable thing about the woman is the black eye, discoloured and puffy, already yellowing around the edges.

This is obviously the woman Ben came to me about last week. His attraction to her makes perfect sense. She is everything that society requires of beauty, except for the black eye.

'Sorry, Lana.' Ben's face flushes. He is embarrassed at not being able to control the situation, I'm sure. Our practice specialises in helping people who are struggling with everyday life. We don't have violent or very disturbed patients. It's unusual to ever hear shouting in our office, although voices are sometimes louder than usual during marriage counselling sessions.

'No, you're not sorry!' the woman yells. 'If you were, you wouldn't be abandoning me.' Tears fall and she scrabbles in her bag for a tissue. I grab one from the box on the reception desk and hand it to her. There are boxes of tissues everywhere in the office. Tears are a by-product of a therapy session. I've shed a fair few myself in conversations with SueEllen. The woman takes a tissue from the box and dabs at her eyes without acknowledging me.

'I am sorry,' says Ben firmly. 'This is just not working for me anymore or for you. I have given you the list and you will find someone who can help you, I promise.'

The woman blows her nose dramatically, more tears falling. 'Please, Ben,' she says, defeat in her stance, 'please, I can't explain to anyone else, I simply can't. I would rather die than start this process again.'

Ben shrugs his shoulders and glances at me, anguish on his face. I should never have come out here. I should just have left Ben to sort this out himself, but now that I'm here, I can feel this woman's desperation.

'Please, Ben,' she begs, her voice just above a whisper. 'I can't go on like this.'

'I'm just so sorry, I will try and help you find someone else.'

'I can't.' She shakes her head. 'I will never talk to anyone again. I don't care anymore. I'll just—'

'Perhaps you can come and have a chat with me,' I say, dragging the words from inside myself. 'I'm a therapist as well.'

She's in a bad way and who knows what decision she will make in such a state. It's important that she calms down before she leaves here. I would hate to send a distressed patient back out into the world without at least trying to help them. 'Please come into my office and we can talk for a bit.' I try really hard not to let her hear the disappointment in my voice. This is my break and I wanted some time off. I have a full patient list but I can feel that I'm being pulled into this. I'll just talk to her until she can think straight and then suggest a new therapist.

The woman looks at me and then back at Ben. She seems to be considering the possibility that Ben will relent but he won't meet her gaze, instead looking down at his shoes. Her tears won't stop coming and she blows her nose again and then nods.

I can see the relief in Ben's face. He wants someone else to deal with this problem.

I'm angry with him for not handling this better but I can't let this woman leave in the state she's in. One of the worst things about being a therapist is my inability to leave my patients at work. I worry about them all the time, so much so that SueEllen and I have come up with a plan for fifteen minutes each day where I worry about everyone I have seen that day without trying to stop myself. Having official worry time does help me focus on Iggy better after I'm done.

I know why I worry so much, of course.

Before I was a therapist, before university, I was a normal person. A friend. Just someone who should have listened to someone in my life – but didn't. I chose not to listen because I was busy with my own life. I chose to turn away. It could be argued that I was too young to know what I was doing or that I was a teenager and so naturally selfish, but it's something I will always regret. And because of that, I will always worry about all my patients – about anyone who opens up to me. Even if I really wanted to – and I do – I don't have the ability to leave this alone and let this woman get on with the rest of her day. I won't be able to focus until I know she's okay. And some small part of me is intrigued. She's so beautiful. I just know she was the most popular girl at her school, the one with every boy's attention, the one every girl wanted to be and every boy wanted to date, and yet here she is, crying in my practice because her life is a mess.

I turn and she follows me into my office. I gesture to the sofa and then I go to close the door as she sits down. Ben is still standing in reception and he mouths, 'Thank you,' and I shrug. I don't have much choice.

'I'm Lana,' I say, sitting down in front of the woman, who is dabbing at her face. She has stopped crying so that's something.

'Sandy. Has Ben told you about me?' she asks. She is dressed in a navy-blue jumpsuit, an outfit that would make me look like an overgrown toddler but one that is casually elegant on her. This is not someone who has ever obsessed over her weight.

I bite down on my lip, debating what to do. Ben should not have been discussing her with me but perhaps if she feels I know some of what is wrong, she will understand that another therapist can easily help her.

'He told me that you are struggling in your marriage. And I'm sure that if you want him to, he will be able to talk to whoever your new therapist is and explain everything so you don't have to feel like you're starting again.'

'And I'm sure he told you that I'm in love with him.' Her voice is tight with anger. She crosses her arms over her chest, her chin jutting out. It's a lightning-quick transformation and something I take note of.

I deliberately relax in my chair, letting my arms rest by my sides. 'He told me you have some feelings for him but I know that he also explained about transference.'

Sandy nods her head. 'He did, so I don't know why I can't still work with him. It's not like I'm going to attack him.' She smiles ruefully and I can't help but return her smile. Her smile lights up her face and I can imagine that her whole path through life has been eased by that smile. I remind myself again that she is here because she is in trouble. Her smile has not made her life perfect.

'No, but it may interfere with your therapy.' I don't mention Ben's feelings for her, of course.

She shrugs her shoulders. 'Maybe...' She looks around my office, her eyes focusing on the wall where my degrees and extra diplomas are all hung in matching wooden frames. 'Maybe you can...' She shrugs again. 'I don't know. Can you help me? I mean can you treat me?' She looks back at me, her eyes wide. 'I... don't want to start again and maybe if I like... give Ben permission, he can tell you everything? It won't be the same as starting with someone completely new. I think... it would be easier.' She leans back against the sofa, more relaxed now.

'Well,' I hesitate, not wanting to say yes. 'How about this... We can have a quick chat now and you can tell me as much or as little as you want and then I will give you a list of names of people who may be able to help, other therapists. But if you don't want to talk to them, then you can talk to me.' This is not what I want. I don't need more work. But I do want to know who gave her that black eye.

Kirsty will have to squeeze her into my schedule some-where. I can see that she is not going to want to find another therapist.

'I don't want to talk to anyone but Ben, but at least if it's you, I mean, you're part of the same...' She gestures around the office. 'I feel like I've spilled enough secrets.'

'The best person to tell your secrets to is a therapist. I promise I won't tell anyone else. But I need to tell you that if I feel you are in danger or you are a danger to others, I have to report it to the police.'

'Okay' – she waves her hand – 'Ben gave me that whole speech when I started seeing him. But can you... listen first, just listen. I'm not' – she shakes her head – 'not ready for...' She waves her hand again without telling me what it is she means.

'I'm going to listen, I promise you,' I reassure her.

She takes a deep, shuddering breath and dabs at her eyes again. 'God, it's so complicated... My husband... Things are not good between us. I think he's gaslighting me, making me think I'm crazy, you know?'

'How does he make you think you're crazy?'

'He tells me he's coming home at a certain time and then doesn't. He tells me I've had too much to drink when I know I haven't. He tells me that I agreed to things like where to eat or what to do with the kids when I know he's never mentioned anything. He's trying to drive me crazy.'

'Does he... hurt you?' I ask.

'What? No, no, nothing like that. I guess you could call it emotional abuse.'

I wait for a moment and then she laughs. 'Oh this' – she gestures to her eye – 'I walked into a door.'

'Okay,' I reply. I don't believe her but then why would I? And I can see from the way she is looking at me that she doesn't really want me to believe that clichéd excuse.

'He says that I drink too much, and I know that I should cut down, I know I should, but life is so... Everything is so hard, you know, like every day is...' She stops speaking and I wait for her to tell me what she is thinking. Softly, she says, 'Do you ever get the feeling that you're just waiting for death? I mean barely getting through one day and then the next day and just waiting for it to all be over?'

I can hear her pain but I don't answer her because she's looking at the picture I have on the other wall in my office of a beach in the sunshine with bright blue, white-crested waves lapping at the shore. A little girl is digging in the sand with a pink bucket and matching spade. It was painted for me by a friend of mine, Amy, as a present for when I opened my own practice.

'My daughter, Lila, loves the beach.' She takes a deep breath. I can see that she's calmer, which is better for her. I'm not going to ask about how much she drinks. Not yet. 'My husband is the one who drinks too much and sometimes he...'

'Sometimes he...?'

She frowns. 'I'm not... ready to talk about everything. I barely know you.' She seems angry at me and I take note of that. There is obviously a lot more going on here than just gaslighting.

'Do you still love him, your husband?' I ask her, sitting forward in my chair.

'I do. I know that I have a thing for Ben, but I also know why that happened. I love my husband, Lana, and I wish I didn't but I really, really do. I'm thirty-six. I don't want to have to start again.'

Outside the office I hear the phone beginning to ring and then I hear Kirsty answer it, 'Calm Minds Clinic, hold please.'

I can't help thinking that this woman's life should have been perfect. I know that beauty doesn't guarantee anything but even now, at my age, I cannot help but envy her looks. She's as old as I am but she looks much younger, even with the black eye. If she can't have the perfect life, what hope is there for anyone else?

'Why don't you start at the beginning?' I tell her as I remind myself that I can't be 'Lana the woman' now. I need to be 'Lana the therapist', neutral, unemotional and certainly not jealous of another woman's looks.

I listen while she talks, letting her tell me the story of her marriage, of how she met and fell in love with her husband.

After half an hour, I know that I need to stop her because I have another patient coming soon.

'We can meet again,' I say. 'I'll talk to Kirsty and get her to contact you with a time.'

'Thank you,' she says as she stands, 'thank you so much.' She clutches her matching navy bag. 'At least you're prettier than Ben.' She laughs and I am at once flattered and concerned. It's an odd thing to say to your therapist.

I stand as well, deciding to ignore the remark, opening my office door as she throws her crumpled tissue into the garbage bin by the door.

The waiting room is empty; my next client has, thankfully, not arrived yet.

'Kirsty will be in contact,' I tell Sandy.

Closing my office door, I take a deep breath and then I look down at my garbage bin where Sandy has thrown her tissue. Something seems off and I bend down to get closer, actually picking up the tissue she was using, even as my stomach churns at the idea of what I'm doing.

There are marks on the tissue, not only the black streaks of running mascara from all her tears but blue, yellow and purple smudges as well. From her eye make-up? Surely, I would have noticed purple? I study the tissue. Where did all the colour come from? She only dabbed at her eyes.

I screw up my face and drop the tissue back in the bin, using the hand sanitiser on my desk quickly.

There's no way that black eye was fake – is there?

FOUR

Sandy

I didn't do well at school. Truthfully, I had so many other experiences that I wanted to enjoy. I didn't need to bury myself in repetitive rubbish, foisted on us by bureaucrats. I spent a lot of time in the bathroom, preening in the mirror, reapplying my delicate pink lip gloss, making sure my hair was perfect and waiting for the lunch break, which was when I was the most important person in the place. Girls watched me wherever I went and boys simply stopped talking when I walked past, their mouths gaping open with desire.

The fact that I failed to get into university doesn't mean I'm stupid. I like to consider myself a student of the human condition. Mostly, I'm fascinated with myself, with the reaction others have to me. But I do like to watch other people, to get to know them, to find out what makes them tick and then maybe figure out what it would take to destroy them. If I hadn't been stupid enough to fall into infatuation with 'the husband' and then end up pregnant and trapped, I would have destroyed him as well. I hate that I was weak, that I let him get to me, and that now, sometimes, I am afraid of him.

Needless to say, my parents never understood me. They didn't have the capacity and were delighted when I got married and became someone else's problem.

I stopped working when I got pregnant, and I did enjoy the months of growing the first child inside me. I liked the attention, the smiles and benevolent looks I received from strangers. I liked that people stood up when I was near, offered me their chairs.

I was a beautiful pregnant woman, my hair thick and glowing, my skin perfect, my bump neat. I was envied. I could see that.

But then the baby arrived and it was all so... so boring.

I should never have tried again to capture the feeling. The second one is never as good.

But at least I never had to return to work.

Instead, my work became trying to survive as I waded through the mud of everyday life.

Until I can figure a way out of this, I am doing my best to survive. Once I settled on the idea of therapy for entertainment and for my other needs, I went to my first therapy session bubbling with excitement, a feeling I had sorely missed.

I chose his name, the name of my therapist, from a website and I imagined him overweight with bushy eyebrows and wearing a brown waistcoat. I saw the way he would respond to me, how easy it would be to turn him inside out with a little flirting. I wanted other things from him, needed him to listen to my story, to agree with it. But I was going to start with a little light flirting.

I chose my outfit carefully, making sure that the pants moulded to my form, that I left my white shirt open one button too many so that he would be able to glimpse the pink lace bra I was wearing.

It was expensive, but 'the husband' – that's what I call him in my head, 'the husband' – was willing to pay for it.

I had to push him a little, goad him into an argument and wait for him to get nasty and vicious, which doesn't take much. And then I had to cry so that he would be sorry.

He doesn't like me to talk about our arguments and he hates the idea that I will be discussing them with a therapist, which is exactly what I want. The therapist is as important as what's in the cookie jar for my future.

I chose a familiar argument to push him on, something I complain about a lot, which is the nasty state of the kitchen. I want to redo it and he says we can't afford it.

'You could figure out how to get the money if you weren't so useless,' I spat at him.

'You're a bitch,' he drunkenly threw back at me. A shocking, horrible word and one that he pretended he hadn't said the next morning.

'I would never use that language. Why are you lying?' Beer goes to his head very quickly. He drinks a lot when we're together, perhaps hoping to capture the feelings of our first years with each other when the infatuation was so strong, he would turn me on with a look.

I cried then, talked about how my father used that word on my mother and how devastated I was to hear it from my own husband.

He felt guilty and apologised, even as he still denied using the word. 'If I said it, I'm sorry, but I don't think I did say it.'

It meant he was primed and ready when I brought up therapy. 'Maybe it will stop you making all this shit up,' he said.

Run away, I tell myself every morning but you cannot run away with nothing. I will not run away with nothing. I am biding my time, waiting for an opportunity. I will know it when it comes.

But for now, I have therapy.

I walked into my first session ready for the old man I assumed would be waiting. But I got someone very different. I got someone unexpected and I was a little thrown, a little disconcerted. But I righted myself soon enough.

And after one hour with me, I could see that he would be easy. They all are, aren't they?

It was so good for a while but then he told me it wasn't working, told me that it wasn't right for us to be talking.

And now I have to adjust because I am talking to someone else, to a woman who I can see envies me even as she feels sorry for me and my poor, messed-up life. I think she believes I'm stupid but I'm not.

I don't like the way he switched things on me but I understand why it had to happen. I'm biding my time and making my plans.

They think they're so clever but they're not as clever as I am.

I dress as carefully for my first full therapy session with her as I did with him, choosing a tight black skirt and thigh-high boots. I like the way she looks me up and down. I can see her comparing us, see her judging her own looks. And there is always the possibility that I will see him, that he will walk into that waiting room to call in a patient he has deemed to be someone he can keep talking to. I want him to know what he's missing. I want him to think about me when he's talking to someone else, to be distracted.

I make sure to smudge the make-up perfectly under my eye. I have a time lapse on my computer so I know exactly what it should look like today.

I have been collecting stories to take to her.

When we talked for the first time, I told her about meeting 'the husband' at a sales conference. I explained how he sat down next to me and didn't look at me until we were told to introduce ourselves. I remember that moment clearly. It was the moment I slipped into infatuation and ruined my life. His eyes were so blue and he had taken off his jacket so I could see the movement of his muscles under the crisp white business shirt.

He asked me if he could buy me a drink and I told him he could. I chose a glass of expensive champagne and he happily paid.

It wasn't like I had never dated a good-looking man before. I'd been through plenty of them but this one caught me. Perhaps it was the way he looked at me, as though he were drinking me in. Perhaps it was the stories he told of his ambition. He wanted the biggest house, the nicest car, the most expensive vacations, and he wanted to have someone at home that he could give all of it to. I knew that would be the perfect role for me. I was born for it.

The company he worked for at the time was growing and it seemed that the sky was the limit. 'We'll be turning over millions soon,' he told me, 'millions.' I didn't even struggle as he lured me into the net, and then I was filled with his baby and stuck.

I finish my make-up, dismissing my past mistakes. Perhaps if she asks about the eye today, I will give a different excuse. I need her to know 'the husband' is dangerous. I need her to understand that my safety is my concern. My safety and the safety of the children I adore.

That's the plan now, the one that has come together in my head perfectly.

I am in danger from 'the husband', and whatever happens now, I had no choice.

I glance in the mirror as I leave the house, watch the way my eyes fill up with tears that I have to blink away.

I am far away from sixteen with my whole life ahead of me. But I can't let that upset me. I have to keep moving forward with my plan. One day I will have everything I want if I keep moving forward like a shark. In the mirror I smile, baring my teeth that are not sharp and dangerous. I close my mouth, practise a pout, lick my lips so they shine.

Actually, I think I might be dangerous – just dangerous enough.

FIVE

Lana

Every Monday morning, at 8.55 a.m., I allow myself a full minute of resenting Ben for putting me in this position. The only time I could fit in a session with Sandy is Monday mornings at 9 a.m., which means that every Sunday night I have to check to make sure that either my mother or Oliver remembers that they have to get to my house at 8 a.m. so that I can leave in order to get to work on time. Since Iggy started school, I have prided myself on dropping him off every morning he's with me, even though he has to stay in after-school care or get picked up by my mother or Oliver in the afternoon.

I have seen Sandy twice now, delving into her marriage and her relationship with her husband and seeing clearly the classic pattern of the abuse cycle she is in. I want to help her but it has meant giving up a part of my day that I value, and last night Oliver told me he couldn't make it but Becky would be there.

This morning as I struggled to get myself ready and get Iggy's lunch packed, Becky arrived, clad head to toe in skin-tight exercise gear with her auburn hair in a high ponytail and a broad grin on her face. She was literally fizzing with energy. I've met Becky a couple of times and she seems determined to be friends with me. I am determined to find a way not to hate her on sight every time I see her because she's actually really nice. I understand my feelings and where they come from but that doesn't mean that I can stop them entirely. I'm working on it, which is about the best I can do.

'Oh, you look great,' were Becky's first words to me. 'That colour red really suits you,' she said, complimenting my jacket. 'Is there anything I can do to help? You can leave it all to me. Iggy will show me what to do, won't you, little man? I may be coming more often now that Oliver has a new client because they can only meet on a Monday morning. I hope that's okay with you because I'm so happy to help. But if it's not, I totally get it and Oliver will just have to work something out. You're the mother and you get to decide.' She spoke quickly, almost breathlessly, determined to get the words out so that I would know she was not trying to tread on my toes. I managed a tight grin and, 'It's fine. Thank you for helping,' before I dropped a kiss on Iggy's head and headed out the door so that I could be here before nine and take some time to resent Ben before I see Sandy.

People might think that therapists have the ability to sail smoothly through life because they've studied the human condition in such depth, but in the end, we're just trying to get through the day like everyone else. I am having to work particularly hard to stay on an even keel when talking to Sandy. I feel like everything she says and does is a performance for my benefit and I can see exactly why Ben fell for her. If I were a man, I would have a hard time resisting the head tossing, the delicate tears and the beautiful smile that replaces them.

What I am not sure of is why. Why is she doing this? I want to get at the real reason, find out what is really going on in her marriage. Is she actually unhappy? Is her husband actually emotionally and possibly physically abusive? Or is that what she wants me to think?

I know that there are things Ben hasn't told me, things that he is keeping to himself about exactly why he didn't want Sandy to just leave the practice, and that's something that I have been thinking about. He's attracted to her but there's more than that and I'm not sure exactly how to ask him the question.

A buzzing sound tells me that Sandy has arrived and I open my eyes, allowing my resentment of Ben to dissipate into the air.

I take a deep breath and get up, opening my office door and smiling at my patient.

I notice that the black eye is nearly completely gone now, just a faint smudge of yellow. If she did fake it, she was really committed to the process as I have watched it fade over the last couple of weeks.

'So, you need to meet Mike,' Sandy tells me before she's even sat down.

I bite back some resentment at the command. She talks a lot about how much she loves her children and her husband and how desperately she wants to save her marriage. And she seems very distressed a lot of the time, but sometimes, I feel like she sees me as someone who works for her rather than someone who is working with her to help her.

'I don't think that's a good idea,' I reply as she settles herself on the sofa.

'Why?'

'You've told me he's emotionally abusive and I don't think there would be any value in bringing your abuser here.' Each time I see Sandy, I study her carefully, aware, as I have been from the first time I saw her, that she is hiding something. I feel like every session with her is a test of my abilities as a therapist and it is becoming important to me to prove to myself that I can figure this out.

'You know, I feel like you want me to leave him because you know how hard it will be for me.'

I shake my head. 'Not at all, Sandy. I am giving you the same advice I would give any other woman in your situation. And I'm not telling you to leave him, just that I don't think it's a good idea for him to come to a session until you know what you want and you're feeling stronger. This room should be your safe space, something for you and only you.'

'It feels like you have a direction you want me to go in and you're pushing me that way.' She looks down at her hands and then casually pushes a cuticle back on a nail as though what she has just said is not a pointed critical accusation. The words sting as she must have known they would.

'I would never push you in any direction. This is your life and all the choices are yours.'

Sandy looks up from her hand and then she nods and sniffs like she's about to cry. 'You're supposed to help me, Lana, and I'm telling you that I want to save my marriage,' she says. Grabbing her blue leather bag, she finds a tissue and dabs at her eyes delicately.

Squashing some irritation at the way she is talking to me and the way she seems to be using tears to manipulate me, I say, 'I only want to help you.'

'Please just meet him,' she says, her tone changing as she smiles at me. I can see that she is used to getting everything she wants. It must be hard for her to find herself in a situation that she can't control completely. 'I know that it will make a difference if you do. I think that you're really good at what you do, and I would never have believed this but you're actually a better therapist than Ben is, maybe because you're a woman. I feel like you really understand me and what's going on and I think that meeting Mike would really help things.'

It's a calculated compliment but I can't help the good

feeling that comes from her words. I know I'm a good therapist but it's always nice to have it confirmed.

'Okay,' I decide to agree, against my better judgement. Perhaps meeting her husband will allow me to understand exactly what she's hiding.

And I am curious to meet Mike, to see how he presents himself to the world. Abusers can be incredibly charming to strangers and it's only behind closed doors that they let their true selves come out.

'But, Sandy, you know from our discussions that change may not be possible for Mike. If he is gaslighting you, he needs to be able to acknowledge it and get help so that he stops his pattern from repeating.'

'I know, I know.' Sandy flaps her hand. Today she is dressed in tight blue jeans and a soft navy jumper. She looks lovely in everything she wears and I know that if she got divorced, she wouldn't struggle to find someone new to share her life with. I need to get to the root of what is tying her to this man.

'I do understand your feelings and you have every reason to want a functional relationship.'

'Doesn't everyone?' She cocks her head to one side. 'Are you married? Or... divorced, yes, I think you're divorced.' The barb pricks but I maintain a neutral façade.

I've noticed this about Sandy over the last couple of sessions. When she feels I am pushing her to leave, she begins asking personal questions and it makes me wonder if she did the same thing with Ben. I know enough to steer her away from my life.

'We aren't here to talk about me,' I say in reply to her question. 'We've never really discussed your parents. Do they or did they have a good marriage?'

Sandy glances at the clock on the wall as though ascertaining how much time is left in her session. An expression I've never seen crosses her face, a kind of shutting down.

'They have a fine marriage. They live on the South Coast so we don't get to see them as much as I would like. I don't think they understand me or that they even want to. They're happy enough although it's a very, like, 1950s marriage. My dad goes to work and my mum stays home and it's always been like that. I mean, I don't work so it's not only about work, more about how they behave with each other. When I was a child, Dad always had to be served dinner first and Mum always made sure that the house was clean and my sister and I were behaving nicely before he came home. He ruled the roost but he was a good father, except for... I mean he drank some.' Her gaze darts from side to side and it's obvious to me that she's uncomfortable now.

I make a note on the pad in front of me. *Grew up keeping the secret of abusive father? Has chosen to repeat.*

'What did you just write down?' Sandy asks, irritation flickering across her features, and I have a feeling she has inadvertently revealed something about herself, something true.

'Exactly what you told me.' There's no way she can read what I've written from where she is sitting. I am in my usual leather tub chair, a present from my own father when I completed my studies.

'Every good psychologist needs a comfortable chair to sit in,' he told me on the card he wrote to go with the gift. However terrible my teenage years were, I always knew that I had the love and support of my parents. I still do.

If Sandy doesn't want to discuss her parents, there's something there that I need to pay attention to.

'Anyway, my parents have nothing to do with anything. I see them on Christmas and we visit over the summer holidays but I can't count on them for help or anything. It's not like they have a lot of money and so... if Mike and I get divorced, I will be one of those single mothers living in poverty. I know that for sure. And I refuse to live in poverty.'

'You can get help; the government has a lot of programmes available to help single mothers and he would have to pay child support...' I try to imagine Sandy having to watch every penny but can't. Her clothes look expensive, her nails are perfect and diamonds sparkle on her hands. She looks like a woman who spends time and money on herself.

But money can't buy the happiness and peace she is desperate for. The therapist in me takes a step forward. *Why are you being so harsh?* I sit up straight in my chair, dismissing the judgemental voice inside my head.

'Yeah,' she snorts, 'I've read about all the men who *pay* their child support. It's so easy for a man, you know, they can leave, they can just leave and make another life for themselves and that's not fair. We're stuck with the kids and having to worry about feeding them and caring for them while we work – I mean, some women.' She waves her hand again. 'You wait till you meet Mike; he's really good-looking and charming and he will have someone else in his life like that.' She snaps her fingers.

'But is that a reason to stay with someone who you claim gaslights you?'

'Claim?'

I clear my throat, a little ashamed of myself. 'I guess I'm wondering what is tying you to someone who makes your life very hard.'

'I still love him.' She shrugs. 'I wish I didn't. But I do.'

Again, I wonder if this is true.

There is a lot more to this situation than what she's telling me and it will be a good thing to meet her husband so that I can be sure of what is and isn't the truth.

We sit in silence for a few minutes as Sandy plays with the gold link bracelet she has around her wrist.

'Mike gave this to me on our first anniversary,' she says, smiling. 'We already had a baby and I was... Felix was not a sleeper and I thought that I wasn't going to survive. I hadn't even remembered it was our first anniversary but he came home early in the afternoon with flowers and this gift and he told me he'd booked me a hair appointment and he had a dinner reservation.'

'That sounds like a lovely gesture.'

Sandy nods and she sniffs, reaching for a tissue from the box on the coffee table in front of her.

'I don't know how we got here.' When she feels the session is not going the way she wants it to, like when my sympathy and attention do not seem to be as concentrated as she would like, Sandy resorts to tears. I know this about her. I know a lot more about her than she would give me credit for.

'And now, he's all freaked out about losing his job and he's getting angrier and angrier and the drinking... well, that's getting to be over the top.'

'It must be stressful to be in that situation,' I tell her, 'for both of you.'

'He wants me to get a job. He says that now that the kids are at school, I can work and contribute. He told me he would give me the world, and to be honest, all he's given me are two kids and a shitty house.' The tears have dried very quickly and I can see anger on her face at where she finds herself.

'Perhaps it would help things if you did have some part-time work. It might be something that you enjoy and it would mean that, if you do decide to leave, you already have something in place so that you can support yourself and your children.'

'What kind of a job am I going to get, Lana?'

'Well...'

'Can I tell you something weird?'

'You can tell me everything weird.' I smile.

'I was looking for something in Mike's things last week, like his bedside table. I was looking for nail clippers because I wanted to clip the kids' nails and I have one for them but of course that goes missing regularly.'

In my pocket, my phone vibrates with a reminder that the session is ten minutes away from ending. I have no idea where Sandy is going with this.

'And so, I was searching through his stuff because I know he keeps a pair in there and I found...' Sandy hesitates, her fingers returning to the bracelet. I wait. The normal desire to fill in a silence is something I battled with when I started my training but I have endless reserves of patience now.

Sandy looks directly at me. 'I found a life insurance policy for me... like on me.'

I swallow. 'And you didn't know about it?'

'No. We've never really discussed something like that, and even if we had, wouldn't it make more sense to have one on him? I mean he earns the money and statistically men die before women.'

'Did you ask him about it?'

'No, I was... too scared to. I just put it back. I mean I'm sure there's a logical reason. There must be, mustn't there?'

A thought I can't help having is that it's possible that there is no life insurance policy. Based on what I've seen, it would not be out of the question for Sandy to make it up. But what if I'm wrong and it does exist because if it does, that's not good. It's problematic and very concerning. I am pleased that I get to meet this man next week now. Why take out a life insurance policy on a thirty-six-year-old woman without a job? Perhaps I have been misreading this situation?

My phone vibrates again. The session is over. I would let it go on longer but I have another patient.

'Sandy, perhaps this is something we should discuss between us another time.' I don't want her to bring it up with Mike when they are alone and she has no protection, not until I know what's really going on. I suppress a shudder as I wrap up the session.

'You're right,' she says. 'It's better not to confront him about anything the first time he sees you. I want him to feel relaxed, you know.'

'I understand.' I glance towards the door.

'Oh God,' she says, pulling out her phone, 'we've gone over, sorry. I could talk to you all day.'

'It's fine, it's only by a few minutes. I'll see you next Monday with Mike.'

I open the office door to let her out into the waiting room.

Kirsty and Ben are standing together, each holding a cup of coffee, gazing at each other in a way I find perturbing. I raise my phone a little and snap a photo of the two of them although I have no idea why I do that, probably to torture myself with later. I really do need to talk to SueEllen about a lot of things.

I clear my throat, flushing a little at the idea that I have done something so strange. What if they'd caught me doing it? Kirsty jumps when she sees me. 'Oh, Lana, Ben got me coffee.' She giggles as though I have said something funny and then she darts behind her desk and sits down, ready to process Sandy's credit card.

'Same time next week?' she asks Sandy, who is staring at Ben, her arms folded across her chest.

'Same time next week?' asks Kirsty again, and Ben meets Sandy's eyes and then immediately drops his gaze to the floor.

'Yes, same time. Lana is so good to talk to,' says Sandy, her voice loud in the quiet office. And then she leaves quickly.

Ben turns and walks towards his office. It's unfortunate that he was out here. He has back-to-back patients on a Monday like I do so I'm surprised he's not in his office since Sandy and I went over time. Was he waiting to see Sandy? Or perhaps his next patient cancelled?

'Come in,' I say to Christina, my next patient, and then I

glance at Ben, who is standing at his office door, staring at Kirsty.

Christina follows me into my office and sits down on the sofa. 'I volunteered to be part of the school fundraising committee,' she tells me with a triumphant smile.

'How wonderful,' I reply, knowing that she struggles with social anxiety. And as she tells me what else she has done with her week, I let my mind wander a little.

I think about Ben bringing Kirsty coffee. There's nothing unusual about it – he often brings me and Kirsty coffee. The more unusual thing was the way they were looking at each other, and in front of a patient as well. It felt like an intimate moment between the two of them and I hope there is nothing to it. It would be very unprofessional.

Admit you're jealous. Kirsty is young and free and pretty, everything you are not.

And then I think about Sandy, who will come in with Mike next week. I have no idea what he looks like. In my head he is a faceless man, someone who is treating his wife unkindly, but he will probably be nice and charming, ordinary. I bring my attention back to Christina, who is talking about ideas for fundraising.

At the end of the day, I'm grateful to get away a few minutes early to pick Iggy up from after-school care. The sun is setting and the wind chilly when I get to the school.

I peek into the classroom where the after-school care group is and see my son sitting alone in a corner, something that's unusual for him. Iggy is always surrounded by friends.

Opening the door, I call, 'Iggy,' and he turns and sees me. He's been crying and my heart instantly thrums with alarm.

'What's wrong?' I ask as he barrels into me, clutching my

legs tightly. He doesn't reply, just buries his head as the teacher in charge comes towards us.

'Could I have a quick word?' she says, taking off her glasses and letting them hang from the chain around her neck.

I crouch down and hold my son by his shoulders. 'Let me talk to Mrs McDougall quickly, love. Go and get your stuff. We can get pizza for dinner tonight.'

The promised treat brings a smile to Iggy's face and he darts off to pack up his bag and get his coat.

'What happened?' I ask the teacher when I am standing away from the other children. 'He's been crying.'

'Yes, yes, but his tears are perhaps because I had to have a few words with him about his behaviour.'

'What?' I am instantly furious. Iggy is very well behaved and whatever he may have done, there was no reason for this teacher to make him cry.

'He called Abigail "stinky breath", and he got everyone else in the class to call her the same thing. I had to ask her mother to come and get her early because she was so distressed.'

My fury disappears and humiliation appears in its place. 'Oh... I'm sure he didn't mean... I would never accept...'

Mrs McDougall stares at me as I try to find the right words. She knows I'm a therapist and I can feel her questioning my abilities in my chosen profession and as a mother. The school has a zero tolerance policy for bullies, not something I enjoyed while I was at school being tormented by the pretty girls and the popular boys who called me 'Llama Lana' and 'Lame Lana' and 'Lumpy Lana', and as we all got older 'Loathsome Lana'.

'I'm sure it won't happen again,' she says, rescuing me from having to say anything else.

'Please tell the little girl's mother that I'm sorry and I will definitely be talking to him about this and it is unacceptable,' I tell her as I finally find my voice.

'Mum,' says Iggy and I turn and leave, not taking his hand and forcing him to follow me to the car.

Once he's buckled in, I get in and then turn around to look at my child. 'Why would you have said such a terrible thing about that little girl?' I ask, my voice rising. 'That was a terrible, awful thing to do and I never want to hear of you doing anything like that again, do you understand me?' I am yelling now and I bite down on my lip to stop myself.

'I...' His eyes fill with tears. 'I... Her breath was stinky and...' He shrugs as tears fall. 'Sorry, Mum. I'm sorry and I said sorry to Abigail, I did say sorry.'

He sniffs and I root through my bag, handing him a tissue. 'It's okay, it's okay,' I tell him, my anger at my child disappearing. My yelling isn't about him and what he did, and I don't need to be a therapist to know that. My school years just came hurtling back to torment me.

'But Iggy, that was not a nice thing to say and you made her very sad.' I soften my tone and he nods.

'I won't ever say it again.'

'I know you won't because we don't hurt people's feelings, do we? That's not nice.'

Iggy nods his head vigorously. 'We don't say nasty things that we wouldn't want people to say to us,' he says, echoing what I have told him many times.

I turn around and start the car.

'Can we still have pizza?' he asks in a small voice, and I feel like someone has punched me. Neither Oliver nor I yell at Iggy. It's never really been necessary. He must be confused by my over-the-top response.

'Yes, we can,' I tell him and I start driving.

I know that I will need to discuss what just happened with SueEllen. It was not a normal reaction, obviously.

The older I get, the more distant school seems until something like this happens or until a client like Sandy, cloaked in beauty, walks into my office and suddenly I am the overweight teenager with a single friend who was bullied as badly as I was, actually worse than I was, much worse. I try to push away thoughts of Janine, my one school friend, short with red hair and freckles and terrible skin but a very kind heart. I feel like she could be sitting right next to me in the car.

I don't want to think about her, about how she called me one night and needed to speak to me but I wasn't in the mood and told my mother to tell her I was busy. If we were teenagers now, she would just message me and I would be able to respond with an emoji or a single sentence. If we were teenagers now, she would be able to find a Reddit forum and discuss her problems. But this was before smartphones and I didn't feel like a conversation. I have regretted that decision for twenty years now.

I still have a long way to go to put my teen years behind me.

I think about Sandy telling me that she could talk to me all day. I certainly couldn't imagine that, and I would never think of approaching a woman like her for friendship. But now that I am tasked with helping her and guiding her, I worry that my own issues may be preventing me from doing the best job.

'Rubbish,' I say aloud.

'What, Mum?' asks Iggy.

'Nothing, sweetheart, nothing.'

A terrible thought occurs to me as I make my way to our local pizza place. Maybe it's not Sandy who can't be trusted. Maybe it's me. What if I can't trust myself and the way I'm dealing with her because of my own personal history?

I need to find a way to bring my best self to my sessions with Sandy, regardless of what I think or know about her.

With that thought in my head, I park and get my son out of the car, grabbing him in a quick tight hug before we go and order pizza.

'I love you, baby,' I tell him.

He wriggles in my arms. 'Yes, Mum, I know, I'm hungry, put me down.'

A happy little boy bounces into the pizza store. I need to borrow some of that and make sure I'm bringing my best self to work when I next see Sandy. I do want to help the woman, after all.

Of course you do, I reassure myself, *of course you do.*

SIX

Sandy

Today is the next step of the plan and it's all going so well. Ben telling me that he could no longer treat me was a bit of a spanner in the works but I've adjusted.

It took more effort than I would have thought to get 'the husband' to agree. But I managed it in the end.

I waited until the children were in bed and definitely asleep. He likes to do the bedtime routine, to play the 'good dad'. He reads a story to Lila first, lies next to her on her bed with the princess pink duvet cover and reads about fairies and creatures who live in a magical tree. I enjoyed creating my daughter's bedroom. I made her the kind of space that I wished for growing up, when I had a room with a bed and a chair, a desk and a bookcase filled with books that I never had any interest in reading. Sometimes, when the children are at school, I go into that bedroom and lie down on the bed and imagine a different childhood for myself, one with glamorous wealthy parents whose only desire was for me to shine brightly and look beautiful. I know it's fashionable to blame your childhood for the person you are but I think that I am who I was always going to be. My mother, Maureen, with her sensible short hair and a chunky body, was never quite able to believe I had come from her.

'People used to stop me in the streets,' she has told me, 'just to say what a beautiful baby I had.' They never said that about my older sister and that's because she looks exactly like my mother. And she has grown into the same kind of woman, lumpy and practical. She's a librarian in a small country town, and when I see her, I can't help looking at the rough skin on her hands or getting irritated by the fact that she doesn't wear any make-up. She has two children with her husband, who's a farmer, and I don't think I've exchanged more than a perfunctory greeting with her for years.

I think my mother would have preferred it if my beauty had diminished as I got older, rather than blossomed.

I know she felt that if she could keep me on the straight and narrow, direct my interests towards working hard and doing good, then I would become a worthy human being despite my looks. Beauty seemed to be inherently problematic to my parents, as though it was an indication of something lacking in the person, something that took away from who they could be rather than something that added to a life.

My father had his own brand of keeping me on track to becoming a good person. But there was no way either of them could change the path I was on. Only I could do that with a stupid infatuation. They were delighted when I got married and then had two children because they thought I had finally settled into an acceptable life. 'You'll never love anything the way you love your children,' my mother told me when I was pregnant with Felix and I wanted to believe her but I knew it wasn't the truth. Children require sacrifice, demand you give them everything you have and everything you are, and I was never cut out for that.

But I'll make sure things are put right now.

In preparation for the conversation about him visiting the therapist with me, I poured myself a third glass of wine and waited for him to be done with story time, scrolling my phone, admiring a green silk dress priced at over a thousand dollars, thinking about how much better it would look on me than it did on the model. I heard him move to Felix's room, where he reads to the child about wizards. My son's room is all in blue with wooden boat decals bobbing on pale blue walls. When I knew story time was over, I poured a large whisky for him.

He was somewhat surprised when he came downstairs but happy enough for the drink, and I was just buzzed enough on the wine to know exactly how to get him to do what I wanted him to do. I need him to come with me to meet Lana. I need the therapist to see exactly what I'm dealing with.

I started by explaining that we were dysfunctional, damaged, and that we were damaging our children. He is attached to the children. I care for the children's physical needs because that's what I have to do. But I won't have to do it for much longer. Everything is falling into place. I have the cookie jar and I have Lana, who is desperate to help me.

I can see a future where I am not here, tied to this stagnant pond of a life.

'We need to go to therapy together,' I told him.

'I don't need therapy. I have enough shit to deal with. I told you that the factory is closing down. I know it's going to happen and I'm going to need to look for a new job. I need some support, not you attacking me all the time. And maybe you could start thinking about cutting back on your spending and getting a job.' He has said this before, many times, but I just ignore him when he mentions the idea of me working. That's not going to happen.

I didn't like hearing his refusal to go to therapy with me and I wanted to yell at him for trapping me, for making me ordinary, for giving me this tiny life with nothing to hope for. But shouting at Mike is not as effective as belittling him so I drank down my glass of wine instead and took another approach to get him to do what I wanted him to do.

'It's not my fault your company is failing. You're probably a shitty salesman,' I said and he lunged towards me, his hand up and ready to strike, and I thought of how perfect it would be to turn up with a real bruise. How much would it hurt? How much damage could he actually do and would he? It felt like the possibility of him unleashing his anger on me was getting closer every day. I could see a time when the gaslighting would not be enough for him, when he would need to take it further.

'Go on,' I said softly. 'I know you want to.' And then I offered him a sad little smile. 'And that's why you need to come with me, Mike. Because you want to hit me, you really, really do.' It was exciting to watch him wilt, to drop his hand and hang his head. And I knew that I had him exactly where I wanted him.

He doesn't like being reminded that he is a failure, not when he once thought success was within his reach. I don't know how he gets up every day and leaves the house, knowing that he is achieving nothing, absolutely nothing. But I also don't care as long as the money keeps coming in. It's disturbing to realise that money may not be coming in. But that is why I have the plan.

'If you care about our children, you will come with me,' I told him, making sure that he could see how upset I was, tears appearing on cue. I was gratified to watch him pour himself another whisky, throw it back and then pour another. I like to watch him lose control. I like the idea that others think he loses control even more.

'I'm not coming, leave it,' he told me.

'I found your little insurance policy,' I said, and I watched how he carefully arranged his face.

'My policy?'

'Yes. You took it out on me. I don't earn any money. Why would you need it?' My tears had dried up quickly because I could see he wasn't paying attention to them.

'We both agreed to those policies, Sandy. There's one on you and one on me. We agreed to them, remember?'

He looked confused and I could see him questioning himself. He was wondering if we actually did agree to them. We had such a brief conversation over them and he signed what I told him to sign because I'm the one who deals with all the finances. He poured another whisky, spilling a few drops because the alcohol was taking effect.

'I would never have agreed to that,' I told him, speaking slowly as though he lacked the ability to understand me. 'Why are you making things up, Mike?'

'You're the one making shit up. This is what you do.' He lifted the glass, drained the drink in one swallow and poured himself a refill. He was close to passing out so I knew I needed to get him to agree quickly.

'My therapist thinks you might hurt me,' I said. And that was the truth because she does think that and I believe that as well. The easiest way to maintain a lie is to sprinkle in some truth. I grew up in a house where my mother was hurt and I'm not going to wait for that to happen to me. I can feel him on the edge of doing something all the time and I won't be that woman. I have my plan and I will not be forced to turn into my mother.

I never said this to him, and I never would. I just needed him to agree to seeing Lana.

'Why would she think that? That's ridiculous.' His face paled and he slumped down onto the dark blue sofa, a colour I don't love but one that at least hides the messy stains that come with children.

'Is it, Mike? Is it?' I watched him rub his face.

'Did you hear what I said about work?' he asked, his words

slurring. 'Paul fired two of the office staff today. He's worried about making rent,' he said, referring to his boss. When we met, he told me it would not be long until the old man retired and sold him the company. That has never come to pass, and instead of fighting it, he has lazily accepted it, and that makes me so angry – angry for myself and what I imagined would be my life.

'You don't care about our marriage,' I whispered as I sat down on a grubby armchair, one that I would love to get reupholstered. My wine bottle was finished and I didn't want to open another one just yet. I knew it was time for a retreat, to back off and let him think I was terribly sad, defeated. And dropping my head in my hands, I sat in silence for a minute, letting him watch me.

He didn't get up from the sofa and come over to comfort me. There was a time when he would have done so but he was woozy with whisky and exhausted from his day. I could see that but I needed him to come with me.

'Please, Mike,' I begged, looking up at him again. 'Please.'

He was quiet for another minute, his gaze moving around our living room, landing on the collection of pictures on a glass and metal console. Our wedding picture is there and we are a beautiful couple: young, perfect, filled with something like hope. I wasn't showing yet and the lace sheath I chose clung to my curves perfectly.

'We were happy once, weren't we?' I said softly and he sighed.

'I'll come if it means you will give me a break, a small goddamn break from all your shit.' He can be so unkind, so detached. Once, he would have taken me in his arms; once, he would have told me it would all be okay. Once, he promised me the world.

'Thank you,' I said, knowing that this was the best way to end the conversation. His eyes were already closing when I left the room.

He often falls asleep on the sofa, which suits me because it means I have our marriage bed to myself.

This morning, I didn't remind him about the appointment. I wanted to see if he remembered.

He took the kids to school without saying anything and then he came back.

'I told Paul I won't be in until lunch. I think I should take my own car to this appointment. Can you text me the address?'

'I think we should go together.'

'No, I need to get back to work afterwards. Things are getting really tough at the office and I need to be there.'

I waved my hand at him, not wanting to hear any of that.

'Please, let's drive in together. We need to talk about what we want to achieve with therapy.'

He sat down at our small kitchen table, picked up half a piece of toast that Felix had left and chewed his way through it, disgusting me.

'Whatever you want, Sandy,' he said and I smiled. That's exactly what I needed to hear.

'I'll get dressed,' I told him.

And now we are on our way through early-morning traffic and I find myself excited and worried at the same time. What will happen in the appointment, and more importantly, who will Lana believe? There are three sides to every story: his, mine and the truth. I need Lana to believe that my story is reality, mine is the one she can trust. That's what I need.

SEVEN

Lana

'Thank you for coming in, Mike,' I say as the man shuffles uncomfortably on my sofa. He doesn't want to be here at all, and I wonder how Sandy got him to come, what she said to make him turn up here.

Her husband is tall, blond and square, like a well-muscled Ken doll. I cannot help the thought that they make a beautiful couple. I know they have two children and I imagine they are as lovely as their parents are. Whatever is going on in their house, I hope they are safe from it.

'No problem,' he says, clearing his throat. He wrings his hands together, forcing me to look at them. He is a lot bigger than his wife. He could do a lot of damage with those hands. But would he? Has he already?

'Did you come together?' I ask, choosing an innocuous question so that he relaxes a little. I'm not actually sure what the goal is here but I'm going to let Sandy lead the way.

'We did,' Sandy answers for him, 'and I told Mike that I'm

really hoping this can help us. I want us to be better at being married and being parents, being people.'

Mike shoots his wife a look. What was that – disbelief? Disdain?

Sandy is sitting on the opposite end of the small sofa, her fingers pale as she squeezes her hands together in her lap. She seems to be afraid of him, even sitting in this office with me, she is afraid of him. Or that's what she wants me to think.

He looks around, studying the picture of the ocean on the wall, and then his gaze flicks over to the window, where a bright winter sun shines.

We all sit in silence as I wait for one of them to say something but neither does so eventually, I say, 'Perhaps you can tell me why you agreed to come.'

'I want to help Sandy,' he says, folding his arms across his chest.

'And I think that Sandy would like to help you,' I say, and he looks at his wife.

'Why would I need any help?' He uncrosses his arms and shuffles some more on the sofa.

'Please, Mike,' says Sandy, her voice soft and cajoling, 'please try, for both of us.'

He takes a deep breath and it's easy to see that this has an effect on him. She is so soft and quiet that he cannot help but respond to her. There is a meekness about her in this moment.

'I'm not sure what you want me to say here,' says Mike, opening his arms wide.

'Perhaps you can tell me how you view your marriage,' I suggest.

'Well, it's... I mean it's not the greatest right now... We're not happy. I know that neither of us is happy. But we have young kids and I think... I want to make everyone happy and I work hard and I... Work is really a mess right now so I'm really stressed and...' He stops speaking.

'It's okay,' I tell him, leaning forward. 'Go on.' I have a feeling that we are getting somewhere and I risk a quick look at Sandy to see that she is also sitting forward.

There is something about him, something simmering underneath the surface. It's so strong I can almost feel it in the air. Barely concealed rage maybe? Or is it something else?

'We argue a lot,' he says, 'about stupid stuff mostly.' He doesn't look at his wife.

'And what happens when you argue, Mike?' I ask.

'Things get heated,' he says.

'Right.' I sit back. I doubted Sandy's decision to bring him here but she obviously knows her husband well. It seems possible that he may even admit to the abuse and that's what she wants. She needs him to admit to it. And if he does, she wants to move forward as a couple. At least that's what I believe Sandy wants. I look at her, gauging her reaction to his statement. Her eyes are wide, her shoulders tensed. Is she afraid, right here, right now? Her mouth twitches slightly and I reassess. Is she happy? Triumphant at his confession that things get heated?

'I know that Sandy gets frustrated. I get that it's hard with two young kids and...'

'Go on, Mike,' says Sandy, encouraging him. 'Tell Lana what happens when things get heated.'

He turns to look at his wife, who nods. 'There's nothing more to tell.' Mike scratches at his jaw. He looks around the room again, conveying his disinterest in continuing the conversation. I wait a minute to see if he will say anything else but he doesn't.

I can see that we've hit a brick wall. Sandy sits back against the sofa and looks at the painting and I watch her blink quickly, keeping away tears. I can see her hopes of some kind of confession or acknowledgement of his behaviour dissipate.

I wonder why he has come and what he hopes to achieve

out of this appointment, if anything at all. From my point of view, I want to know what is really going on, if I have any right to doubt Sandy.

The silence in the room grows. I try again.

'I want you to know, Mike, that this is a safe place,' I tell him. 'I can help but, as with all problems, you can't get help unless you acknowledge what's really happening.'

'I've told Lana everything,' says Sandy. 'I told her that I still love you and I want to be able to work it out with you. I want to try and make our marriage better. I think we can both be better, for us and for the kids.'

'You've told her everything?' asks Mike, and I watch his fists clench. I am glad that Ben is here today and that he's just next door with one of his own patients. I wouldn't know what to do if this got out of hand. I have no doubt that this man could hurt both Sandy and me without even breaking a sweat. But would he? Is he capable of it – not physically because he obviously is, but mentally? Is this a possibly violent, abusive man sitting in front of me or a confused husband?

'Everything,' Sandy confirms.

'And can you help her?' Mike asks. 'I mean, can you help her get her anger under control?'

'Her anger?' I ask, confused.

'I'm not the one who needs to control my anger, Mike,' says Sandy as she shreds a tissue in her hands. 'You know what happens when we argue, how you go from zero to a hundred in a minute and then you...'

'Then I what?' says Mike as he sits forward, planting his legs wide apart.

'You know what,' says Sandy and then she gestures towards her eye.

'What the hell are you talking about?' he asks, his voice rising, and I can feel his frustration with his wife.

'My black eye,' says Sandy, her voice filled with defiance. 'I told her about my black eye; well, I mean she saw that, didn't you, Lana?' She sits back and I can see that her body is trembling as though it has taken a great deal to say these things out loud. I doubted that black eye but was I right to? Maybe the make-up on the tissue was just her trying to cover the black eye?

If it was real, was that the first time? Is it ongoing? Do I need to get the police involved here?

Mike looks bewildered. 'You never had a black eye – what the hell are you talking about?'

'Lana saw it, Mike, she saw it.'

It becomes clear to me now that Sandy has been waiting to confront her husband because she needed someone else to hear this information when she did it, knowing that he would not attack her in front of someone else because abusers rarely do, especially ones who deny the abuse. I look at Mike, whose whole body is tense, and I wonder how quickly Ben could get in here if things went awry.

But am I only seeing what Sandy wants me to see? My thoughts are giving me whiplash.

He shakes his head. 'Look, I don't know what you've told Lana, but I'm not the one who lashes out.'

'Liar,' says Sandy quietly.

'You're the liar,' he replies, his voice rising.

There are always three sides to every story. Everyone knows that. I have always prided myself in being able to ascertain, fairly quickly, who is closer to the truth when I undertake marriage counselling. I have never had a situation where I am as unsure as I am now as to who to believe.

'Okay, I feel that this is not the best way to move forward,' I tell them both, hoping that the tension I can feel smouldering in the air can be tamped down. I cannot have this session get out of control.

Mike looks from Sandy to me and back again. He won't do anything in here, surely? I can see that he's getting angry. He jiggles one leg and cracks his knuckles. But I also sense a lot of confusion from him.

I watch him take a deliberate breath and I can almost see him counting in his head. 'What exactly has Sandy told you?' he asks me.

'I told her that when you get really angry, you hurt me,' whispers Sandy, looking down at her lap, where she has started on a fresh tissue, moving it from hand to hand and tearing off small bits. 'I told her that you black out when you drink and that's when you hurt me.' Sandy has not told me this. She has told me about the drinking and the gaslighting and she has also told me she got the black eye when she walked into a door. The explanation didn't make sense but I get it now. She feels safe enough, with me here, to say what she needs to say. But he seems puzzled as well as angry. Even if he blacks out and hurts her, he must have seen the results of his violence. It cannot be that she has never said anything at all about his behaviour to him until now. She's talking as though this is something they both know. Is his puzzlement all an act? Are her accusations of abuse a lie? I hate that I am still not completely sure who is telling the truth.

He raises his hands and runs them through his neat blond hair and then he closes his eyes. I wait again in silence for him to say something. Finally, he looks at me and says very slowly, 'That's a lie. Everything she says is a lie.' His tone is even, as though he is simply stating a fact.

I find myself questioning everything I know about this situation again. Who should I believe?

'You're the one who makes things physical,' he says as he looks at me although he is obviously talking to Sandy.

'Oh, Mike,' says Sandy, shaking her head as more tears appear. 'If you can't even admit you have a problem, how are we ever going to make things better? I don't want to go to the police. I really don't want to. I don't want to get divorced either but you have to admit...' Her face pales. 'You have to admit what you do in order for anything to change, isn't that right, Lana?' she says, raising her head and looking at me, and I nod. I am gifted one of her glorious smiles for agreeing with her and I realise that I am being manipulated here. I am supposed to be neutral.

Mike shoots out of his seat and I feel myself rearing back as my heart rate speeds up. He comes towards me, waving his clenched fist in my face. 'How stupid are you to fall for this crap?' he says. 'She's the one who gets physical.'

I push myself further away from him and he drops his fist, mutters, 'Shit,' and goes to the door. 'I knew this was bullshit,' he says and he opens the office door, slamming it behind him as he leaves.

And Sandy bursts into tears. 'Do you see?' she wails. 'Do you see what I'm dealing with?'

I wait while she sobs, giving her time to get a hold of herself – and if I'm honest, for me to get a hold of myself, too. I saw that surge of anger. Is that what happens? Does she goad him into hurting her? It's not something we are ever supposed to consider but it can happen. In relationships where domestic violence is part of things, one partner sometimes does push the other into violence. Most of the time, it's the woman pushing the man because at least, once he has hit her, she gets some relief from the cycle of abuse. She gets to have him move into the apologetic phase. And that appears to be what I have seen today but I also watched Sandy push her husband, watched his incomprehension at her accusations. He didn't say that she forces him to hurt her, that it's her fault. He just denied it was happening and instead called her the aggressor.

Finally, she stops, blows her nose and then sits back and takes a deep breath. 'I had such hope,' she says.

I'm not sure what to say to her. Her husband has accused

her of being the one to lash out physically but everything about him seems to indicate that he is the one who hurts her. Whatever the truth is, these two people cannot be together until things are sorted out, especially not tonight after what just happened.

'I think you should find a safe place to be tonight,' I say. 'He does seem really angry. Maybe get the children from school and go somewhere else, give him time to cool off. There are places I can call... people who will help...'

'No... no, it's fine,' she replies, shaking her head vehemently. 'You don't need to worry about me. I know him and I know he's going to be upset about walking out. He'll probably be really... nice for a few days.'

'But maybe some more time apart would be good for him. It will give him time to think. I can get Kirsty to organise somewhere for you to stay tonight with the kids. I can speak to the police with you. I promise you that I can help you get free of this man.'

'And I'm telling you, Lana...' she begins, her demeanour changing quickly. I see the shutting down in her eyes again, the quick change in her personality when she wants to end a discussion. 'I know my husband and I'll be fine. You don't want to be someone who pushes a patient into doing something she doesn't want to, do you?'

'Of course not,' I reply, feeling like I'm being accused of something. 'But I want you to be safe. You will be safer away from him.'

'No,' she says firmly. 'No,' she repeats, returning to the tissue in her hand. 'It's fine for you to tell me what to do, Lana, but you don't know everything about my life and my marriage. You don't even know everything about him. He's a good man, a good provider. He loves the kids and I'm not willing to blow up eight years of marriage because he's struggling right now.'

'I understand but you shouldn't be afraid of your partner.

You know that.' It's difficult to keep myself from getting exasperated. I'm not sure what Sandy hoped to achieve here, but I remind myself that domestic abuse – emotional or physical – is complex and Sandy has been with this man for a long time. Unravelling how she got here and why she stays will take many hours of work. I cannot push her to make any decisions until she is strong enough but I would like her to put some distance between herself and Mike tonight.

'Just for tonight, take some space and time,' I try.

'You don't' – she turns to stare at the door to my office as though she is contemplating leaving – 'you don't get it. He had a hard childhood. His parents, particularly his father,' she says, 'was brutal.'

'We all carry baggage but it's not an excuse to hurt someone.'

'He once told me a story about his father teaching him to swim or not teaching him, just throwing him into the pool and waiting for him to surface. I mean I've heard of people doing that before but Mike never surfaced; he sank like a stone every single time. He was only four years old and he almost died. He used to hide whenever his father told him it was time for a lesson. Isn't that terrible? I mean can you imagine?'

It does sound awful. My mind flashes back on Iggy's first swimming lesson, both Oliver and me in attendance with our phones ready to snap pictures and a sweet teacher who turned the whole thing into a game and rewarded him with a small chocolate afterwards.

'It's still not an excuse, Sandy. He can get help for his past trauma. He can heal and be better but you can't *make* him do that. Your priority is yourself and your children.'

'The kids love him. I can't take them away from their dad. I shouldn't have ambushed him in the session. I should have told him what we were going to discuss. I don't blame him for the way he feels.' She looks directly at me, a desperate appeal on her face.

I take some time to think through my reply. If her husband is hurting her, she needs to get away from him. Even if she is the violent one as he has suggested, she still needs to get away from him. He is so much bigger and stronger than she is and I don't want to think about what could happen if an argument between the two of them got out of control. 'Sandy, when a person is in a domestic abuse situation, they need to find a way to leave to keep themselves safe. Your children need to be safe. There are, as I've told you, so many resources, so many people who can help. I can go with you to the police right now to report him. You will be supported all the way.'

I've never laid it out as clearly for her before. And part of me is hoping that she agrees to go to the police so that I can be certain that she is the one telling the truth. She wouldn't take the chance of getting them involved if she was lying. At least, I don't think she would.

'No... no. And you should know, Lana' – she looks at me with defiance in her eyes – 'that if you go to the police, I'll deny anything is happening. They can't do anything unless I agree to press charges and I won't. Don't think I haven't looked into this, because I have.'

'I won't do anything you don't want me to do, Sandy.' I can almost feel her pulling my strings to get me to respond the way she wants me to, but I don't know how to stop it happening.

'I'll talk to him and it will be fine.' She sits back against the sofa and then she giggles. 'But if I don't turn up next week, you can assume he's killed me.' Her giggle turns into a full-throated laugh.

I stare at her, wondering why she would say such things and what kind of a reaction she is expecting from me. It's such a contrast to only a moment ago that I feel like my head is spinning.

'Oh my God, Lana, I'm joking obviously. I know how to handle him.'

'It doesn't seem like it,' I say quietly, shifting in my chair.

My phone buzzes to indicate the end of the session and I have to admit that I'm relieved. I'm exhausted.

'Okay then,' she says as she stands up. 'I'll be fine. You don't need to worry about me at all.'

I have another client in the waiting room and there's nothing more I can do now. 'Call me anytime,' I say, standing and going to my desk to grab a piece of paper that I write my mobile number onto. Not something I have ever had to do before, but I'm very concerned.

'Okay,' she says, 'I'll see you next week, Lana.'

She opens the office door and closes it behind her with a soft click.

I drop onto the sofa and then turn and lie down, stretching my legs out and resting my head on a plump blue pillow. I need a minute or two. None of my patients ever do this but the sofa is big enough in case they ever want to. A ping on my phone alerts me to a text message and I pull it out of my pocket.

I'm sorry I got upset with you. I know you're only trying to help. I'll be fine. Mike and I are fine. He's a good man.

I stare at the text. It doesn't sound like Sandy at all. It sounds like something you say when you're being told what to say. The see-saw of my belief between Mike and Sandy tips wildly back and forth.

I'm really not sure what I should do here, and if Ben didn't have such a complicated relationship with Sandy, I would go and ask him.

Instead, I email SueEllen.

Free for a catch up?

Sunning myself on a glorious beach in Greece right now. Back in two weeks. I'll tell Pete to schedule it in.

Thanks, enjoy. Lucky you xx

I can handle the situation for the next couple of weeks and then SueEllen will have some input.

Nothing is going to happen in two weeks.

EIGHT

Sandy

In the middle of the night, I open my eyes and he's standing next to the bed, staring down at me.

'What do you want?' I ask, keeping my voice low so he doesn't think he is scaring me. I know he wants me to feel scared. And under my warm duvet, my body is tense, real fear freezing my muscles. He wins.

'What the hell are you trying to... to do? What was that... about?' His words are slurred, his body swaying slightly.

The session with Lana is all I can think of. I know that's what he's talking about. I haven't spoken to him since he came home. I have stayed away. Because I'm not quite sure of what his reaction will be.

Have I made a mistake? Have I pushed this too far? Is it all going to work out the way I need it to? Or am I going to pay for exposing him?

'You need to go,' I tell him, conscious of his size, of the anger, marinated in alcohol, coming off his body.

'Just go,' I say firmly.

But he doesn't leave.

Instead, he leans down and places his hands on my neck.

And now I know the answer to my questions.

NINE

Lana

I arrive at the office at eight o'clock on Monday morning. Iggy went with Oliver and Becky to visit her parents last night and it seemed easier to let him sleep over since Becky is taking him to school this morning. I didn't sleep very well because I never really do when Iggy sleeps out, and when I opened my eyes at six thirty this morning, I decided I might as well use the time to catch up on case notes at work. When I walk into the office, Ben and Kirsty are standing at the desk, both looking at his phone.

'You have to tell the police,' I hear Kirsty say.

'What's up?' I ask and Ben turns to me.

'It's um... look, can we talk in your office?'

I nod my head and walk in, putting my laptop down on my desk and stowing my bag in a filing cabinet.

Ben sits down in a chair near my desk so I take a seat opposite him, growing concerned about how pale he looks.

'So, there's something I haven't told you,' he says and I feel my heart flutter a little at what he might say. He looks so serious and his eyes seem dull, as though he hasn't slept well.

'Okay. Is it to do with a patient?'

'Not exactly.' He shows me his phone.

*You don't get to abandon me and survive it. You just don't. I've
found your number now, and soon, I'll know where you work
and then I'll know where you live.*

'I don't understand, who is this from?'

Ben locks his phone and puts it down on my desk, turning it
upside down.

'Back in the UK, there was a patient, a woman. I was
treating her for depression and anxiety. She had recently gotten
divorced and she was struggling. And she fell for me, told me
she loved me and' – Ben waves his hand – 'the usual that we
get.'

'Right.' I nod, agreeing with him.

'When she told me, I gave her the information on transference and a list of other therapists and I told her that I couldn't
treat her anymore. I had zero interest in her, I want to say that
right now, it was all her and none of it was me. I gave her a list of
great therapists to contact.'

'Which was the right thing to do,' I say, sitting back and
crossing my arms. I don't like where this is going.

'Absolutely, and she seemed to accept it at first but then
things got very weird. She began turning up at my office every
morning, begging to be taken back. She told me she didn't love
me and she'd just made it up. Obviously, I still refused to treat
her and then she began turning up at my house at odd hours of
the night. I don't know how she got my address but she did.
She would ring the bell and wake me and demand to be
treated, in the middle of the night.' He shakes his head at this
absurd idea.

'I can imagine that was a very frightening experience,' I say
softly. I can see how disturbed he is by the memory and I'm

thankful something like that has never happened to me, especially since I am a single mother now.

'It was and eventually I had to call in the police. It's one of the reasons why I left the UK and came to Australia. That and the weather,' he says with a dry laugh.

'Oh Ben, I am so sorry, how awful for you.'

'It wasn't great... and now she seems to have found me.'

'Kirsty's right,' I say, 'you should report it to the police.'

'She's in the UK and I'm hoping it's just an idle threat.' He shrugs his shoulders, and I can see that while he is hoping that's the case, he's also worried that it might not be.

'But what if it's not? Please tell me you'll go to the police.'

Ben takes his glasses off, squeezes his nose and rubs his eyes. 'You're right. I'm being stupid.' His accent is stronger when he's distressed, the words more clipped and pronounced.

'It's absolutely the right thing to do and I know how awful this is for you. I would be terrified if someone turned up at my house.'

'Yeah,' he agrees, 'especially since you have Iggy.'

I bite down on my lip, feeling a shiver run through me at the idea of a patient coming to my house, seeing where I live, knowing I have a son.

'I will contact someone today. Anyway...' He stands. 'I'm sorry I didn't tell you sooner. I should have.'

'It's fine, Ben, it sounds like a horrible experience.'

'It was,' he says, standing by my office door, 'and it's part of why I really didn't want to send Sandy off to another therapist. I needed someone I could trust taking care of her so I wouldn't have to go through it again. I think if this woman, Carla, if she had found the right person, a new therapist, immediately, it would have been fine. But you can't always trust a patient to find someone else or to do the right thing for themselves.'

'I understand,' I tell him and I do. You can show a patient a path to take but you can never guarantee they will take the first step. I knew there was more to what he told me when he asked me to take on Sandy. And now that I know, I feel deeply for him. It would have been very traumatising.

'I'm here for you if you need to talk,' I tell Ben as he opens my office door.

'Thank you,' he says with a smile. 'Working here has been kind of a blessing really. It feels safe and the patients are interesting and I'm just really grateful you took a chance on me, so thank you.'

'No problem, Ben,' I reply with a smile and I am suddenly glad that I did take a chance on him. He needed someone to give him some help and it feels good that I got to do that. I'm so glad he confided in me since it explains a lot about the Sandy situation.

Looking at the time, I see I have twenty minutes until she gets here so I power up my laptop and put all other thoughts aside as I get some work done.

At 8.55 a.m., I close down my computer and sit in my chair with my notebook, ready to speak to Sandy. Kirsty usually lets me know when a patient is in the office so I know Sandy hasn't arrived yet but I'm sure she'll be here soon.

She is not here at 9 a.m. and I find myself staring at the clock on the wall in my office. Sandy's words haunt me with every minute that passes and she doesn't appear.

I'll be here next week unless he kills me. But she laughed after she said it, told me it was a joke, and then she sent me a text reassuring me everything was fine. *But that text didn't ring true.*

I should have reported it, both the statement and the text that I didn't quite believe. It's my duty as a therapist to talk to the police when someone is in immediate danger but all along, Sandy has asked me not to. And all along, especially after what her husband said last week, I have been unsure about the truth. I am still, even now, unsure about which of these two people, Sandy or Mike, is telling the truth.

Sandy is ten minutes late. Just caught in traffic, I try to reassure myself, but it's an average Monday and I have scrolled through the latest news on my phone. If there had been an accident big enough to cause traffic delays, it would have been reported. Perhaps she's not coming because she's afraid that I'll try and convince her to go to the police.

I shift in my chair, uncomfortable with that thought. I've been suspicious of her but I should have made her feel more supported. I should have told her that I was going to the police and she needed to come with me. I shouldn't have let her veiled threat get to me but should have seen it as what it was: a cry for help. I should have forced the issue but even as I think this, I know that doing that could have been a terrible mistake.

Sandy is now fifteen minutes late.

I take out my phone and call her number.

'Hey, it's Sandy. You know what to do at the beep.'

'Hi Sandy, this is Lana. You seem to be running late for our session. I just wanted to make sure everything was okay.'

When I end the call, I immediately regret making it. I've had plenty of patients not turn up for their sessions and it's only irritating because it wastes my time. There is always an explanation and they are charged for the missed hour anyway. But something about this feels off, wrong.

I get up and go to my desk, press down on the intercom.

'Yep,' answers Kirsty.

'Sandy didn't happen to contact you and you've forgotten?' I ask.

'Have I ever forgotten?' Kirsty replies and I can hear the edge in her voice. She thinks I'm questioning how she does her job.

'No,' I answer quickly, 'of course not, I'm just a little worried.'

'I promise if she calls, I will let you know immediately. I'm watching my email as well.'

Seventeen minutes late.

I leave my office, knock lightly on Ben's door. We have sliding signs on our office doors to let each other know when we're with a patient so I know he's alone, probably doing paperwork.

'Come in,' he calls.

'Hey, do you have a minute?'

'Sure.'

Ben is at his desk, his computer open, and sunlight streaming through the window behind his chair. He smiles when he sees me, running his hands through his hair. 'So many case notes,' he says ruefully.

'It does feel like more paperwork than anything else.' I shrug and then I sit down on his sofa, identical to mine except his plump pillow is grey instead of blue. I furnished both offices when I got the lease.

Ben hasn't added anything to his office and so the walls are bare, which I find quite jarring. Angela took her two paintings of vases of flowers with her when she left, along with the knick-knacks she kept on her desk, including a Newton's cradle and a whole lot of stress balls. Ben's desk is bare except for his computer and a notebook.

'Did you contact the police?' I ask and he nods.

Looking down at the notebook, he says, 'After a bit of a runaround, I spoke to Detective Sergeant Peterson, who deals with online stalking, which I think is what this falls under because she is in the UK.'

'And?'

'He told me there's not much they can do, but at least I've reported it.'

I bite down on my lip. Logically there is not much they can do to someone who is in a different country.

'Is that all you wanted to ask about?'

I shake my head. 'Look this is a bit hard but... Sandy didn't turn up for today's session and I'm...' I don't finish the sentence.

Ben sits back in his chair. 'Concerned?' he asks.

'Yes, and I wouldn't discuss this with you unless... I mean especially with what you're dealing with but I'm apprehensive that something may have happened.'

Ben swings his glasses around as he thinks. His face looks very different without them, as though he's naked.

'It's a cause for worry,' he agrees. 'I'm assuming she's told you everything...'

'Yes, but I am having trouble getting to the real truth of the situation, or at least I was. I find her a little...' I hesitate, 'unreliable.'

'Well, we're all unreliable narrators of our own lives,' says Ben.

'I know... I know that and I have been worrying that I am judging her a certain way when I shouldn't be, and then I met him last week, her husband, and he...' I shake my head. 'He turned things around on her, said she is the one who makes things physical. I mean he seemed to be telling the truth but then so did she and...'

Ben puts his glasses back on. 'That's one I haven't heard before. I mean it's amazing that you even got the guy to come in. But she actually never mentioned physical violence to me... She kind of skirted around it. I always suspected it but she never actually used the words.'

'But you saw the black eye – I mean the first time I met her she had a black eye and when I asked about it, she told me she walked into a door... not that I believed that.'

'Yeah, right, she told me' – Ben runs his hands along his

desk as he thinks – 'she told me that her son had a temper tantrum and threw a toy at her.'

I sit with the vastly different reasons Sandy has given us for a moment.

'That's disturbing.'

'Yeah, I agree with you,' says Ben. 'It's a sure sign that something very wrong is going on.'

'Well,' I say, 'I did advise her to take some time away from him. Things got pretty heated in our session and I told her to contact the police.'

'Probably not bad advice. I mean I don't like to tell patients what to do normally but when it's a question of personal safety...' Ben drums his fingers on the desk.

'Yes, that was my thought.'

'And now she hasn't turned up,' says Ben and I can hear some anguish in his voice. Do we both carry responsibility for this? Sandy was his patient. He's invested in this as much as I am. Any good therapist would be troubled.

'She's also not answering her phone,' I tell Ben.

'What do we do?' he says, standing up and going to the window.

'Can you use your mobile to call her? She has my number and she must know the office number, but if you didn't give her your phone number, she may answer. Perhaps she's angry with me for pushing her to report.'

Ben turns around and grabs his mobile from his desk, and I watch as he bends over and taps on his computer keyboard, pulling up Sandy's number from when she was his patient. He dials and we wait but I can hear the sound of the phone ringing and ringing before he shakes his head and ends the call.

'Maybe you should have left a message. Perhaps she would get back to you.'

'I don't think she would. She may be angry at you but she was really mad at me.' I can see how much this bothers him, and

in light of what he told me about his stalker, I completely understand and I'm feeling some guilt as well now. He entrusted me
with this patient and I may have screwed up. I can't let Ben take
responsibility for this. I was in the room with Sandy and Mike. I
advised her, possibly more than I should.

I look at my phone. Half the session I was supposed to have
with Sandy is now over, but if she turns up, I will still see her,
not something I would do for any other client. I have left Ben's
office door open so I can hear if Kirsty greets anyone at
reception.

'What would you do?' I ask.

He sits down in his chair again. 'Honestly, I don't know.
Maybe... Look, all you need to know is that she's okay. Maybe
give it until tomorrow and then if she still doesn't answer, try
and go to her house. I mean, if you do decide to go, I could come
with you because you shouldn't go alone. I know it's weirdly
unprofessional but if I was that concerned, I would go, just to
make sure she was okay.'

I can't imagine what Sandy would think if I turned up at
her house, but at the same time, what other choice do I have?

'Should I call the police maybe?'

'And then what?' Ben asks.

'They would do a welfare check and then I could relax
without having to get involved at all.'

'But that might inflame things,' he says, 'and she would
probably stop coming if you did call them and then there's the
matter of exactly how violent Mike is.'

'Well, at the session she brought him to, he seemed
almost... shocked at the idea that he hurt her. Which makes me
think he's even more dangerous than the usual abuser,' I tell
him. This has just occurred to me. What if Mike hurts his wife
but is able to mentally distance himself from his actions
completely? It means that he might be capable of anything.

But also, what if Mike is telling the truth and maybe the

session that he came to has made everything worse and Mike has simply... snapped?

I feel sick as these two possibilities tumble through my head. I have not been my best self in this situation. I have looked at Sandy, who is so beautiful, and allowed that to cloud my judgement because of my own insecurities. But I know that she is manipulative as well. I've seen evidence of that when she turns her tears on and off.

Ben's intercom buzzes and he answers, 'Yep.'

'Mr Surry is here,' says Kirsty, and I glance down at my phone. My session with Sandy is nearly over.

'Great, thanks,' Ben replies.

'I'll leave you to it,' I tell him, standing up.

'I wish I could help more, Lana, but I honestly don't know what the right move is.'

'Thanks anyway, I'll figure it out. I may give her until tomorrow.'

'I hope she gets in contact. Let me know if she does.'

I leave his office, walking past the waiting room, where I can see my next client, Violet, is already waiting for me. Violet is never late and I think she uses these sessions for company as opposed to anything else. Her daughter lives overseas and Violet is terrified of the idea of moving, as her daughter wants her to. I'm working with her to embrace the idea of changing her life at seventy but I understand her fears.

I try Sandy's phone one more time and then I open my office door to let Violet in.

The morning passes quickly with back-to-back patients and I try to put Sandy out of my mind so that I can concentrate on doing my best for my patients. At 2.30 p.m., as I finish a late lunch, Kirsty buzzes me and I feel my heart lift a little because surely this is Sandy to apologise for missing her appointment this morning.

'Damien called to say he can't make it today. He's got to go to an emergency dentist appointment.'

'Okay,' I say, thinking of my 3 p.m. client who is, it must be said, a frequent canceller. Damien has a problem with alcohol but because he covers it so well, he doesn't believe he has a problem. He is only seeing me because his wife makes him. It will take me some time to get through to him.

'And he was your last client for today,' Kirsty adds.

'Thanks,' I reply.

It's nearly 3 p.m. and Iggy is spending the afternoon at his friend Jack's house. I only have to pick him up at five thirty. I suddenly have some time spare.

Impulsively, I grab my bag. I need to know that Sandy is okay or I'll get no sleep tonight at all. Visiting her at home will be crossing a lot of lines but I need to do it, just to make sure. And I have to admit that I'm actually fascinated to see where she lives.

'Ooh, early mark,' says Kirsty when she sees me with my bag.

'Yes. Sandy didn't call, obviously?'

Kirsty shakes her head. 'No respect for other people's time. I'll bill her.' She smiles.

'Okay.' I wonder if I should tell her that I'm heading over to Sandy's house now. I immediately decide against it. It's not professional, and what I'm really hoping for is to be able to go to her house and see her without her seeing me. It feels a bit cloak and dagger but I need to know that she's all right.

I glance at Ben's office door and see that he's with someone so there's no way I can interrupt him and ask him to come with me. Maybe I should wait? Leaving via the stairs, I go back and forth with each flight, but finally, I decide that I'm doing this for myself and I don't need to involve anyone else.

And with each step I take, I try to convince myself that
Sandy is fine and that all I'm doing is making sure of that.

I'm just making sure.

TEN

Lana

When I drive out of the parking garage, the sky darkens, rain
threatening. Summer feels an eternity away.

I have keyed Sandy's address into my GPS and I should get
there in about half an hour.

Possible reasons for her missing the session circle in my
mind. Perhaps she and Mike have sorted everything out and he
has promised to go and get help for his violent outbursts. A very
unlikely scenario. It's not that I don't believe violent men have
some hope of changing, of redeeming themselves, but I do know
how much work it takes and that work begins with admitting
what you are doing. Mike is nowhere near close to that, especially if he is accusing her of being the violent one. Unless he's
telling the truth.

Perhaps she was just running really late and decided not to
come, although she should have called to cancel. She could have
a sick child and have forgotten. That's the one that makes the
most sense. I remember when Iggy was five, which is how old
Sandy's daughter Lila is. When they're sick at that age, they are

really unwell and then almost instantly better. Iggy had a bout of tonsilitis at five years old that sent his temperature soaring. It went so high that I called Oliver and told him he had to come and get us to take us to the hospital. I was exhausted from lack of sleep and didn't trust myself to drive.

After two doses of antibiotics, Iggy was his usual self and I felt like I might never recover. I'm sure that's what happened with Sandy.

When I pull up outside Sandy's house, it's started raining, making it hard to see. Checking her address again, I make sure I have the right number and then I wait in my car, watching the house. The home is typical of the older suburb with red bricks and white painted timber window frames. Red roof tiles look like they need to be repainted but the front garden is nicely done with a stone path and flower beds surrounded by wood palings. There aren't a lot of flowers but I'm sure there will be in the spring. I wonder if when she was at school, this is where she expected to end up, and then I chide myself for the unkind thought.

As I watch, a black Toyota pulls into the driveway and the driver's door opens. I slouch a little in my seat, certain that this is Sandy and not wanting her to see me.

But it's not Sandy who gets out of the car. It's Mike. He moves quickly, opening the back passenger doors and getting the children out of the car. I watch as the children – a little boy who looks exactly like Mike and a little girl who shares Sandy's delicate features – run for the front door.

The children are not with Sandy so that ends my sick child theory. So where is she?

Mike and the children disappear into the house, the door slamming hard enough for me to hear it across the road. At least none of them even glanced in my direction.

What now?

I can leave it or I can go to the police. What if nothing is wrong and Sandy is simply out? Reporting a patient missing because she didn't attend her therapy session will surely sound unhinged. I should go home and forget about this but I can't. I need to know that this woman is okay. I can't see another car anywhere but there is a single garage at the front so perhaps it's in there?

I sit in my car for another five minutes, debating what I should do as the rain gets heavier. When a small hailstone hits my car, I am tempted to drive away but something keeps me sitting there, and finally, I stop trying to reason myself out of action and open my car door, forgoing an umbrella and simply dashing through the rain to the front door of Sandy's house. On the covered front step, I take a deep breath and push down on the bell, listening as it chimes through the house.

No one comes and now the hail is really heavy. Perhaps he hasn't heard the bell?

I push the bell again, hating that I'm here and that I feel the need to do this. I should never have agreed to take on Sandy as a client. I've never really worried so much about a client like this before. My concern over her is taking up way more than my regulation fifteen minutes every day after work.

I've had a few patients who were in domestic violence situations before but those were emotional and financial abuse situations and I managed to help those women build up enough strength to leave their marriages or to confront their husbands. And I was also absolutely certain those patients were telling the truth. Most of my patients are people just struggling with being in the world and those around them. Someone in actual physical danger is not something I have dealt with, even during my training.

The door opens, startling me from my thoughts.

'Lana,' says Mike.

'Mike, I'm...' Now that he is standing in front of me, I realise how silly this is. I have no idea who this man is or what he may be capable of. I should have just sent the police. 'Sandy missed her appointment.'

'Do you know where she is?' he asks.

'I was going to ask...' I say, confused.

'I don't know where she is. She won't answer her phone. Do you know where she is?' he demands again.

Fear ripples through me. The man in front of me looks angry, and worried. Is it an act? Does he actually know where his wife is, and if so, what does that mean?

'I don't—' I start to say and there is a huge clap of thunder.

'Come in,' says Mike, grabbing my arm and pulling me inside before I can move away, slamming the door behind me. My heart rate speeds up at the aggressive contact. I catch my breath. What on earth have I gotten myself into?

ELEVEN

Mike

The minute he has touched the woman, Mike regrets it. As the thunder booms across the sky and the hailstones hit his house, he and Lana stand in silence. He can read naked fear on her face. He should not have grabbed her but he only wanted her in and out of the weather. An urge to smack his own head rises up inside him. Why does he do things like this?

'I don't...' she starts to say, clutching her black handbag tightly against her body as though it might be able to protect her.

'Daddy, Daddy,' shouts Lila, running towards him but stopping abruptly as soon as she sees Lana, her thumb automatically going into her mouth. She is carrying her teddy.

'Who are you?' she asks, removing her thumb from her mouth to ask the question.

'I'm a friend of your mother's,' says Lana, and Mike can hear, in her voice, that seeing Lila has disarmed her a little. She smiles and Mike knows that she's relieved a child is here because surely a man won't hurt her with a child here. The world is filled with messed-up people, Mike wants to tell her.

'Mummy's having a day off and me and Felix is not allowed to go because she needs a rest,' says Lila, parroting what he told them when he picked them up.

Lana looks from Lila to Mike, scepticism on her face. *Yeah, I can't believe it either*, he would like to say.

Only hours ago, his whole world imploded.

At ten this morning, what was left of the company he worked for was given the news that it was over. Paul, his boss and someone he considered a friend, hadn't given them any warning. He just called a staff meeting with everyone, including the factory staff, and told them that it was done.

'I've been trying to renegotiate the bank loan for a couple of weeks now,' he said, rubbing his eyes under his black-rimmed glasses so he didn't have to look at his staff, 'but they've told me that they can't let it go on. They want their money and they're calling in the auditors. I'm very sorry and I will use what I have left to pay all of you as much of your entitlements as I can. You can leave for the rest of the day, start getting your résumés in order. I will, of course, be giving you all excellent references. The factory will stop production immediately but the office staff need to stay for when the auditors come in.' He had nodded his head as he spoke and Mike had felt his grief but beneath that he knew there was something else. It was relief. Paul was tired of trying to hold his company together in a dying market. Rising interest rates, rising grocery prices, a world in chaos – it was amazing that they managed to hang in as long as they did against cheaper, quicker competition. Once, the mattresses the company made had been in high demand from all the best stores. But for the past six months, Mike knows that people have been avoiding his calls – the mattresses are not worth buying because their retail price has to be so high.

When he was finished speaking, Paul looked around at all

of them and then shrugged and turned and walked away. There was a moment of silence as the staff digested the news and then Paul's office door closed and they all began speaking at once. Jeremy, who was in charge of everything IT, immediately pulled up as many jobseeker apps as he could and began applying. The factory staff left quickly to go to the pub and Mike went to Paul's office and tried knocking on the door, wanting to offer some comfort, but Paul didn't answer. Mike could imagine him sitting behind his large desk asking himself exactly what it was all for. He had sacrificed family time for decades, worked as many hours as he could to build up a business and just like that – it was gone.

Mike had known it was coming, but he had hoped, really hoped, that it wouldn't happen. And his first thought had been about Sandy. She was going to be angry. He knew others in the office would be on their phones, speaking to their partners, gathering support and comfort, but he wouldn't dare phone Sandy. He would get no comfort from her. He would get anger and aggression, blame and hysteria. And he couldn't deal with it.

He had stared out of his small office window at the heavy grey sky and thought about when things were different, about meeting his wife for the first time.

Eight and a half years ago, he met Sandy at a sales seminar Paul sent him to. Sandy had just begun working in a department store and she was there with a few other young salespeople. Mike arrived late and took the first seat he could find, next to Sandy, only looking at her when the guy giving the talk told them to turn to the person sitting next to them and sum up their jobs in a few words that didn't include 'sales'.

'Making women beautiful,' said Sandy to him, and he grinned, suppressing the urge to tell the petite woman that she was beautiful, absolutely beautiful. His whole body wanted to touch her immediately.

'The best night's sleep,' he replied and she smiled, her perfect teeth and soft bronze lips making his heart flip.

'Can I take you for a drink?' he asked as the talk resumed.

Sandy smiled again and touched him lightly on his leg. It was that fast, that instant, for him at least. They got married six months later when they found out she was pregnant, and had Felix eight months after that. They should have dated longer, should have seen each other through good and bad, but they didn't and now they are here, where most discussions, regardless of how simple they are, degenerate into vicious arguments. He wanted a baby and she didn't. But it didn't take much to convince her that they would be amazing parents and that they would have an amazing life. Mike wanted a family where violence wasn't the way of life, and creating his own family seemed like a way to do that. At the time he told her that working in the mattress factory was a stepping stone, that he had ambitions to own the company one day and that Paul was likely to sell to him sooner rather than later. Things were good then and the world was a different place. Mike is a salesman and he used to be good at selling himself. All the things he promised Sandy, like a big house and an expensive car and trips overseas, have not eventuated. He knows she has buyer's remorse in the worst way but somehow, they are still together.

Things between them have been so tense since the appointment with the therapist. Although tense is probably an understatement. Something shimmers in the air between him and Sandy now, something... dangerous.

This morning, looking at his résumé, Mike knew that it was going to be difficult to get another job that paid him what he needed. He's only worked in two companies and both of them have gone bankrupt – both due to circumstances beyond Mike's control but any employer would have to question his sales ability. He had assumed that there was no way his day or, indeed, his life could get any worse.

Looking at the woman standing in his hallway, the whole debacle of an appointment comes rushing back to him. He thought that the appointment would be a neutral chat, just the three of them figuring out a plan to help Sandy feel better and to help the two of them do better at being married. Sandy had called them dysfunctional and he knew they were, but he also knew that a lot of their dysfunction came from her disappointment at how her life had turned out. He wasn't blameless but mostly, he only wanted a quiet life. In his mind, once he agreed to go despite really hating the idea, he hoped that he could find a way to address this in front of the therapist. He could never have imagined that Sandy would talk about the violence between them, about what happens when they argue and things get out of control. That was supposed to be a secret they both kept from the world. But after Sandy's accusations, his whole life feels like a lie because she lied.

He's not the one who hurts her.

The night after the appointment, he remembers getting as drunk as he possibly could and falling asleep on the sofa. And then, some time after midnight, he woke up and dragged himself to the bedroom, standing next to the bed and staring down at his wife.

'What do you want?' she asked him.

He doesn't remember much after that. Only that he woke up feeling like shit the next day. And things have only gotten worse from there.

They have barely spoken over the last week. It's been easier to avoid her so that an argument can't even begin. Two nights ago, he had walked into the bathroom, not knowing she was getting out of the shower, and she had been startled, jumping and wrapping the towel tightly around herself.

'Sorry,' he said.

'You're not sorry; you did that on purpose,' she snapped, grasping the peach-coloured towel closer to her body.

'I didn't – I was looking for...' Words failed him as he actu- ally forgot why he had come into the bathroom. They have been married for close to eight years but he can still remember when him walking into the bathroom when she was showering was a prelude to sex, when she couldn't stop touching him and he thought about her all day.

'You're pathetic,' she spat at him, disgust on her face, and he felt his fists clench. 'Go on, hit me,' she taunted and he had raised his hand but then deliberately lowered it.

'I don't know what's wrong with you,' he said, turning and leaving.

'What's wrong with you?' she shouted after him. She hates him. It's obvious she hates him. Does he hate her? Maybe.

The two of them are so toxic now, so bad for each other and for the kids. But he still went along to the appointment hoping that something, that anything could change.

In his office this morning, he had scrolled through job ads as phones began to ring – customers who had, somehow, already heard the news. He had given up on looking for a job quite quickly, knowing that he had a long road ahead of him. He knew Paul was obviously waiting for everyone to leave and he saw no point in waiting so he grabbed his suit jacket and decided on a few drinks in the pub before he went home to confront his wife with the news.

But at 2.30 p.m. his phone rang, and he answered when he saw it was a call from the kids' school.

'Mr Burkhart?' enquired a woman's voice.

'Yes.'

'This is Janet from the front office. Your wife hasn't picked the children up from school and she's not answering her phone.'

'What?'

'School ended for Felix and Lila at two today because we have some staff training. An email was sent along with text messages to all carers' phones.'

'I don't know anything about that.'

He never reads the messages from the school. That is Sandy's job. Her only job, despite how much they need the money that her working would add to their lives.

'I understand, sir, but the children need to be picked up.' The woman's voice was smooth and clipped and he could hear her judgement over the phone. She was calling him and Sandy shitty parents without calling them shitty parents.

Mike wanted to fling the phone across the bar. 'I'll call her and make sure she comes to get them,' he said and he hung up before the woman could say anything else and called his wife. Sandy didn't answer her phone.

He paid for his last beer and went to his car, calling Sandy over and again, leaving voice messages about the kids needing to be picked up.

'What the hell is wrong with you?' he yelled into the phone as he arrived at the school and it started to rain.

And now they are home and his wife has still not picked up.

'That looks like a lovely teddy,' says Lana, dragging him back to the here and now as thunder rumbles across the sky and the rain falls.

'Lila, your snack is in the kitchen. Can you go and eat it please?'

His daughter looks him up and down and he can see she senses that he wants her away from this conversation.

'Can I watch *Bluey* on my iPad?' she asks, knowing now is a good time to push for what she wants.

Mike sighs. 'Clear boundaries and rules,' Sandy likes to say but there are no rules for this situation.

'Yes, and tell Felix he can use his iPad as well.' Lila runs off shouting the joyous news to her brother. He had already said no to this in the car because the iPads are supposed to be for later when he needs them to calm down and get ready for bed. No wonder the kids don't listen to him.

'Come into the living room,' Mike says to Lana, but she remains at the front door.

'I think it would be best if I left.' Now that Lila is gone, she's jittery again. Mike hates the way she is looking at him.

'I'm not going to hurt you,' he says through gritted teeth. 'Just come into the living room and I can explain. My kids are here. What am I going to do to you with my kids here?'

Lana nods slowly and he turns and walks down the passage and into the living room, where he is momentarily embarrassed by the chaos of dirty plates and toys on the floor, a basket full of clean laundry on the coffee table and a heap of coloured blankets draped over a chair from where Felix was making a fort last night.

After mostly avoiding each other, he and Sandy really got into it yesterday. Things got ugly enough for her to storm upstairs and slam their bedroom door, leaving the chaos of the living room for him to sort out. He opened a couple of beers instead.

Usually, Sandy cleans up. She's home all day, and she likes things to be neat. He dropped the kids off this morning and she was here but she obviously left the house before tidying up. How long has she been gone?

'Sorry,' he says, waving his hand to indicate the mess, 'I've been at work, the company's gone bankrupt and it's been...' He stops speaking, aware that Lana is still hugging her handbag to her chest. He doesn't know why he has shared this information with the therapist. Sandy doesn't even know. Where the hell is Sandy? He needs to check the garage, see if her car's in there, but first he needs to deal with Lana.

'I shouldn't have come here, it's very... I was just worried about Sandy because she missed her appointment,' she says, speaking fast. 'I'll go and leave you.' She starts to walk towards the front door, and for the second time, he grabs her arm.

'Look,' he says urgently as she shakes him off, shocked at the contact. 'I don't know where she is. She didn't pick the kids up from school. They were supposed to be fetched early today and she didn't get them and she wouldn't answer her phone when the school called or when I called.'

Lana stares at him and Mike can see the woman's mind turning. 'I tried to call her as well.'

'She may be... taking some time for herself,' he says, the memory of the terrible argument they had yesterday making him feel slightly sick.

When the kids were babies, he and Sandy had an agreement that each of them got to sleep in one day of the weekend. On Saturday morning he got up and took the kids to the park because for once, it wasn't raining. It was cold and unpleasant and boring but he had consoled himself with the idea that he would get to sleep in on Sunday. But on Saturday night, Sandy went to meet some girlfriends for drinks and left him with the kids, coming home after 1 a.m. Mike had consumed a fair few beers himself so when Felix burst into their bedroom on Sunday morning, he simply turned over and ignored him, knowing it was Sandy's turn to get up.

But Sandy also ignored the kid and so Lila and Felix set themselves up in their bedroom, playing some nonsense Lego game, their voices loud and piercing until Mike roared at them to go downstairs. Sandy got up and stomped downstairs and Mike stayed in bed, wide awake. And then he got up and got dressed and left, staying away for the whole day. He only came home to change clothes and tell her he was meeting Ron for a drink. And that's when she exploded.

It was the first time they had really spoken since the therapist appointment and he would hardly call it a conversation.

The kids were, mercifully, upstairs. Sandy went nuts, throwing everything he had ever screwed up on throughout their entire relationship at him. And he replied in kind and then everything got crazy.

Mike knows, from looking at the therapist, that there is no way he will share any of this with her.

'Have you reported her missing to the police?' asks Lana, and Mike can hear her scepticism.

'Not yet. Don't you need someone to be missing for twenty-four hours before you do that?'

'Um... no, but I do know you have to do it in person.'

'Well, I can't do that now. I have to feed the kids and get them to sleep. I can't go now.' Mike folds his arms, wondering exactly what the therapist hoped to achieve by turning up here. It's a strange thing to do. Therapists don't make house calls. Maybe Sandy told her to come? Does she know something about where Sandy is?

'Have you heard from her at all since last week?' he tries, in case the therapist is lying to him.

'No... not at all. I can go and report her missing. I have to get my son but I can go afterwards.'

Mike had not expected this but then he hadn't expected his whole awful day. Why is she so keen to involve the police already?

'No,' he says. 'I'll do it tomorrow. We had... Things haven't been easy since our appointment with you. Maybe she just needed some time away.' He can imagine Sandy doing something like checking herself into a hotel for the night, ordering room service and leaving him to deal with everything. After last week, he can see that's probably exactly what she has done. He will check the banking app after the therapist leaves, after he checks to see if her car is here, and then he has to figure out dinner and... His mind whirls.

'Isn't there someone you can call to stay with the children? I think you should report it to the police tonight. She wouldn't leave her children.'

Mike looks at the woman and wonders exactly what kind of

a therapist she is. There's no way she has even the faintest clue who Sandy is, that much is obvious.

'She would,' says Mike softly. 'You think you know her but you don't.' He understands it, he really does. It's always the husband, isn't it? Anytime he has ever seen or read anything about a missing wife, his mind automatically blames the husband. Because it usually is the husband. Men are bigger, stronger, angrier. Men are the perpetrators of violence. And women are the victims. But not all men and not all women. Although how is this particular woman to know that? Sandy has had a good few weeks of talking to Lana to convince the woman that Mike is an abuser. And Sandy can be very convincing when she wants to be. But surely a therapist can see through obvious lies?

'What is that supposed to mean?' Lana asks and Mike wishes that he had stuck around at the appointment, maybe convinced this woman of the truth about his wife.

In the kitchen Lila shrieks and Felix shouts, 'No, Lila, that's bad.'

'Give me a second,' says Mike and he goes to the kitchen, where Lila has taken Felix's iPad and is trying to find *Bluey* on his screen. 'Mine is flat, Felix, it's flat.'

Irritation and anger mingle inside Mike. He needs to sort this out. He can see that Sandy's therapist thinks he did something to her and she can believe whatever she wants. He needs Sandy to come home so she can sort out the house and the kids and then they can talk about him losing his job. She's going to be beyond pissed and he just wants to get it over and done with.

'Right, both of you lose iPads now,' he yells, hating that he can't control his anger even with someone in the next room who thinks the problem is that he can't control his anger. But that's how it goes sometimes. It rises inside him, a tsunami of rage that he can do nothing about.

'But, Dad!' shrieks Felix.

'Go to your room,' bellows Mike, and Felix darts out of the kitchen, followed by his sister. He is the worst parent in the world. He groans and feels a sharp stabbing pain join the low-level tightness in his head.

In the living room Lana has her phone in her hand. 'I'm calling the police,' she says and Mike lunges forward and grabs the phone. 'Just wait,' he snaps. 'Let me explain.'

And now he can see she's not just scared but terrified. He has grabbed her phone and she's no longer close to the front door. Outside, the hailstones hit the house, clattering as they smash against windows and the roof, and it occurs to Mike that Lana could scream as loud as she liked and no one would hear her. If the kids are in their rooms with their doors closed, they wouldn't hear her either, and if they did, they would probably be too scared to come out. Right now, he could do anything he wanted to this woman.

'There's nothing to explain,' says Lana, her voice rising over the noise outside. 'Your wife is missing. The police need to know.' Her face is flushed and he can see her eyes darting from side to side, seeking out an escape.

Mike would like to roar his frustration but instead he takes a deep breath and hands her phone back to her, which she takes with two fingers, like he's made it dirty. 'Lana, you need to let me explain, and after I explain, if you think we should call the police or go to the police, we will, okay?'

He can see she wants to leave but she nods slowly, stepping back, the phone in her hand, where she taps the screen and then turns it to show him. 'All I need to do is hit the call button.'

'Do you want to sit down? Can I get you a drink?' he tries.

'No.' She steps back again, closer to the door of the living room. 'Just tell me what you have to say. I have to go and get my son, and if I'm late, everyone will worry. They know I would never be late. And I've told... I told the receptionist at the practice that I was coming here.'

He knows that's a lie. Therapists don't visit their patients at home. She wouldn't have wanted anyone to know.

Mike shakes his head. 'You think I hurt her right, that I hit her?' He locks eyes with Lana.

'I need to go and get my child.'

Mike knows he's going to get nowhere now. This woman is not going to believe a single thing he says.

Upstairs he hears Lila shout at Felix and he gives up.

'Fine,' he says, going to the door and opening it, letting rain blow into the entrance hall.

'I'm going to the police tomorrow if you don't,' says Lana.

'Before you do, you should know: I don't hurt her. It's actually the other way around.' He feels the heat of a blush on his face. He's a man but he doesn't feel much like a man right now. He feels like a boy. A scared stupid little boy. And he hates feeling like that because that's when he does things he knows he's going to regret.

TWELVE

Lana

As I stand in the entrance hall, the rain flying at me as the wind blows in, I have no idea how to respond to what Mike has said. He must be at least six feet tall, if not more, and he has broad shoulders. He looks like he works out and like he could lift his wife in a single hand. How stupid does he think I am?

'Before you laugh at me, let me explain.'

My instinct is to run, to get out of this house and go straight to the police, but there is something in the way he's looking at me that makes me stay. I step forward, allowing him to close the front door, relieved to be out of the cold and the rain. Is this a lie, and if it is, why? What kind of a person says something like this and thinks they will be believed? And if I stay and listen, will he tell me where his wife is?

I glance down at my phone and see that it's nearly 5 p.m. 'I have to fetch my son,' I tell him again. 'It's at least a half-an-hour drive, talk fast.' I lower the tone of my voice and try to sound calm, in control.

'I understand,' he says. 'But please, this is very important.

You need to understand about Sandy before you call the police. You need to know that I've never hurt her, not ever.'

I swallow. 'I have a few minutes.' I could ask Oliver to get Iggy, of course, or my mother but there's no way that I'm stupid enough to put myself in a position where no one is expecting me.

'Okay, okay.' He raises his hands. 'Just let me explain. He steps towards me and I instinctively step back, feeling the handle of the front door dig into my back. I push harder, move one hand behind me, so that I can open it fast. I will need to run. I think I will need to run.

'I know that she and I are not good together,' he says, pulling his phone out of his pocket. 'I don't know how much she's told you about her childhood but it wasn't the greatest. She's believed all her life that her mother was jealous of her looks and so they were never close. But she had some horrible experiences too.'

'Okay,' I say, unsure where this is leading.

'Like when her father was teaching her to swim, he refused to get her lessons, refused to let anyone else teach her. Instead, he would just throw her into the pool, just chuck her in, and every single time, she would sink like a stone. She was only four years old and each time, she panicked and sank and he left her there until she nearly died. She can't go anywhere near a pool or the ocean because she's terrified of dying.'

I can hear alarm bells ringing in my head at the repetition of exactly the same story that Sandy told me about him. Why is he making the story about her or did she make it about him? She was very reluctant to discuss her parents. So is he telling the truth?

'I didn't have the greatest childhood either. My dad... liked to hit, both me and my mother. What I'm saying is that both Sandy and I are damaged and I know, especially now, that we are not good together. But because of what my mother went through, what I went through, I would never hurt her.'

I don't know what to say to him. Does he think that I can believe him? His wife is missing and he's here.

'Look,' he tells me, opening his phone. 'I never wanted to... I hate that I have to do this but I'm going to show you some pictures, okay?'

I nod, glancing down at my phone. I only have a few more minutes.

He finds his photo gallery and flicks through his pictures until he finds what he wants. 'Look.' He turns the phone around and I see a picture of him with a gash on his forehead and what looks like a few stitches.

'She threw a mug at me and it hit me in the head. We were arguing about money and I told her that she needed to get a job but she really doesn't want to go back to work. We were standing in the kitchen and it was a Saturday morning and the kids were in the other room. They were watching television and we were talking... arguing. I said she needed to start contributing because both kids are in school and she chucked the mug at me. It had coffee in it and it burned my face a little but it also hit me on the temple and caused this gash.' He lifts his blond hair away from his forehead with his other hand and I see the raised scar, still red and healing.

I study the picture, where I can see that, in addition to the gash, one cheek is a bright, angry red. It looks painful and real but you can create anything on the internet these days. He could have gotten the gash anywhere at all.

'And here...' He flicks through the phone again and then shows me another picture. In this one his lip is swollen, crusted with dried blood on one side. 'We were arguing about money again because she wanted to go on vacation and I told her we couldn't afford it. It was a couple of months ago, in our bedroom and late at night. We were both in bed and she was reading a book, a hardback, and I said, "The answer is no, Sandy," and she swung the book at my face.'

'Can I see?' I ask, holding out my hand for his phone. It means I have to slide my own phone into the pocket of my pants and let go of the door handle. If he hands me the phone, I can blow up the picture, try to figure out if its real or not; if he hands me the phone, I will be more inclined to believe him. You don't hand over your phone to someone if you have something to hide.

We lock eyes and then he gives me the phone. Using my fingers, I blow up the picture but I still can't tell whether it's fake or not. He drops his gaze and pushes his hands into his pockets as I look down at his screen, quickly flipping through the last few pictures.

I expect to find pictures of his children but there are only pictures of mattresses, and then I stop on one that is not a picture but rather a screenshot of an email of a few lines.

We can't be together anymore. We both know that. I don't want one of us to get hurt. You need to grant me a divorce, Mike. You need to let me go.

I cannot help gasping and he looks up, grabs the phone away from me and looks at what I've seen.

'I've never seen that,' he says, gritting his teeth. 'I don't know how that got on my phone. I've never had a message from her like this.' His voice rises with panic as I stare at him and then he looks down at the screen again. 'That bitch,' he whispers.

I have no idea what to say to him. In my pants, my phone buzzes with the alarm I set so I would have enough time to get to Iggy.

My heart is racing and I struggle to take a deep breath. I don't know what to say, what I should say so that I can get out of here.

'You need to go,' he says quietly, 'and I understand you may not believe me. I mean, who would?' He shrugs his shoulders and offers me a sad smile. 'But Sandy is not the one being hurt here and I haven't told anyone because, well, to be honest, it's humiliating as hell. I love her... loved her... I mean it's complicated now but the truth is she has these rages and she comes at me and of course I can't hit her or fight back because if I did...' He leaves the words hanging in the air. If he did, he would easily kill her. 'I would never hurt her. She knows that. She relies on that. And that screenshot wasn't on my phone yesterday. I promise you it wasn't. She's a conniving liar and you need to know that's the truth.'

'Her eye...' I touch my face. 'When I first met her, she had a black eye.' If this man is telling the truth, I need to know, and if he is lying, I need to know that too because if I can determine that he's lying, I'm going to the police tonight. As quickly as it began, the hail outside stops and silence abruptly falls, the rain trickling down to a drizzle.

'I didn't do that. I never saw her with a black eye.'

I question the smudges of colour on the tissue again. It's exhausting to be doing this back and forth all the time. But that screenshot? What if it's true and she wants out and he won't let her go? Why take a screenshot of it?

'Dad, Dad, Lila took my Lego,' his son shouts from upstairs.

'I can't...' I shake my head. 'I need to go.'

'Okay, but you need to know that she disappeared because she wanted to. She must have wanted to. I'm sure she'll be... back.'

It doesn't seem like he is that worried about her, or that he wants her back. Maybe that's because he knows exactly where she is.

He says he loved her, what does that mean? Is he no longer in love with her or is she gone?

I turn around and struggle to open his front door. As I pull it open, I look down and a flash of red on the white wall catches my eye. I hold my breath, feel him behind me as I take a giant step out of the house and onto the front path, feeling myself sway and twist as I struggle to find my footing on the wet ground.

I take a deep breath of cold air. Under the now shining streetlights the quickly melting hailstones cover the grass in a crystal sheen. 'Lana,' he says but I don't stop to listen. Was that blood? It could have been blood.

Oh God, it could have been blood and that means everything he has said to me is a lie, a complete lie.

Without stopping, I dash across the road to my car, my keys in my hand. Once I am inside, the doors locked and my heart thudding in my ears, I glance over at the house. He is standing with the front door open, staring at me. His legs are wide apart and his arms folded over his chest. Does he know I saw it?

I pull off slowly, biting down on my lip. I try to calm myself down as I drive to get Iggy, taking deep breaths and repeating, *Nothing happened, nothing happened. Nothing happened to you, not to you.*

I want to go straight to the police but I have no idea what to say, how exactly to explain it, and I need to get my son. I need to be his mother now.

It takes me the whole drive to Jack's house to calm down, but once I am there, I am able to plaster a smile on my face for Marion, Jack's mother, and thank her for having my son for the afternoon.

'I was nice to Abigail today,' Iggy tells me after he's buckled himself into his seat. 'I didn't say anything mean.'

'I'm sure you didn't, sweetheart,' I answer him. He tells me every day that he has been nice, that he has been good, and I wonder how long it will go on for. I did some damage with my reaction to his bullying incident and I am worried about that. Or is it a good thing, that he's learned from the experience? I just don't know. Suddenly, I am questioning myself over everything. I can't trust myself and I hate feeling like that.

Right now, I'm more worried about Sandy and where she is, what has happened to her. I cannot help but go over my sessions with her. How would I have behaved if I did not have my own insecurities tapping me on the shoulder as I looked at her? I think I've messed this up, really messed this up, and now a woman may be hurt or... dead.

'Aren't we going to drive, Mum?' says Iggy and I realise I haven't even started my car.

'Sorry, love, of course we are. Tell me more about your day. What was your favourite class today?' I start the car and pull out into the street, where the heavy rain is taking a break right now.

'It was art because Mr Tate said that we could draw anything we liked and I drew a Transformer and he said it was good. And Jack's mum made chocolate chip pancakes as a snack – can you believe that, Mum, a snack? – and she said that I can come over whenever I want because I'm polite and said "please" and "thank you" just like you and Dad said I should. Do you like chocolate chip pancakes? I do. I wonder if Becky and Dad like them. Can I have them for breakfast on Saturday?'

'I'm sure you can,' I say as I pull into my driveway, where I am glad I have an internal entrance from the garage to the house as the rain ramps up again.

'Dinner will be ready soon,' I tell Iggy once we are in the kitchen and he has dropped his school bag on the floor. 'Do you have homework?'

'Mr Tate said that we have to do two pages of our reading books but me and Jack both read to his mum so it's all done.'

'That's good,' I say, thankful to Marion for taking care of homework even though I usually enjoy the time with Iggy.

'Can I play on my Switch?'

'Only until I call you for dinner, okay?'

'Okay, Mum.' He smiles and dashes out of the kitchen

I am relieved to have a moment of silence as I pull a bottle of red wine out of the cupboard and pour myself a glass before putting on a pot of water to boil for pasta. At least I thought to make Bolognese sauce yesterday so that we could eat it during the week.

While I wait, I sit on a stool at my small kitchen counter as I sip the heavy red wine. Is Mike telling the truth? I know that women are not the only people who experience domestic violence. It's much rarer for a man to be the one being hurt but not something that has never happened. But he is so much bigger than she is. One of them is lying and everyone's first instinct would be to believe her.

But you've been questioning her all along.

I open my phone, calling Ben.

'Hey, Lana.' I'm so pleased he answered, I feel my eyes grow hot with tears. It's been a long time since I was so scared, so panicked in a situation that could easily have gotten out of control.

'I went to Sandy's house.'

'What? You should not have done that without someone with you. I thought you were going to wait or call the police. Her husband is dangerous, Lana, you know that.' Ben has obviously made his decision on who is telling the truth. 'What if he gets angry with her because you turned up at the house—'

'She wasn't there,' I interrupt him. 'He says she didn't get the kids from school and she's not answering her phone. He said...' I take a deep sip of wine. 'He said that she's the one who hits him and he told me that she would actually leave her children and that I don't really know what she's like.'

Sandy has only ever expressed love and adoration for her children. She has admitted in sessions to yelling at them and I know she gets upset with herself when she does, but what mother doesn't yell?

Ben is quiet for so long, I take my phone away from my ear to see if he's hung up.

'Ben?'

'You didn't believe any of that, did you? I mean, look at the size of the guy. And I know she loves those kids. They're the only reason she hasn't left.'

'When did you meet Mike?'

'I didn't. She showed me a picture – a wedding picture if you can believe that. They were happy once but... you should not have gone there alone.'

'Yeah, well,' I say, taking another sip of my wine, 'I'm fine but I'm not sure where to go from here. What if he's telling the truth and she turns up in a day or two?'

'What if he's done something to her? You need to call the police.'

'But...'

'Lana, don't mess about with this. Call the police, report her missing and tell them your concerns. I have to go now, my mother's calling from the UK. I'll see you tomorrow.' He hangs up the phone abruptly. He's angry with me for doing something stupid but I'm angry with him for putting me in this position in the first place. I know what he thinks I should do, but I'm still not completely convinced. If Sandy does turn up and the police are involved, it may make things worse for her. This is such an odd toxic situation.

I try Sandy's mobile again but only get her voicemail. What do I do here?

The water for the pasta is boiling and the same thoughts keep going round and round in my head. I wish I had never taken Sandy on as a client and I am immediately guilty about this thought. I should be happy to help. That's my job.

But she says one thing and Mike says another and I know that the truth is obviously somewhere in between unless one of them is an outright liar. But which one?

THIRTEEN

Mike

He locks up the house, checking the back door and the front door twice as the rain ramps up and dies down. Out in the back garden, the scooters and bicycles are rusting in the rain but he can't be bothered squelching through the downpour to pick them up.

Near the front door, he glances anxiously up at the ceiling, noting that there is a bubble forming, meaning that there's a leak. 'Shit,' he mutters. Roof leaks can cost a fortune to fix. He grabs a bucket to put under the bubble in case it bursts and checks the front door again. He's already checked everything but he's anxious, and when his anxiety kicks in, he has to keep checking things, keep taking care of the things he can control.

And then he gets a rag out and some bleach and goes to wipe the red streak on the white wall by the front door. Lana saw it. He knows she did. And now he knows exactly what she must think.

'It's my blood,' he would like to tell her. But there's no way she would believe him because no one is going to believe him.

Three months ago, maybe more, he and Sandy had a fight late one Saturday night. He was drinking and she was drinking and when her bottle of wine was empty, she hissed, 'I hate you,' and lobbed it at him, hitting him in the face. His nose started bleeding and he turned and left, grabbing tissues and going out of the front door, knowing that he needed to give her an hour to fall asleep before things got even worse. He thought he had cleaned up all the blood but he obviously missed some that dried and stained and now Lana has seen it.

Add to that the screenshot on his phone of an email, an email that he never received. Did he? And why is the screenshot on his phone? When would Sandy have had access to his phone?

Last night, after their vicious argument, Sandy slept in their bedroom and he passed out on the sofa.

This morning, she kicked the sofa hard to wake him and said, 'You take the kids to school,' and he knew better than to argue. She left him in the kitchen with them and he heard the bedroom door slam and then the sound of water running through the pipes, meaning she was taking a shower. He hasn't heard from her since then.

He looks through his emails, trying to see if there's one from Sandy asking for a divorce, but there isn't one and he knew there wouldn't be. That's not the kind of email he would have missed. So how did she get the screenshot onto his phone? His code to unlock the phone is the kids' birthdays, which Sandy knows. He doesn't know how to unlock her phone, but he's never cared.

He picks up some dirty plates to take to the kitchen, wondering exactly how he got here.

He knows he's one of the few people in his friendship group from school who's married. The rest of them are still single, still playing the field and enjoying every minute of it.

All week, since the appointment with Lana, he has thought

about how to extricate himself from his marriage and his toxic wife. He imagined she was thinking exactly the same thing.

At some point during yesterday's argument he yelled, 'You don't want to be a better person, Sandy. If you did, you wouldn't have lied to your therapist like a psychopath.'

And she screamed back, 'You're the one who lied, Mike – you can't hide what you are anymore. The whole world is going to know just what a monster I have had to live with.'

They would have gone on throwing hate at each other but then Felix appeared. 'It's bath time,' he whispered, his little face pale and his blue eyes wide with fear.

'Fabulous, how fabulous. Why don't I take care of this like I do everything else? You drink yourself to sleep,' Sandy said, throwing up her hands, and she stormed upstairs.

And then today, Sandy disappears, just up and disappears, and he can't help wondering if it's for the best. It's a shame that the therapist is involved because Mike can see that the woman is unlikely to let things go.

Did he manage to plant even the smallest seed of doubt in her brain? If he was a woman with injuries like the ones he showed Lana, there would be no hesitation from those around him to offer support. But he has to admit that if a mate of his came to him with the same story, he would find it unbelievable. And the blood on the wall is a problem. But it's gone now, and only a slightly whiter patch on the wall shows that something was there. Maybe he should paint over that? No, that would look way too suspicious. The screenshot is a problem as well so he opens his phone and deletes it and then empties the trash so that it's really gone although nothing is ever really gone.

He returns everything to the kitchen along with the plates and goes to the single garage to check if Sandy's car is still there and of course it is. They are a thirty-minute walk from the nearest train station. Leaning against the kitchen counter, he opens the banking app, checking their shared account. If she had taken a cab or an Uber, it would have shown up on the credit card but it hasn't. Neither has a charge for a hotel or motel, not that Sandy would ever stay at a motel. He checks their small savings account but that hasn't been touched either.

As he prepares a dinner of fish fingers and oven chips for the kids, he tries Sandy's phone a few times, leaving messages just like he did this afternoon after the school called. He knows there's no point but it feels necessary to leave the messages.

'Hi Sandy, please call me back.'

'Hey Sandy, I know that you're taking some time, but the kids really need you here.'

'Sandy, please just call me so I know you're okay.'

'Can you please call me back? This is not fair to me or the kids.'

Her mailbox will fill up quickly at this rate but he needs to keep trying.

He checks the credit card and their bank account again, in case something has happened in the last few minutes, but nothing has been touched.

When dinner is ready, he calls the kids.

'Can we eat in front of the TV?' asks Lila because if anyone can sense a chink in his armour it's his five-year-old daughter.

'Yes.' He takes their plates to the coffee table in the living room and makes sure they have water as well. 'If you argue about what to watch, I'll turn it off,' he warns them.

'I'm not...' starts Felix because he regards Lila's television programmes as 'for babies'.

'We can watch the Daniel Tiger one,' says Lila quickly because she knows Felix loves the show. Mike finds it for them and puts it on, and then he leaves them to it, taking a beer from the fridge in the kitchen and draining it quickly, needing to get to the next one.

After his third beer, he makes himself some toast to eat because he can't be bothered cooking anything. He needs to get the kids into their bath and off to bed but the thought exhausts him and he flirts briefly with the idea of just walking out and going to a pub, but obviously he wouldn't do that.

Felix and Lila know something is up.

Once he has cajoled the two of them into a bath, he reads Lila a story first and then goes to Felix's room to read to him. He's had three beers in quick succession and he's not even buzzed.

'When is Mum coming home?' Felix asks as Mike sits down on the bed.

'I don't know. Soon, I hope,' he replies.

'Why did she go away?' Felix asked this question already but Mike knows he will keep asking it because he finds the answer so unsatisfactory.

'Because she needed a rest. She was tired.' He's sticking to the same answer, which he knows is frustrating for his son. It's frustrating as hell for him too. Sandy will be back tomorrow, of course she will be. Won't she?

'But why is she so tired?'

'I don't know, mate; she needed a break.'

'But mums don't need a break from their kids. They're mums.' Felix picks up his soft toy koala and holds it close to him. Mike wants to tell him he's too big for the toy but he lets the thought go. He can deal with that another day. Who knows how much Felix will need the toy over the coming months.

'Sometimes they do. Now it's time for reading.'

'I don't understand.'

Mike wants to tell him that he doesn't understand either, that he is as confused as a seven-year-old boy because none of this should have happened.

'Where are we up to in your book?' he asks, hoping to distract his son from his line of questioning.

'The part where the children run away,' says Felix and then

he is quiet. He taps his finger on the book. 'Did Mum run away?' he asks.

'No, no, mate, she didn't,' Mike replies firmly.

Maybe Felix is right. Maybe Sandy did run away. He hasn't checked their closets. He'll do that next, when the kids are asleep.

After two requests for water and one more story for Lila, it's after 9 p.m. but the house is finally silent and Mike is exhausted. He has to drop the kids at school early tomorrow morning so he can get to work on time and it takes them ages to get ready. He's forgotten to pack lunches and do whatever else needs to be done. The laundry pile seems to have grown in the few hours they've been home and the house is a mess but he doesn't have the energy for any of it.

The temptation to stay home from work tomorrow is over-whelming but Mike needs his last pay cheque. Everyone does. And it feels like that may not come to him if he's not there.

In their bedroom, he goes to Sandy's closet and pushes aside her clothes, trying to figure out if stuff is missing, but it's still jammed full. He has no real idea if she has taken anything or not. He feels a surge of fury when he comes across a black jumpsuit with the price tag still on: four hundred dollars. No wonder he always feels like he can't get ahead. He's talked to her more than once about her spending habits but it seems to make no difference to her at all.

Exhaustion creeps up from his toes. He needs to shower and sleep.

He stands in the shower for a long time, trying to work out a way forward. Until Sandy returns, he can do nothing. Will she return? Does he want her to come back? Despite how hard it is to deal with the kids, the house is, at least, peaceful without her here.

When he's in bed he switches off the light and stares into

the dark until he understands that sleep is far away. He's too wired.

He climbs out of bed and lifts the mattress, taking the phone out from underneath, the phone he found there this afternoon when he walked into the bedroom, calling his wife. It was charging so it has a full battery.

As he found it, the doorbell rang and Lana was there so he didn't have time to look at it properly. All he could do was turn it to silent to make sure it couldn't be heard. But he studies it now. There are lots of missed calls listed on the screen, from him, from the therapist, from the school, from Sandy's friend Emma. He tries a few lock patterns, knowing that he will probably never guess what Sandy has used, but he keeps going until the phone locks him out of trying again, so he throws it back under the mattress and gets back into bed.

If the therapist tells the police, the first thing they will do is trace Sandy's phone. How long does that take to do? Why did she leave it? She's glued to the thing all day long. Should he have taken it to the police or given it to the therapist? No way.

'Has Mum run away?' his son asked him and what Mike is hoping is that she realises that she shouldn't have left, that her conscience pricks at her and she comes home and then he'll tell her they need to get divorced because he's not staying in this marriage for one moment longer, but in order to start the process of divorce, his wife needs to turn up.

And she will turn up if she has chosen to leave, if she hasn't been forced to go, but by who? And if she's not hurt, but also, by who? And if she wants to come back.

That's a lot of ifs, Mike, he tells himself. *A lot of ifs*.

FOURTEEN
TUESDAY

Lana

I wake with an already pounding headache after a restless night filled with horrific dreams of Sandy's body, bloodied and bruised, floating in a dam somewhere.

Was that blood I saw on the wall? Why was the screenshot of Sandy asking him to let her go on Mike's phone, and were the pictures of him hurt real? More or less real than Sandy's black eye?

Grabbing my phone, I check to see if, somehow, Sandy has messaged me but there's nothing from her.

'I don't want Vegemite sandwiches for school,' Iggy shouts from his bedroom.

'What do you want?' I call back, wincing as the headache intensifies.

'Cheese and jam. I'm getting my breakfast now.'

I hear him jumping down the steps one at a time to the first floor of our small terrace house and then the clatter of dishes as he gets himself a bowl of cereal.

Sandy's son is the same age Iggy is, and I can't help

touching my chest over my heart as I think about a little boy who has no idea where his mother is. Children rely on their parents, especially their primary carers, to make the world a safe place filled with routine and predictability. Sandy was the one who took care of the children, staying home and dedicating her time to them. Her parents live hours away and I know that she has mentioned that Mike doesn't speak to his family much at all. It's such a mess.

Swinging my legs out of bed, I opt for a long hot shower to shake off the terrible night. I run late as a consequence and then have to hustle Iggy out of the house with a piece of toast in my mouth.

Iggy's chatter along the way to school keeps me distracted until I've dropped him off and he's waving enthusiastically from the gate. And then I am alone with my thoughts.

There's no question about what I'm going to do. I keep letting the thoughts go around in my head but, ultimately, I think I've already made a decision.

I drive to the nearest police station and park. Before I go inside, I call Sandy's mobile again, hoping that she will pick up and ask me what I want. But as I have done since yesterday morning, I only get her voicemail. I could call Mike and ask if she's home, if she's returned, but I don't want to do that. I don't want to have to speak to him again. I don't have his number in my phone anyway, although it is on Sandy's records at the clinic.

Before I can talk myself out of it, I get out of the car into the bright September morning. It's cold but at least the sun is out.

Inside, the police station is empty, no one behind the counter, and I stand awkwardly looking around before a door opens and a policeman comes out.

'Sorry,' he says as a greeting, and he flushes slightly. 'How can I help?'

'I need…' I stop speaking, aware of how warm the room is.

The policeman leans slightly over the counter towards me. 'Take your time,' he says softly, his dark eyes focused on my face.

'I need to report someone missing.'

I had imagined that I would simply walk into the station and report Sandy missing and leave the police to do their job. That's what I imagined and even that felt like an impossible thing to do. But it's a lot more complicated than that.

The policeman, who introduces himself as Constable King, asks me what feels like a hundred questions. *How do you know Sandy Burkhart? Have you tried calling her? Why is her husband not reporting her missing? What makes you think something has happened to her? When did you last see her? How did she seem? Why are you concerned? Is there no one else who may know where she is? Have you spoken to her friends, her family? Have you called the school today? Why didn't you report this earlier?*

I am glad I have a late start at work as the questions keep coming, but eventually, I seem to have satisfied the constable that I have a legitimate reason to be concerned and he shows me into a small room with a chipped laminate table and three plastic chairs. A stale odour permeates the air and there is a garbage bin filled with paper cups in a corner.

I don't know if I should sit down or stay standing.

I send a quick text to Kirsty.

Something has come up. I don't think I will make my 11 a.m. Can you cancel for me, please? Apologise for me.

Peter actually just called to cancel you so all good.

She adds a thumbs up emoji. I'm happy Peter cancelled. I had forgotten he was on my schedule for today as he comes in every few weeks depending on how he feels.

I sit down, wondering how many other people have sat on this chair and what kind of people they were. A few years ago, I was stopped for a roadside breath test, and after I drove off, I realised that it was the first time I had had any interaction with the police since I was a teenager and my small world fell apart.

As the minutes tick by, I remember two constables coming to my front door one hot February morning. I had just started year eleven, just turned sixteen, and even though I had hoped, all through the summer holidays, that this year would be different, the bullying had begun on day one. *Loopy Lana, Lardy Lana, Lame Lana.*

Each morning that I got up for school, I comforted myself that at least I had Janine, my one friend who was as much of a target as I was. She was taunted for her bad skin, for her red hair and her freckles. I never understood why the pretty, popular girls in our year needed to do it. I didn't know what they gained except for laughs but maybe that was all they wanted. As an adult and a trained therapist, I now know that each of those young women was suffering in her own way, as we all are as human beings, and taking it out on me and Janine, the easy targets. But as a teenager, you can't think about anyone else's pain, only your own, and Janine and I were in pain every day, making our way around the school looking over our shoulders and hoping that we did not run into the beautiful clique of girls who made fun of us.

Despite this, it felt like we would be okay because we had each other. We would meet outside school every morning, each waiting for the other to turn up so that we wouldn't have to walk in alone. We had a calendar countdown in our school diaries for how much longer we would have to endure the experience – how many days until graduation and the shining star of our futures at university where everything would change. I wanted to study something in the medical field and Janine wanted to study fine art. She was a beautiful artist. The bullies at school had been particularly relentless with her at school the week before. She was in her element in art class and all the girls who took the subject because they thought it would be easy to simply float through the year doing nothing disliked how much the teacher praised her and her work.

She had called me the night before but I hadn't felt like talking. I was reading a novel, a fantasy, and I was lost in a world of dragons and knights with no desire to leave. I thought I would see her on Saturday afternoon. We were meeting up to go to the library and study for an English exam on Monday.

The sound of our doorbell ringing early on a Saturday morning pulled me, my mother and my father out of bed because it was so unusual.

The two constables spoke to my mother first and I heard her cry out at what they said. And then the constables and my mother took me into the lounge, where I sat, still in my pyjamas, wrapped in an old dressing gown covered in pictures of cupcakes, while they told me that my best friend was dead. They had questions for me about why it might have happened.

'She was bullied at school all the time,' I told them. 'We both were.' It was a different time and I don't think they thought that was enough for someone to take their own life. They assumed there had to be more. Maybe there was. I knew Janine well but no one knows everything about a person and their life.

I have never forgiven myself for not taking her call, for not being able to help her to hold on through what must have been a very dark night. When I returned to school two weeks later, I was shielded from the bullying by teachers and other students who were watching me intently. When they eventually forgot about Janine and everything started up again, I felt able to deal with it because I had a plan in place. I was going to be a psychologist. I was going to help people who were suffering. It had been my intention to focus on adolescents but I found that too hard and so moved to working with adults.

I have been conscious, since I lost my best friend, that people can be struggling even when they are winning praise and they seem to have everything to live for. The pretty girls didn't get away unscathed by life. Two of them left in the middle of year twelve to deal with eating disorders and they never returned to school. Being pretty doesn't make your life perfect. If it did, I wouldn't be here to report my beautiful client missing and to tell the police that I suspect her husband of hurting her.

Only ten minutes have passed but I stand up again, feeling a cramp in my back. I hate revisiting my past failures. I need to make sure that Sandy is safe and that she does not become someone else that I've failed, and I worry that I have not worked hard enough to make sure that happens.

The door swings open and a man walks in, casually dressed in jeans and a jumper. His brown hair is cropped close to his head.

'I'm Detective Franks,' he says, holding out his hand for me to shake, and I surreptitiously wipe my own on my grey work pants before doing so. The room isn't heated but I'm hot.

'Lana Stanton,' I reply and Detective Franks gestures for me to sit down.

'I'm going to give you a case number for this conversation and a number to call if you do hear from' – he looks down at his notepad – 'Sandy Burkhart. This is my card and I'm the officer in charge for the purposes of communication.'

I nod my head, taking in the information as I grip the white card in my hand. I can feel my day ticking away.

'Now why don't you detail your concerns for me,' says Detective Franks.

I go through the whole thing again, answer all his questions, even telling him about my visit to the house last night. I know I should probably mention the pictures on Mike's phone and the screenshot but it all feels too complicated. I have told the first policeman that I'm worried about her safety because I think her husband is both emotionally and possibly physically abusive. That should be enough. I hope it is.

'That's a bit unusual, isn't it?' says the detective.

'What?'

'Going to visit a patient. I've never really heard of a therapist turning up at someone's home to check on them. I mean she saw you once a week, didn't she? Why would her missing one appointment bother you so much?'

I realise that this is a method of questioning. I have already answered this question but it will be asked again until the detective is satisfied.

'I was worried about her because I believe that her husband has the capacity to be violent. It would have been remiss of me not to check on her. And a couple of weeks ago she...' I hesitate, not wanting to break patient confidentiality, but if ever there was a time when it was permissible, it's now. 'She told me that her husband took out a life insurance policy on her and she doesn't work so it's...'

'Well, my wife stays home with the kids and we have a policy for her as well so I wouldn't really take that as an indication of anything. But can I ask you why you didn't think to call the police last night?' he asks.

'What do you mean?'

'Well... it's very unusual to do what you did. If you were that concerned about her, surely you would have just called the police. Why would you have gone over to a house where you were worried about who the husband was and what he might do?'

I stare at him, not sure exactly what he wants from me and worried now that I have done entirely the wrong thing. He's right. I should have called the police last night. What if Sandy is somewhere in that house? What if she is being held by Mike? What if she's hurt and I could have saved her by coming here earlier? I realise why Ben was so angry with me last night. It was a terribly stupid thing to do and I may have put Sandy in even more danger.

'I should have called the police,' I say to Detective Franks and he nods his head.

What if Sandy is actually dead? I think about the splash of red on the wall by the door. Was that blood? Should I mention it? It could have been paint.

'Maybe she has done what Mike says and just taken some time off.' I rub my hands on my pants, hating that they are damp with sweat.

'Perhaps, but her kids are, what, seven and five?' he says, looking down at his pad again. 'Her husband should at least know where she is.'

I cross my arms over my chest, feeling like a child talking to an adult. 'I realise I may not have made the best decision last night, but I'm here now and I think it's something that you should check out.'

'Right,' says Detective Franks, standing up, 'I have all your details and I have all of her details. I'll definitely go and check this out. Thank you for coming in, Ms Stanton.' He holds out his hand again.

I have been dismissed so I stand and it is only when I am out of the police station and back in my car that I realise how fast my heart is racing, how worried I have been and how fearful I am about what happens now.

At work Kirsty and Ben are standing together by the reception counter, their heads close as they whisper to each other.

'What's going on?' I ask, fearful that in the time it has taken me to drive to work, the police have found something and Ben and Kirsty are working out how to tell me.

'Nothing,' says Ben as he steps away from Kirsty. 'I thought

Kirsty should know what's going on in case... Mike turns up here or something.'

'Why would he do that?'

'I don't know, Lana,' says Ben with a shrug. 'I have no idea what he's capable of – do you?'

I shake my head. 'I went to the police,' I tell them. 'I've told them everything and they're going to investigate.'

'That's good,' says Ben, 'and look, I hate to do this to you, especially now, but I have to leave for a couple of days.'

'Why?' I ask, acutely aware that it's actually none of my business.

'It's a' – Ben waves his hand – 'a family thing... My mother called and it's... I don't really want to get into it.' He stops speaking, waiting for me to acknowledge his right to privacy, which I do with a nod. I am not his boss and he can do as he pleases. But I know he was worried about Sandy, and I also don't want to be here alone. I never considered Mike turning up here because why would he? But now that Ben has mentioned it, I know it will sit in the back of my mind, a worrying thought that will make me jump at every sound.

'Now that you've told the police, I'm sure this will all be sorted out. You just need to sit tight.'

Ben rubs at the stubble on his chin which is normally very neat but I can see that he's neglected to shave this morning. He must be stressed about his family situation. I'm lucky that both my parents, who moved to Sydney to be closer to me after I got pregnant with Iggy, are still strong and healthy.

'Kirsty and I have been talking about this and I think...'

'You think?'

Ben looks at Kirsty and she gives him a quick smile. They've obviously been discussing this for a while. I am reminded of how much time they spend talking to each other. They seem closer every day. Does Kirsty know why Ben needs to take time off? I think it's possible that she does, from the way they are interacting.

Does that mean they are having a relationship outside of work? It would be problematic, especially because of the difference in ages and the fact that Ben is essentially Kirsty's boss. But I can't deal with that now. And anyway, I could be imagining things.

'Come into my office,' he says and I follow him, standing next to his desk as he closes the door softly behind us.

'Look, this is probably me being over the top but I'm worried about you. You live alone and I'll be gone for a couple of days...'

'I'll be fine, Ben; the police have been told. Mike is not going to come here. I spoke to Detective Franks at Wiltshire police station.'

'Lana...' Ben hesitates. 'Did Sandy tell you that she found a life insurance policy Mike took out on her?'

'Ben, are you still talking to her? She only just told me that a couple of weeks ago, or at least she told me that she only just found that. So how do you know?'

Ben holds up his hands. 'Now wait a minute,' he says and he goes behind his desk to grab his phone. 'She texted me, more than a week ago, to tell me. I knew immediately that she was trying to draw me back into treating her and I told her that she needs to discuss this with you or the police since I am no longer her therapist.'

He opens his phone and shows me a text conversation with Sandy that reads exactly the way he has said it would.

'Sorry... sorry... this situation feels out of control,' I say.

'Did you tell the police about the life insurance policy?' he asks.

'I did, but the detective didn't seem to think that meant much.'

'Well... I mean maybe but it's good that you told him. Look,

I have to get going but I wanted you to have this.' He bends down and opens his bottom desk drawer, and when he stands up, I take two steps backwards. He is holding a small handgun.

'Are you insane?' I am unable to keep from sounding shrill. I have never seen a real gun in my life. 'Where on earth did you get such a thing?'

'I'm a member of a gun club. I had to jump through a million hoops to get it and it's just for target shooting but it is a real gun. It's a sport I'm involved in, that's all. It helps me destress.'

'You shouldn't have it here. It shouldn't be anywhere near people. Aren't you supposed to keep it locked up?'

'Relax, Lana. It's a precaution.' He comes around the desk to stand next to me and then he puts a hand on my shoulder. 'I'm worried about you,' he says, 'you mean a lot to me. It's just to scare Mike if he comes here. He won't do anything if he sees it. I'm not asking you to use it, only wave it around as some sort of deterrent.'

'I'm not really alone, Ben, Kirsty is here.' I take another step backwards, not wanting to be anywhere near the small black handgun. It looks like a toy but I know it's not, and to me it seems to have a larger presence in this office than its size should dictate. I can feel it in the air.

'Yes' – Ben waves the gun around casually, irritating me – 'but this is a big guy, an angry guy. And what about at home? You have Iggy to think about.'

'He's not going to come to my home, Ben.' But suddenly, now that the words are out there, that seems like something that could happen. I turned up at his house after all. I have never been worried about a patient turning up at my house. But it's happened to Ben. It could happen to me.

'You don't know that for sure... and... you don't know everything about him.' He looks away as he says this.

The conversation is beginning to drive me crazy and I wish

again that I had never gotten involved with this woman. 'Are you saying you know something I don't know, Ben? Is that what you're saying?'

'Look, I never wanted to tell you this – I mean Sandy told me when I was treating her and it should have stayed between us if she didn't mention it to you, which I assume she hasn't – but...'

'But?'

'The guy has a record. Mike has a record. I mean not officially anymore because it was for something he did when he was sixteen so it's considered done with because he hasn't been arrested for anything else ever but he did hurt someone, pretty badly.'

'Oh God.' I cover my mouth, my stomach churning. 'What did he do?'

'I don't have all the details but what does it matter? That's why I'm giving this to you. It's filled with blanks so worst-case scenario it will make a loud noise. It's just to show him if he turns up here or at your house.' He holds the gun towards me but I still can't take it.

'This is ridiculous, Ben. Even if he... did something in his past, I still can't have a gun.' My mind is whirling with what he has told me. How dangerous is Sandy's husband? What is on his record? What did he do?

'Look,' says Ben, his eyes on the gun, 'you've never had a negative experience like I had back home in the UK and I hope you never do, but I hate the idea that he could come to your house and scare you or...'

'Ben... I do understand how hard that was for you. I can't imagine going through something like that but I really don't think I need a gun. It's so extreme.'

Ben runs his hands through his curls. 'I didn't tell you everything, Lana, not everything that happened.'

'Then tell me now,' I say, touching his arm. 'I'm listening.' I need to know why he is suggesting something so over the top as me having a gun. It's not logical.

Ben sits down behind his desk with the gun in his hand. 'The woman who stalked me, Carla, made my life very hard, and something I've never...' He hesitates and then he looks up at me. 'I was in a relationship, a good one, and we were going to get married, and then Carla found out and she terrorised Bianca, my fiancée. She posted about her on social media, saying all sorts of ugly things, and Bianca was a nurse so Carla called the hospital where she worked and reported her for sexual assault – an absurd idea but it still had to be investigated. Bianca took it all as well as she could but each time Carla did something else, I could feel her withdrawing from me and all the drama. The police weren't much help. We filed protective orders but Carla was too far gone to care. And then one day Carla turned up at Bianca's apartment with a knife. I wasn't there.'

'Oh my God, that sounds awful... Was Bianca hurt?' My stomach sinks with each new fact he offers and I understand his desire to have a gun, to use it to destress. It must help him to feel in control of a life that, at one point, felt very out of control.

He shakes his head. 'No, she managed to call the police and Carla was arrested but she was out after a day, on bail, and still accusing me and Bianca of a whole lot of crap. She told the police we stole from her; she accused me of sexual assault.' Ben turns away from me to look out of the window behind his desk, clutching the gun close to him. 'The police weren't sure who to believe, and to be honest, they weren't much help.'

'Why didn't you tell me any of this?'

He turns around again. 'Because that incident was the last straw for Bianca. She broke up with me, and after the police cleared me, I knew I needed to get away from Carla, as far away as possible. I'm a dual citizen so I came here. And fortunately, I was lucky enough to find you and you gave me a job and you'll never know how much I needed that.'

'I am so sorry that happened to you.' I move to go and touch him, give him a hug or squeeze his arm, but then I stop, not wanting to cross any professional lines. I do feel dreadful for him. During my training I heard stories about therapists who were hurt by their patients, physically and emotionally, but I never thought I would have to confront such a thing.

'Thanks, but I only told you because you need to know that I understand patients can be dangerous, and the violent husband of a missing patient is... capable of anything.'

'I understand.'

'Hopefully nothing will happen. This is just in case or until she turns up or... just keep it, okay? I'll get it from you when I get back in a couple of days.' He holds the gun out to me again.

'Okay.' I reluctantly take the small weapon from him. I will put it in a drawer in my desk here at work and hide it somewhere Iggy will never find it at home. This whole thing feels absurd and I'll probably never have to even look at it until Ben gets back and I return it to him.

'I'll see you in a couple of days.' He smiles.

'I hope everything works out with your family,' I say. 'Are you actually flying home?'

I know I'm being nosey but his parents are in the UK and that would mean he needs more than a couple days off.

'I'm not but I have to deal with a lot of stuff over there and I can only do it at night. I'm completely exhausted and I know it means I won't be the best for my patients so I need to take the time off.'

'I hope you sort everything out.'

'I'm sure it will be fine. I hope that this whole thing with Sandy... goes away.'

'That's what I'm hoping for too.' Clutching the gun in my hand, I leave his office, making sure to conceal it at my side so that Kirsty doesn't see it.

I put it in my desk drawer, hiding it under a folder, and I am more relaxed when I can't actually see it anymore.

Once it's hidden, I decide on getting a coffee and stand up. Picking up my bag, I open the office door and see Ben and Kirsty enclosed in a tight hug. 'I'll miss you,' I think I hear her say but I'm not sure because I step back and close the door to my office quietly.

Are he and Kirsty involved?

After a minute, I decide I'm being ridiculous and open my office door. Kirsty is sitting behind the reception desk, her gaze concentrated on her computer screen.

'Has Ben gone?' I ask her.

'I think so... but he may have left when I went to take my mug back to the kitchen,' she says with a small smile, and I don't stop to question her, just say, 'Getting a coffee,' and leave via the stairs.

Why would she lie to me?

Back in my office, as I wait for my next patient, I know I should use the time to catch up on paperwork but I don't feel like it.

Instead, I sit in my chair, staring at nothing, and allow myself a brief fantasy that Sandy turns up tomorrow, angry that I spoke to the police but alive and well.

That's the best-case scenario. But the worst case... could be things unfolding the way Ben thinks they might.

What if Sandy is hurt? What if she's trapped somewhere?

And what if Mike does turn up at my work or at my home?

All the terrible possibilities circle in my mind, and all the while I'm conscious that I'm in possession of a handgun that I have no idea how to use.

FIFTEEN

TUESDAY

Mike

He's late for work but he doesn't care. The morning was as chaotic as he had imagined it would be, with the kids sleeping late because he was passed out on the sofa.

Once he had replaced Sandy's phone under the mattress, he had found himself unable to get comfortable, like the princess with the accusing pea underneath him. Lana, the therapist, had not believed a word he'd said. That much was obvious. Her pale face, the way her eyes focused on the blood on the wall and then him went around in his head until he thought he might go a little mad.

He had gone downstairs, and even though he'd known it was not a good idea to drink any more, he had turned on the television, slumped onto the sofa surrounded by the kids' toys and started with one beer that led to two and then to three.

Eventually he had passed out. And he had only woken up to Lila hitting him on the head with her teddy. 'I want breakfast, Dad, and I can't find my school dress and Felix is in the bath-room and I need a wee.'

He had tried, as he did four things at once, not to yell at the kids because he knew they were unsettled by their missing mother. The lunchboxes needed to be packed and the uniforms found. Felix seemed only moments away from tears all through breakfast and Mike ended up throwing chocolate bars and small bags of chips into both lunchboxes, not caring that he would get a call or email from the school on the topic of *Healthy Lunches*. When he walked out the door and finally had them both in the car, he knew that he had left the house in a dismal mess. If Sandy returns while he's at work, she will have a lot to say about that.

He sent her a quick text after he dropped the kids off at school.

Sorry about the mess. Will clean up when I get home.

He knows it's better to send it, better to have it on record in case. *In case of what?*

As he walks into the office, a woman wearing a name badge that says 'Kellie' catches his eye and virtually runs over to him.

'Hi, I'm Kellie, and I work with the firm of Arthur and Gorman. We're the auditors and we're here to help wrap things up and see if we can get as many suppliers and staff paid as possible.'

She has brown hair in a pixie cut and a wide smile on her face as though this is all a delightful adventure.

He can't believe how quickly she has appeared and it seems to him that Paul has probably had this in the works for a while.

'Um hi,' replies Mike, wishing that the day was over already.

'Okay if we have a quick chat in your office?' she says and Mike can do nothing except nod. She is filled with questions about every sale he's made over the last two years and wants every single dollar accounted for, and eventually he holds up his hands. 'I'll get that all to you, just give me some time,' he says.

'Right, but we are going to also need—'

'Can you just give me some time?' he repeats, and thankfully, the woman takes the hint and leaves.

Mike sits in his office for two hours doing nothing at all, staring out of his window and occasionally calling his wife's phone.

At noon he can't actually deal with it anymore. It's his lunch hour anyway and he has a right to some time off. He leaves his office like a thief sneaking out of a house he's robbed, desperate not to draw Kellie's attention again. He needs to do what she says because he needs to make sure he gets his last pay cheque and that he gets as much money in severance as he can. How is he going to survive this?

Once he's outside in the cold air, he breathes a sigh of relief.

As he's crossing the road, making his way to the café where he can usually get a reasonable sandwich, his phone starts to ring. He shoves his hand into his pocket, desperate to get it because it could be Sandy on a borrowed phone, but as he pulls it out, it slips out of his hand and drops onto the road, forcing him to stop and pick it up, a car hooting at him for the delay.

With the phone in his hand, he darts to the pavement and then tries to answer but he's missed the call. Frustration bubbles inside him and he swears. He doesn't recognise the number but then Sandy doesn't have her phone and he goes to hit it on his missed call list before he stops, wondering if this is one of their suppliers or customers. Since yesterday, as news of the factory's closure spread like wildfire, Mike has been getting a lot of calls from people who have placed orders and he's sick of having to tell everyone that there is nothing he can do and that the auditors will be making sure that people get their money back if that's possible. It's been a shitty, shitty time.

And the worst part of all of this is not being able to adequately explain to his kids what's going on.

'Will Mum be home this afternoon?' Felix asked when Mike dropped him and his sister off at school.

'I don't know,' he replied, trying not to sound angry. She's been gone for over twenty-four hours now because he knows she was there yesterday when he left to drop the kids off at school. She's probably really enjoying the idea that he's worrying about where she is and that he has to take care of the kids.

One of her frequent complaints about her life is that he has no idea how difficult it is to take care of young children and that he never gives her enough help, and he has to admit that she's right. It's exhausting and boring and the hours seem to stretch on forever before bedtime. But what kind of a mother leaves her phone behind?

'But you know everything,' said Lila softly when Mike said he didn't know if their mother would be back or not. Mike wanted to scream with rage. He is supposed to know everything but right now, he feels like a kid again, caught up in a chaotic world over which he has no control. The urge to hit something runs through him.

'Chicken and salad, thanks,' he says to the man behind the counter in the sandwich shop, and then he pays and steps away to wait. His phone beeps with an audio message and he shoves a finger in one ear to block out all the other lunchtime customers and listens.

'Mr Burkhart, this is Detective Franks calling in relation to a report of a missing person we've had. I'm trying to get in touch with you or your wife, Sandy Burkhart. She's not answering her phone. If you could please return my call at—'

Mike stops the message, his heart racing and his palms sweating. She's gone to the police: the therapist bitch has actually gone to the police.

'Chicken and salad,' the man behind the counter calls, and Mike steps forward, grabs his sandwich and gestures his thanks.

Then he walks out of the shop into the cold air, thinking that he should have brought his suit jacket. Spring has arrived but it has brought no change in the weather.

He takes a bite of the sandwich as he walks towards a pub that he knows he can get a lunchtime drink at and then he stops and has to concentrate on swallowing. She went to the police.

After chucking the sandwich in a nearby bin, he feels in his pocket, glad that he has his car keys. There's no way he's going back to work now. The police are going to want to speak to him. They are going to want to trace Sandy's phone, to search the house, to dissect their lives. Is this what Sandy wanted? Did she know that things would go this far? Is this her sick, twisted way of punishing him?

He thought there was some hope that Lana would wait and that Sandy would turn up. Obviously, that was idiotic. The therapist turning up last night was weird but it meant that he should have understood exactly what the woman would do today.

And perhaps he should have been the one to contact the police. He should have done it for the same reason he's been ringing Sandy's phone, even while he knows it's under their mattress. It would look better if he had contacted the police and reported his wife missing.

He walks through the back entrance of the building, going into the garage where his car is parked, finding the silence unsettling. The noise from the factory next to the garage is usually tremendous but everything has fallen silent now as the company is slowly buried by the auditors. Mike gets into his car, knowing exactly where he's going.

What has the therapist told the police about his marriage? He needs to get her on side. Maybe if she understands, if she will listen to the truth about Sandy without running off, really listen and understand, then she will call the police and tell them that Sandy really is the kind of person to just up and leave her kids, because she is. He needs the therapist to understand the truth.

It's a few minutes after 1 p.m. and he has a couple of hours before he has to get the kids. He will go to her office and talk to her.

Perhaps he should call the detective back and explain but he's afraid to do that. What if he says something wrong? What if the detective asks a question he can't answer? No, the best way forward is to speak to the therapist.

A small part of him knows that what he's doing is irrational but it's overridden by fear and worry and by his need to be understood, by his need for the truth to come out.

He needs to convince her that he hasn't done anything to Sandy and that she left of her own accord. He knows how weird it sounds. Women generally don't leave their children but Sandy is a very different kind of woman.

It's not just the violence but the detachment as well. She doesn't really seem to care about the kids the way he had always imagined a mother would, although what would he know? His mother never protected him from his violent father. But he does remember some good moments with her, moments when his father was out and she was not busy trying to save herself by putting Mike in between her and her violent husband, and he thinks she did love him. She still loves him even though they speak so rarely, and she adores Felix and Lila, calls them 'the babies'.

When he was a child, there was a way his mother used to look at him sometimes, used to stroke his hair and gaze down at him that made him understand she loved him. He's never seen Sandy look at their kids that way, and she touches them as little as possible. Although when she talks about them to other people, she practically gushes her love for them.

Maybe she does love them; maybe he's the problem because he has no real idea of what a mother's love is really like.

The contradicting, questioning thoughts threaten to send him insane.

He always put it down to the fact that she wasn't ready to be a mother when Felix was born but she seemed happy to be pregnant with Lila, seemed proud of her growing bump and the way people treated her. But when the baby arrived, there was the same detachment. She did all the right things, talked to the baby, smiled at the baby, but sometimes when he was watching her interact with Lila, it seemed to him that his being witness to her interaction was what mattered, rather than the interaction itself. He's never wanted to ask her about it or discuss it with anyone else. He barely speaks to his mother, and Sandy's mother is on the South Coast and sees the children even less than his mother does. Mother and daughter seem to have little interest in each other. But maybe Sandy has gone there?

He pulls over to the side of the road and picks up his phone, scrolling through his contacts to find his mother-in-law, Maureen. He can't recall ever having called her before but Sandy gave him her number years ago.

His stomach rumbles as he waits for Maureen to pick up and he regrets throwing out the sandwich.

'Hello,' she answers.

'Hey, Maureen, it's Mike,' he says and then because she says nothing, he feels compelled to add, 'Sandy's husband.'

'Oh right, of course, how are you? How are the children?'

'Good, good, everyone is good but Sandy... Have you seen Sandy? I know she wanted a bit of time away so I thought she might be there.'

'Here?' Maureen replies and she seems surprised. 'Sandy would never come here.'

'Oh right, right... sorry.'

'How long has she been gone?'

'Only a day, but I haven't heard from her so I was... worried.'

Maureen sighs. 'She used to run away when she was a teenager. This was before she had a mobile phone. James and I used to be frantic. I think she liked... I think she enjoyed knowing we were fretting.'

'Oh,' says Mike, unsure how to respond to this. It explains a lot.

'She once disappeared for three days. We were completely mad with worry. The police were called and there was a story on the news and then she just turned up and got angry with us for involving anyone.'

'Oh, I didn't know about that.' Sandy has never told him this. He knows that, like his, her childhood was difficult and he knows that he contemplated running away from home many times as he grew up. But he would never have gone back and he would have understood if his worried mother had called the police. What if she has done exactly the same thing now? Maybe she gets some kind of kick out of it, out of knowing that people are concerned about her and searching for her?

Maureen pauses then starts speaking quite slowly, as if she is thinking about what to say or how to phrase it. 'I'm sure there's... lots... you don't know about Sandy.' Another pause. 'I mean I love my daughter but she has always had a very different way of looking at the world. Her father and I were probably too gentle with her.'

Mike thinks about Sandy's story of being taught to swim, her father throwing her in the water. That didn't sound gentle. Was that a lie? It could have been a lie. How much of what his wife has told him about her past is true? He has always found the juxtaposition between what Sandy told him about her parents and the way they behave towards her now somewhat confusing. When they come over, they seem fearful of upsetting her in any way, almost afraid to ask for so much as a cup of tea. Has she just made a lot of stuff up? He wouldn't put it past her.

She told her therapist he was a violent abuser. Lying doesn't bother her at all.

'Well, if she does turn up there... could you let me know?'

'Absolutely, but she won't. When she left to work in Sydney, she told me she would never return to our house to live. And we were so happy when she met you and got pregnant with Felix. You really helped her settle down.'

'Right,' says Mike, although he doubts that's the truth. He didn't help her settle down. He 'trapped' her as she likes to tell him.

'We didn't think she would find someone. She was so... difficult when she was a teenager' – her voice softens – 'almost cruel really.' Mike can hear that Maureen has forgotten that she's speaking to him. He clears his throat.

'Listen to me going on about something silly,' says Maureen, who has obviously realised what she said. 'All teenagers are difficult. I'm sure Lila and Felix will challenge you as well. I'm sure Sandy is—'

'I know, I know,' interrupts Mike. 'I just wanted to check, but thanks, Maureen.' He's eager to be done with this conversation now. There's no way Sandy would have gone to her mother's home and only a minute's more thought would have made him realise this. But he's not really letting the rational part of his brain lead the way at the moment. Sandy's father is struggling with his health and being at home would have meant that Sandy was expected to help, something she deeply resented whenever her parents were around.

'You know, Mike, we've always thought you were a good man, James and I,' says Maureen.

'Oh thanks... thanks.' He has no idea what else to say.

'And I know that you and Sandy have a bit of a... strained relationship and I wouldn't say this to her but I feel like I could say it to you.'

'Right.' He sighs, regretting calling Maureen with his whole being.

'You need to protect those children, both of you. Whatever goes on between the two of you, you shouldn't let the children get hurt.'

And then she hangs up, leaving Mike open-mouthed. What the hell was that about? Maybe Sandy *is* there and she's saying things about him?

He can't think about this.

Right now, he needs to get the therapist to tell the police there's nothing to worry about. He pulls back into the traffic. Sandy will turn up, full of smug smiles and explanations about needing a rest. He's more convinced of this now.

As he parks near the therapist's office, he can feel anxiety building inside him. The desire to turn around and go home is overwhelming. His phone is buzzing with texts and calls from work. Paul wants to know where he is. But he needs to speak to Lana above all.

If he could speak to her calmly without the kids interrupting, he can convince her of the truth about Sandy. Maybe they can go to the police together and then the detective will back off. Even if he can't convince her of anything, he can find out exactly what Lana told the police so he knows how to counter everything she said when he speaks to them.

He will be reasonable and he will be logical and he will not let his temper get the better of him. He will talk, just talk. That's all he needs to do. But will she even speak to him?

Sitting in his car, he cracks his knuckles as he wonders about exactly how he will get to Lana. He can't force his way into her office. And the moment he turns up, she will probably call the police, and if Ben, Sandy's old therapist, is there too, Mike will be shown the door very quickly.

Holding out very little hope, he calls the practice.

'Calm Minds Clinic, this is Kirsty.'

'Yeah, um, hi... um, my name is Don... Don Burns and I need to see a therapist. I mean I need to see someone as soon as I can... I...'

'Okay, Mr Burns, I can send you one of our patient intake forms and once you've filled that out, I can see when Lana or Ben has their next available appointment. Do you have a preference for which of our psychologists you would like to see?'

'Um, the woman but... you don't understand, I need to see someone now, like today.'

'Oh right, well, if this is an emergency I can give you the number of a mental health support line and they'll help you find someone right now to help.'

'No... it's not an emergency.' He sighs – this is so much harder than he thought it would be. He really didn't think this through. 'I'm afraid that if I don't see someone today, I'll chicken out and never see someone. I've been struggling with this for a long time and today... I feel like today's the day but... Look, don't worry about it. I probably shouldn't talk to anyone anyway,' he says, laying it on thick.

'Okay... wait... look, I'm going to put you on hold for a minute,' says the young woman. He knows she's quite pretty with curly dark hair but he didn't really pay much attention to her the first time he was at the practice. How much attention did she pay to him? Will she recognise him when he walks in?

What an idiot you are. This is the dumbest thing to try.

There's no chance this is going to work. He should probably just turn around and go home. Maybe he can figure out where Lana lives and speak to her there. But that would be a weird stalker thing to do. Her turning up at his house was definitely a weird thing to do.

'Mr Burns,' says Kirsty, coming back on the line, and Mike holds his breath, knowing what she's going to say.

'Yup.'

'Lana has just had a cancellation at two. It's very unusual

but if you could get here in time to fill out the form, that would be great and she can see you today.'

'Thank you, thanks so much. I'll get there as soon as I can,' replies Mike and he feels like the universe has given him a high five. He's doing the right thing. Relief is warm inside him and he feels more positive than he has done for days. He can even imagine that Sandy will be home soon and all this will be over.

He will walk in just before 2 p.m. so he doesn't have time to fill out the form and so that if the receptionist recognises him, she may dismiss it as a coincidence, thinking he looks like someone who was there more than a week ago. He will get to say his piece to Lana without interruption. And he will quiz her on what she's said to the detective.

He needs to speak to her alone.

That's all he's going to do – just speak to her.

SIXTEEN

Lana

'Just going to the loo,' Kirsty says through the intercom, 'and is it okay if I get a quick coffee from the café as well?'

'Sure,' I reply even though I would like to tell her not to leave her desk. I don't want to be here alone when a new patient that I know nothing about walks in. Jessica, my usual 2 p.m. client, cancelled at the last minute because she forgot she has a facial. If I had been able to speak to Jessica, I would have tried to make her understand that she was avoiding therapy because she doesn't want to discuss her new relationship, in case she is forced to confront any red flags in the process. But she left the message with Kirsty and happily paid for the missed session. Jessica frequently misses sessions, but she always pays. I haven't yet confronted her about her avoidant behaviour. I'm hoping to find a way to get her to acknowledge it when she does actually turn up.

There's a bell on the counter for my new client to ring if Kirsty is not back. I shouldn't have said yes to seeing the man but since I was cancelled on by both Peter and Jessica today, I felt the need to actually do something good with my time. This whole situation with Sandy and my handling of it has me feeling unmoored, as though I have lost my way as a therapist as old feelings of insecurity creep in and I doubt myself at every turn. It would be nice to see someone with a problem I can help with.

'He sounds really worried and like he's made this big decision to get help but if he doesn't see someone today, he may go back on it,' Kirsty told me when she buzzed me to tell me about the new client. Usually when someone cancels, Kirsty goes down a list of all my other patients waiting for appointments and asks if they want the slot, but Jessica didn't leave us with much notice.

I turn my chair around and look out of my office window that overlooks a park. There aren't many people around and those that are there are rugged up against the cold. Sometimes the beginning of spring brings a burst of warmer weather but not this year it seems.

I hear the door that leads out of the office suite slam shut as Kirsty leaves and I am on my own. It's 1.45 p.m. I can eat my yoghurt and the muesli that I so carefully packed last night in a special Tupperware, but the thought of it is unappealing. I am supposed to be trying to lose some weight so of course all I want is food that I shouldn't have. That's why diets don't work.

Instead, I root through my handbag and find a chocolate chip protein bar that I usually keep for Iggy in case he gets hungry somewhere I can't readily find food. The protein bar is at least six months old because that has never happened but I open it and eat it anyway, the slightly plastic taste somehow more satisfying than anything truly filling would be. I know it's filled with sugar and is only masquerading as health food but I don't care.

Outside my office I hear the tinkle of the bell on the reception desk and I stand, quickly swallowing down the last bite of the protein bar. The new client was supposed to have time to fill out the intake form but it's nearly two now so there's no point. Kirsty can get all his details after the appointment. I have his name, Don, which is all I need.

I open my office door, a smile on my face. There is a man standing in reception with his back to me looking out into the corridor as though seeking the receptionist. I take a few steps towards him, clearing my throat. He closes the door to the corridor as I open my mouth to greet him which is an odd thing to do but before I can even question that, he turns around and I freeze.

It's Mike.

'Mike,' I say because I can't think of anything else. Every nightmarish scenario that has been running through my head about Sandy takes another turn, but this time, I am the dead body floating in the river, the bruised face, the broken bones. I should have anticipated this but my senses are off, my abilities dulled, and now I can feel I'm in trouble. This is exactly what Ben was worried about.

Mike looks jittery as his eyes dart from the reception desk to Ben's closed office door and back to me. Does he know I'm completely alone right now?

'Sorry,' he says and then he wrings his hands together. 'I gave a fake... I'm Don, but not. I just needed to see you.'

My heart is pounding so hard, I fear he can see it in my neck, and I raise a hand and touch where the skin is moving.

'You shouldn't be here.' It takes everything I have to sound calm and in control.

'You shouldn't have come to my house. And you shouldn't have gone to the police.' His voice is low, threatening, his fists clenched.

'You're scaring me,' I tell him, again forcing myself to sound controlled. I want to shriek the words, to turn and run into my office, locking the door behind me, and I consider how quickly I could do that. Not fast enough. Honesty might work here. He seems like he wants to be scaring me, but does he? Sometimes when the reality of our behaviour is pointed out to us, we are forced to stop and address it.

Mike unclenches his fists and lowers his shoulders. 'I just want to talk to you. I know you talked to the police but I need you to understand that I didn't hurt my wife. I've done nothing to her. She'll turn up, I'm sure she will. I need you to tell the police that and you need to tell me what you've said to them because you have no real idea what's going on here.'

I take a small, hopefully imperceptible step backwards towards my office. I think about the handgun that I have there from Ben. I think about how quickly I could get to it, but do I need it? Surely, I can speak to this man and figure out a way to get him to leave. Although right now, I'm not sure about any of my skills.

'I'm worried about your wife and I'm obligated to report that to the police if I fear she may be in danger or if I think something may have happened to her.' I keep my voice steady, even, making sure not to betray my fear. I wish Ben was here; I wish Kirsty would return. How long will she be?

'I assume you haven't heard from her?' I ask.

'No, of course not.' He shakes his head, looks around the office. Is he trying to figure out if anyone else is here? My phone is on my desk, only a few steps away, but it feels like I have to cross a vast space to get there. I take another tiny step back.

'Then perhaps it's a good thing that I've reported it to the police. Something may have happened to her and I'm sure you want her to come home safe.' I watch his face as I speak, seeing if his expression changes but it doesn't. It's strange that he hasn't considered the possibility that something bad may have happened to her, that he is not frantically calling hospitals and everyone else he knows. That makes me think that he is aware of where she is and of exactly what has happened to her. Somewhere along the corridor, another office door opens. There are lawyers on this floor as well, only a few offices away, and a dentist. If I scream, would they hear me?

'You don't believe that she's the violent one at all.' He's not asking a question but making a statement. There is no aggression in the words, more like defeat.

'Mike...' I take a deep breath, calculating how long I need, but as I do, Mike takes a small step towards me. It's only small and perhaps he is hoping I won't notice but all my senses are on alert. What is his agenda here?

'If anything happens to me, the police will come to you first,' I say, my voice betraying me with a small wobble. I think about the fact that this man has a record, that somewhere on a police computer, it has been recorded that he did something violent. And now he's here.

'Nothing is going to happen to you, Lana. What kind of a person do you think I am?' Another expression crosses his face. Is that anguish or desperation? Desperate people do desperate things. If he did hurt his wife, why is he here? If he hurts me, the police will look to him first because I reported Sandy missing so he must know that this is a fool's errand and yet he's here, needing to know what I said to them and trying, once again, to convince me he didn't hurt her, that in fact she hurts him. I try to slow my mind down, to calm myself so that I can reply to him in a way that will defuse this situation.

'That's just it. I don't know. It may be that even you don't know what kind of a person you are. You need help, Mike. I'm willing to... find some names for you but the first step to getting help is acknowledging that there's a problem.'

'My only problem is that you don't believe me,' he says, shaking his head.

'You're making it very hard for me to do that. Coming here was a bad idea as was using a fake name.' I take another tiny step backwards but Mike moves as well and my heart pounds in my ears, my stomach twisting.

'I didn't hurt her and if you were open to really listening to what goes on in our house, like I told you, you would know that.'

'Then where is she?' I ask him and he shrugs his shoulders. Who do I judge to be the person I should trust, who is telling the truth? A woman's life is at stake.

'I... don't know. Maybe she left to start again. She doesn't love being a wife and a mother. She just doesn't. If she's told you that her kids are the most important thing to her, she's lied. If she's told you she loves me and wants to make our marriage work, she's lied. I know what you think – you look at her and she's so pretty and seems so nice that you can't believe she would lie about anything. But she does lie.'

I can't help glancing at the clock on the wall. It's two fifteen already. My limbs feel stiff because I've been standing with my muscles tensed for so long. Where the hell is Kirsty?

'Can we just go into your office and talk?' he asks.

'I don't... No,' I say firmly. 'We're not going to do that.' Letting him into the space where there is a door he can lock will be a bad idea. Although the gun is in my desk drawer and I would be closer to it. Could I get it out and use it to scare him? I'm not even entirely sure how to hold a gun and would only be able to imitate what I've seen on television.

'You can't say that! You don't get to just dismiss me!' he yells, his voice rising sharply as he steps towards me, and I put my hand up to stop him from coming near me but it doesn't stop him and he is suddenly right next to me, so close I can smell the fresh ocean scent of his cologne. He grabs my wrist and I can feel the dangerous strength in his hands; his blue eyes darken and his cheeks glow red. Intense anger is emanating off him and hot tears fill my eyes.

Iggy, Iggy, Iggy.

Mike looks down at his hand gripping my wrist and I can

see the horror of what he's done, what he's doing, slowly dawning on him. We stand in a moment of silence with only the warm air from the air conditioner making a slight whooshing sound.

The door to enter our offices opens and cold air from the corridor fills the warm space.

'That took forever,' says Kirsty as she walks towards the reception counter and then she seems to register what she's seeing.

'Hey,' she says, her voice a terrified squeak, and Mike drops my arm, steps back and shakes his head.

'I'm sorry, sorry, sorry,' he repeats and then he looks at Kirsty and then back at me, distress on his face. He pushes his hands through his blond hair and then pulls, muttering, 'Idiot, idiot, idiot,' and then he turns and is out the door before I've even had a chance to breathe out.

Kirsty puts her coffee down on the desk and comes over to me, laying a hand on my shoulder. 'Oh my God, are you okay, are you okay?'

'That was Mike,' I say, holding my hand over my heart as though I can somehow slow it down. 'He said he was Don but it was Sandy's husband. Sandy who's missing. I have to call the police.'

'Okay, oh God. Okay, what do you want me to do?'

'Nothing... nothing, I just need to speak to the police.' I can feel my body starting to relax now, can feel that the immediate threat is over. I am trembling all over as the adrenalin leaves my body. How close did I come to getting hurt? Would he have done something?

'Should I cancel your three o'clock?'

'No, it's fine, it's fine,' I say. 'I would rather be distracted.'

'I'm so sorry, I shouldn't have let him come. I mean I shouldn't have—'

I hold up my hand to stop her speaking. 'You weren't to

know but no more new male patients until I know what's happened to Sandy, until all this is... over.'

'Right, of course, do you want a coffee, some water, some juice?'

'No, thanks.' I shake my head. 'I just need to talk to the detective.'

I turn away from her and go back into my office, closing the door behind me. Sitting down on my sofa, I drop my head down onto my knees, taking deep breaths to try and regulate my nervous system. *Nothing happened, nothing happened.*

But something could have happened. I go to my desk drawer where I have left the gun and I take it out. It doesn't feel heavy enough to cause any damage but it would scare him if he tries to come near me again. It would definitely scare him. Knowing I will have to take it home I think about where I can put it in my house so that Iggy never knows it's there but so that I can get to it if I need it. Hating the way it feels it my hand, I return it to the drawer. I really, really hope I will not need it.

If everything Mike said about Sandy is true, if she lies and she's the one who hurts him, then what might happen to a woman married to a man with a temper like that? How far did Sandy push Mike, and was it one step too far? Is that what has happened here? Is Sandy, who lied and manipulated a violent man, now a woman who has paid the price for those lies?

SEVENTEEN

Mike

In his car, he struggles to breathe in and out slowly. Deep breaths are supposed to calm you down but he can only manage to take in small amounts of panting air as his fury mounts. 'Idiot boy,' he hears his father say, 'useless piece of shit.'

The man's voice will always be inside Mike's head, always. He knew from the time he was small that his father didn't like him and it only got worse as Mike got older. Once he turned fourteen, everything became his problem. His father told him he needed to pay for his school uniform, his books, his clothes and his after-school activities.

'Just like I had to,' he told Mike as he slumped in an armchair, a beer balanced on his potbelly. 'Made a man out of me.'

Mike knew what kind of a man it had made out of his father but he dutifully got himself a part-time job, sacrificing hours of study to keep himself in school shoes and to make sure he had the right textbooks. He worked illegally until he was nearly fifteen and then joined a fast-food giant, flipping burgers and filling orders six afternoons a week.

His mother didn't work because his father didn't believe in that but she saved what she could from her household stipend to give to him. Now Mike sends her money to an account he has set up for her and that they keep secret from his father. He groans as he thinks about what is going to happen now that he doesn't have a job. He won't be able to help her.

The life insurance policy on Sandy floats through his mind. It's enough money to give him time and space and the freedom to work out his next move. Money has always been about freedom for him but it nearly cost him his life.

At sixteen, he grew tired of waiting to get out of his house and he left home carrying a backpack and nothing else. He had a thousand dollars in his wallet, saved up from his part-time job. When he walked out of his home, he had no idea where he was going or what he was going to do. He spent one night on the street, happy enough because it was summer and warm and people were out late. He stayed awake, worried about keeping everything he had safe. The second night, he searched for a place to stay and ended up in a men's hostel, where he sank instantly into a deep sleep only to wake to hands all over him as two men tried to grab his wallet from his pocket.

Mike freaked out at the idea that he was going to lose everything and just started hitting. And he felt, as his fists flew and connected with one man's nose and the other man's cheek, that everything he had repressed was erupting. Every smack, every ugly word, every sneer from his father was at the end of his fists until he was pulled off and held down to wait for the police.

He thought his life was over before it had even begun but somehow, he ended up with a public defender who was very good at her job, and instead of being sent to prison, he was sent to a supervised group home where he was able to finish school and get a scholarship to university, despite having a conviction recorded. His record was cleared after ten years but Mike knows that if anyone was looking hard enough, they would find it. Lana will call the police about him coming to her office and they will find his record and then they will come for him.

Every day that has followed his attack on the men who tried to steal from him, he has reminded himself that he is not his father, that he does not use violence. When he and Sandy had been together for a few months, he confessed this story to her and he remembers her saying, 'You never need to feel like that again.' But that was when things were good, and it seems to him, at times, that she is pushing him to become the man who beat up two people again. And it also feels like she has succeeded, like everything that has happened in his life over the last year has pushed him here. The man he didn't want to be is here. And Mike hates that man as much as he has always hated his father.

Using his hand, he hits his cheeks, repeating the words, 'Useless piece of shit, useless piece of shit,' over and again, feeling the sting of the slap on his cheek, feeling the pain through his body as he hits harder and harder and his breathing gets faster and faster. Sweat collects under his arms as he keeps going until his arm begins to cramp and he stops, his head falling forward onto the steering wheel.

He is exactly what his father told him he was, and even worse than that, he is his father as well. He is both too weak and too strong. All his life he has been fighting the man inside himself, the one who wants to lash out and hurt people. He has tried to turn his anger on himself, tried to let Sandy use her anger on him in the hope that he will keep the monster at bay, keep the animal away, but here he is and look what he's done.

Grabbing his phone, he plays the detective's message again and then he stares down at the number. Maybe if he calls them back, he can get this over with. Maybe they know something already. Maybe they know where she is.

Maybe they already know her phone is at the house. How

long does it take to trace a phone these days? He and Sandy don't have those apps on their phones that allow them to find each other because why would they need them?

But can the police locate a phone in moments or days or weeks? How long does he have? He picks up his phone and calls Sandy again, leaving a version of the same message he has left many times. Her phone is on silent and so he can tell them, tell the police if they find the phone, that he had no idea it was there. Will they believe him? He could have given it to them already. He could even have given it to Lana, but would anyone believe that she just left it for him to find? If he was the police or the therapist, there's no way he would believe that.

An image from the terrible night after their session with Lana pops into his head. He sees his hands around Sandy's neck. But that didn't happen. He went to her room, he was drunk but that didn't happen, did it?

If he hands over Sandy's phone, it will point them directly at him. It's always the husband and Sandy has convinced her therapist that he's abusive. Lana has spoken to the police. If he reveals he has the phone, they probably won't even stop to ask questions before they lock him up. He has to be here for his kids. There's no way he's telling anyone about the phone.

It's getting close to 3 p.m. and school pick-up time so he drops his phone on the passenger seat and pulls off, his cheek burning fiercely. At a traffic light he pulls down the mirror to see what he looks like and is shocked by how bad it looks, as though he has actually been touched by fire.

Will the kids notice? Maybe. He'll just tell them he fell at work. They're too young to question the validity of the statement.

He pulls up outside the school and, mindful of other parents, takes a cap out of his glove box and jams it on his head, pulling it low and keeping his sunglasses on.

Even so, as he walks through the school he can feel some

curious looks but Felix and Lila are standing together instead of playing in separate areas, so they are in and out quickly.

'Is Mum at home?' asks Felix as soon as they are both buckled into their booster seats.

'No, she's still on her... holiday,' he replies. *Maybe she's not on holiday, maybe she's run away, maybe she's with another man, maybe she's dead. I hope she's dead.*

'How come she wanted a holiday without us?' demands Lila.

'Because she needed to rest, I've told you.'

'It's not fair. I need to rest too.' Lila pouts and Mike has one of those moments when he understands that if his life were different right now, he would be able to laugh. If the right Mike was picking up his kids from school, he would try and remember his five-year-old telling him she needs to rest. It would be a cute anecdote to repeat at the pub or work. But he can't go to the pub because he has to take care of the kids, and soon, he won't have a job to go to. There's nothing to smile at or laugh about right now.

Nothing is funny right now; nothing can be.

'How about pizza for dinner?' he says instead and both Felix and Lila cheer at the unexpected treat.

'I'll pick it up now and then warm it up later,' he tells them, mindful of how much cheaper it is to pick up a pizza than to have it delivered.

He has no idea how much money the administrators will allocate to paying off staff. He has a few thousand in his bank account and some money in an emergency fund.

As he pulls away from the school, he can feel his frustration mounting. How can Sandy have put him in this position and why would she have done this? *I think I hate her. I really do.*

Stopping outside the pizza place, he turns around and looks at his kids, two children who would not be here if not for an accident that led to Felix. Who would he be now if he had told

Sandy that he wasn't ready for a baby, if they hadn't both still been in the stupid infatuation phase? She would have happily terminated the pregnancy, he knows that.

He's pretty certain they wouldn't be together; he wouldn't be tied into an awful marriage with a woman incapable of real feelings for him or his children. He would be free, maybe still single.

'Don't move, guys,' he says sternly and both children nod, happy to stay in the car.

Stepping inside the small store, he orders and keeps an eye on the car through the large windows. And he allows himself a few minutes of fantasy, of embracing the idea of freedom from everything.

Picturing himself on a motorbike riding around Australia and working in bars, a sense of calm settles over him. He can almost feel the rush of the wind as he drives through the vast desert. He's always wanted to have a motorbike but he's never had the money to buy one.

'Dude,' he hears, 'dude,' and he's jolted back to reality, where a teenage boy with scraggly hair is standing behind the counter, three pizza boxes in front of him.

'Sorry,' says Mike, the fantasy evaporating as his real life hits him in the face with the smell of melted cheese.

At home, he lets the kids grab junk food snacks from the pantry even though he knows Sandy says they should have a healthy snack when they come home from school but, *Screw that*, he thinks. *I'm in charge now.*

He grabs a beer and sits down at the kitchen table, scrolling through videos until he sees it's nearly 5.00 p.m. He has no idea where the time has gone and he goes upstairs to their bedroom to change and is immediately struck by the lingering smell of

Sandy's perfume, as though she has just been here instead of gone for nearly two days.

The floral musky scent is so strong he feels like he's imagining it. He is compelled to go to the bed, lifting the mattress to check on the phone: it's still there, right where he left it.

If he knew the lock pattern on Sandy's phone, he would have read everything on there, gone through her text messages and emails to try and figure out if anything was going on. He's tried as many combinations as he can think of but after three, the phone freezes up for a few hours.

She could be anywhere with anyone. She could be with another man. That's really likely. She likes telling him about the men who flirt with her and once… a long time ago, he even enjoyed hearing her stories, knowing that she belonged to him. Maybe she's met someone and they've gone off together. Maybe Sandy has been having an affair for some time now and that's where she is. He finds that the idea of her with someone else doesn't bother him at all but the idea that she would simply walk out of her children's lives makes him furious. What if she never returns and he's left taking care of the kids? How will he get a job and manage?

Looking around the room, he tries to figure out if anything has changed or if he's just imagining the smell. He goes over to her dressing table, lifting her bottle of perfume and spraying it into the air, coughing as it catches in his throat, and then he sits down on the small stool she has there and goes through all her drawers, wondering why he hasn't thought to do this before. He should have gone through everything, not just the clothes. The first drawer contains make-up and face creams, small pots of incredibly expensive creams that make him crazy each time they show up on the credit card statement. Why hasn't she taken any of it? Another drawer contains her hairdryer and hairbrushes in different shapes and sizes. It looks like she's actually left everything behind.

He opens her jewellery box, a birthday present from him, timber inlaid with a diamond-shaped mother of pearl decal, creating a beautiful multicoloured sheen. Lifting the lid, he can see that her costume jewellery is still there but her wedding and engagement rings are not. She wears those every day. If she'd left him, would she have left them behind?

Standing, he goes to the door of the bedroom and listens for the kids but he can only hear the television so they are probably zoned out, staring at the screen. He needs to give them dinner and get them into bed. The hours are getting away from him.

He moves over to Sandy's bedside table, emptying everything, throwing nail polish and nail files, an article on plastic surgery that she's torn out of a magazine somewhere, a book on parenting that he scoffs at, all on the bed. There's nothing of value. Sighing, he goes to the closet and feels around on the top shelf, coming across a shoe box that he pulls out.

Inside there are two envelopes. Sitting down on the bed, he opens each one. They are the life insurance policies, one for her and one for him. Did Sandy really not remember the discussion the two of them had about taking policies out? She looks after the household bills and the mortgage and he does occasionally just sign stuff when she asks him to, like he did with this. He remembers her saying, 'I think we need to have life insurance policies in case something happens to either of us.' He agreed with that. Money meant breathing room and stability. Why did she accuse him of doing this without her knowledge?

'Felix, stop it, stop it,' he hears Lila shout and he gives up trying to understand anything, putting everything back and going downstairs before World War III breaks out between his children.

'I'm doing dinner now, guys,' he tells them, 'but if you fight, no pizza. I'll eat it all myself.' The kids are instantly quiet.

Should he call the detective back now? The man hasn't called again but what if he shows up here?

He grabs his own phone from his pocket and googles, 'How long does it take police to track a phone?' and spends five minutes lost in the legal intricacies of police tracking phones and needing permission and using cell phone towers as the oven heats up.

It's not as simple as it's made out to be, obviously. Mindful of what could happen over the next few days, he deletes his browsing history.

The ideal thing would be if she were dead. Then he would have a hundred thousand dollars to help him manage and that's a lot of breathing room. Her being dead would actually be the best outcome.

EIGHTEEN

Lana

I have half an hour until my next patient arrives and all I want to do is get up and leave right now, fetch my child early and lock the both of us in my house, but I already told Kirsty I would wait for my next patient so I have no choice.

At least Iggy is at school and safe. Mike knows that I have a child – someone I will do anything to protect.

I went to his house and I am sure that he's not above coming to my home. Perhaps I should call Ben and talk to him about this but after the way he reacted when I told him about going over to Mike and Sandy's house, I have no desire to tell him that he was right about everything. And he has enough to deal with right now with whatever is going on with his parents overseas.

Sitting down at my desk, I take Detective Franks' card out of my wallet, running my fingers across the smooth flat surface as I bite down on my lip. I wish I didn't have to call him but I know I need to report Mike for coming here. He didn't threaten me exactly but he grabbed me and I felt vulnerable and scared.

Who knows what would have happened if Kirsty had not returned from getting coffee?

Before I call him, I make one last attempt at calling Sandy. She doesn't answer and an automated voice tells me that her mailbox is full. A very bad sign. She hasn't listened to any new messages for a while.

I dial the detective's number, expecting to get his voicemail, but he answers.

'Franks here.'

'Detective Franks, this is Lana Stanton. I came to see you this morning.'

'Ah yes, Ms Stanton...'

'I need to tell you that Mike, Sandy's husband, just turned up here. He wanted me to tell the police that he wouldn't hurt his wife and he... grabbed my wrist. I mean he didn't hurt me but I was scared and I really feel that you should speak to him. I don't know... I was scared.' I know that I sound very unsure but I'm not certain what else to say.

'If he hurt you, you can file charges for assault,' says the detective. 'If he laid hands on you in any way, you can file charges.'

I think about what it would take to file charges, to go down to the police station and spend some time doing that. 'If I do, will you arrest him?'

'Well, we would go and see him and get his version of events. And he may be arrested, yes. Did anyone else witness what happened?'

'My receptionist came in at the end. She had gone to get coffee and she came in and he was next to me and she saw that he was holding my wrist.'

'Okay, well you can come down and report the incident and we will look into it.'

This is not the answer that I wanted. I want the police to

care more, to help me. Maybe they would be able to figure out exactly what's going on.

'Do you know that he has a criminal record?' I ask the detective as I pick up my pen from my desk and begin doodling on my notepad. I feel like I want to jump out of my skin and I'm trying to keep myself grounded.

'Who told you that?' Explaining it all would take too long. 'Sandy – she told me when I was treating her,' I lie. I glance at my phone, seeing that I only have fifteen minutes.

The detective clears his throat. 'Interesting,' he says and I have no idea what he means by that.

'Look, I don't actually want to file charges against Mike. I just want to know that Sandy is okay,' I tell the detective as I stand and begin pacing around my office. 'I'm really worried about Sandy.'

The detective is quiet for a moment. 'Actually, I was going to call you.'

'Oh?' I stop walking, hold my breath.

'Yeah, we had a call about twenty minutes ago from Mrs Burkhart.'

'What?' I don't understand what he's told me and a mixture of relief and disbelief flow through me. Sandy called them?

'Mrs Burkhart just called me; well, she called the station and explained the situation and was put through to me. She has confirmed what her husband told you, which is that she needed some time away. She was apologetic about any waste of police time.'

A thousand questions and scenarios run through my mind. 'But why didn't she call me or her husband? He was just here. Are you sure it was her? Maybe she was coerced? Maybe he's got her locked up in that house and he's... hurting her. Why would he have come here if he knew she was safe? Does he know?'

'Ms Stanton,' says the detective firmly, 'you need to slow down. Mrs Burkhart called us from her phone. She confirmed her details and she also said that you have taken a more than usual interest in her as a client, something that was beginning to make her feel uncomfortable, and that's why she did not come to her session and she has not returned your calls.'

'But how did she know that I'd gone to the police?'

'I called her this morning and left a message on her phone, asking her to contact me and informing her that there was a concern for her safety. She must have assumed that you were the one making the report.'

I sit back down in my chair and I can feel my mouth opening and closing as I struggle to find a suitable reply. I cannot believe what I'm hearing.

'Her mailbox is full,' I say. 'I tried to call her again and her mailbox is full. That doesn't happen – I mean she must have listened to her messages if she's okay and if she listened to your message, it wouldn't be full.'

'She did tell me that you have called her a lot and of course her husband did as well but as Mrs Burkhart said, she just needed a couple of days away. That's hardly a crime. I know my own wife has a girls' weekend every now and again and it really helps with her mental health. You're a therapist. I'm sure you understand that sometimes rest is needed.'

I feel patronised, condescended to, humiliated. There is no point in continuing this conversation. 'How come she hasn't told her husband then? Why did he just turn up here and ask me to speak to the police?'

He sighs. 'Mrs Burkhart did tell me she and her husband had a disagreement and she felt some time apart was a good idea. She said that she would let him know that she's safe and I'm sure she will do that shortly. I assume she has her reasons for not contacting him right away and while that may not be the best way for her to handle the situation, police do not get involved in people's marriages unless there is a reason.'

I think about the dying months of my marriage to Oliver when I would contact him ten times a day sometimes, getting all my anger out over text, and he would simply ignore every message.

Is this the same thing? No, I think this is different. 'There is—'

The detective doesn't let me finish. 'If we interfered in every argument, we would have no time for anything else. I'm sure you understand.' I can hear the background sounds of phones ringing and people talking. He must be in an open space.

'But Mike...' I mutter, unable to process this.

The detective clears his throat, unable to conceal his desire to end this conversation. 'Again, Ms Stanton, Mrs Burkhart has said that she will speak to her husband and that she expects they will resolve their disagreement. I imagine she will go home soon and all will be well. But he should not have come to your office and threatened you. If you would like to press charges, I advise you to go to your nearest police station and they will be able to help you start the process.' The background sounds grow muffled and I know that he's taken the phone away from his ear to talk to someone else. He's done with me and whatever has been going on here.

Mike did not look like a man whose wife was just taking some time away, so Sandy had obviously not called him yet. And Mike looked like an angry man who was worried about the police catching him. Unless that was all an act.

'You should be relieved that this situation is sorted out, Ms Stanton. I would ask that you do not contact Mrs Burkhart again. I'm sure you understand.'

I imagine the man is smiling, enjoying this. 'I do,' I say

shortly. 'I'm glad she's okay, thank you.' I end the call before he can say anything else. Pompous arse.

It's incredibly rude of Sandy to not reply to my messages and I feel like I have been manipulated into behaving like an idiot.

'Vanessa is here,' says Kirsty through the intercom.

I take a deep breath, pushing everything that has happened today away for one more hour. 'Send her in,' I tell Kirsty and I stand, ready to greet my next patient.

Has Sandy been lying to me all along? Or is Mike lying? Does he know where Sandy is and this whole charade is to make me back off? Why did Sandy call the police?

I rub my hand across my eyes, wishing the next hour away as it occurs to me that maybe Sandy and Mike are doing this together. Maybe this is a game to the two of them and I have been taken along for the ride? This makes sense to me in a way that nothing else has.

My skin prickles as I realise that I have been made a fool of, that I have been turned into a joke. As though no time has passed, I am back at school, standing on the stage, holding up my award for English as my fellow students laugh and jeer. I was so nervous to be up on that stage, so happy to have won despite my grief over Janine that I couldn't help some tears. And that made me even more of a joke. I was the girl who thought winning a stupid award was worth crying over. They had all forgotten about Janine by then, as though she had never even existed at all, and I had spent the last months of school alone in the library once again.

I hate feeling like this.

The door opens and my patient comes in. 'I had another argument with my mother,' says Vanessa without even saying hello, and I am pulled away from my thoughts, but as I sit down, I know I am not going to just let this have happened to me. I can feel the anger inside me at this woman and her husband, even at

Ben, who pulled me into this weird situation; I can feel it growing and getting hotter. I hate to be made a fool of and it's not something I will tolerate.

I think about the gun in my desk drawer. It's not something I will tolerate at all.

NINETEEN

TUESDAY NIGHT

Mike

Mike lets the kids eat in front of the television again, because why not?

He sits in the kitchen with a beer and his phone, scrolling through Facebook and Instagram, looking at stupid videos of people falling over. He checks Sandy's Instagram but she hasn't posted anything on there.

It's only Tuesday night but it feels like she's been gone for a really long time.

Maybe something has actually happened to her. Is that possible? Her car is here so it couldn't have been an accident.

The police know she's missing now so they are probably checking the hospitals. There's really nothing for him to do but wait. Surely if they found her, they would call him, although perhaps that's why the detective left a message for him. He should call him back right now. But he can't quite bring himself to do it.

It feels like that will start a chain of events over which he has no control.

Even though he's done it a few times, Mike checks the credit card purchases again but Sandy hasn't used it since Sunday afternoon, when she did some online shopping for new bath towels, which have yet to turn up.

'Stop hitting me, Felix,' Lila screams and Mike grinds his teeth. He really doesn't want to have to sort them out. He wants to wipe out this day with beer. But he stands and goes to the living room. 'Right, no more fighting, bath time for you two,' he says.

'Me first, me first,' shouts Felix. 'I want bubbles.'

'I want bubbles too,' says Lila, jumping up and down, her argument with her brother forgotten.

'Everyone can have bubbles,' says Mike.

An hour later, the house is finally quiet and Mike is slumped at the kitchen table, shovelling cold pizza into his mouth in between sips of beer. Sandy would be horrified at how they are eating. He's going to need to get his shit together and start cooking and do some shopping as well. The fridge is nearly empty because Sandy usually does a big shop on a Monday, and from what he can see, tomorrow he is sending both kids to school with processed crap to eat again.

He's on his third beer when his phone rings. It's his mother, and he considers not answering it, just letting it go to voicemail, but she doesn't call often so he worries when she does.

'Mum?'

'Sweetheart,' she says.

'Everything okay?'

'Yes, yes, fine, fine. Dad is, well… you know. His doctor told him he needs to cut out the alcohol and start exercising but he said that he's seventy-two years old and he doesn't care if his time is now.' Mike doesn't say anything to this although he cannot help the thought that if his father's time was now, it would be a good thing. The violence in his parents' marriage has stopped but only because his father is weaker and his mother generally makes a plan to stay out of his way. Since he retired, Mike's father, Vince, sits on the couch watching television and drinking beer. Mike has told his mother, Rose, to leave him many times but she claims to be too old to make the change and to have to live by herself. Any time Mike suggested having his mother come live with them, Sandy vetoed that idea immediately. The only thing Mike can do for her is send her money each month, something that really pisses Sandy off.

'How are the babies?' she asks and Mike smiles, because he can hear how much she loves her grandchildren. His parents live nearly two hours away, which isn't so far, but they don't get to see their grandchildren as much as his mother would like, and to be fair, Mike doesn't really want them near his father.

'They're good, growing up, you know.'

'And... Sandy?' his mother asks tentatively.

'She's...' Mike takes a long sip of beer. 'Fine.'

'Good... good, that's good.'

'Mum, is anything wrong?' Usually she talks without him needing to say anything, telling him about her friends at bridge and the library and her outings with the community centre.

'Well... look, darling, I didn't want to say anything... because it really wasn't my place and I can't understand why she called me anyway.'

'I don't understand, Mum, who called you?' He lifts the beer bottle to take another sip but finds it empty so he gets up and takes another from the fridge.

'Well, I might as well tell you everything. Sandy called me last week and, you know, she doesn't call me at all. I mean I think I've heard from her five times in the last eight years.' Mike knows this is the truth. He has, over the time he and Sandy have been together, tried to encourage his wife to give his mother a call on her birthday and sometimes just to check in but Sandy always has the same reply to his requests which is, 'She's your mother and I have to call my parents and I am not asking you to speak to them at all.'

'What day did she call, Mum?' he asks, his heart beating a little faster as he grips the beer bottle.

'Oh, it was last Monday, I think. No, yes actually, definitely last Monday because there was a meeting at the library where we had a talk about ageing gracefully. They encouraged us to exercise and lift weights but honestly, I feel like—'

'Mum,' he interrupts, 'you said Sandy called you on Monday?' He can only assume that since the therapy appointment with Lana was in the morning, it was after the debacle of a session where he walked out.

'Yes, and you know I was very surprised, sweetheart, but I was even more bothered by what she had to say.' His mother does this when there is something she is afraid of saying. He knows this from his childhood, when she had to give his father bad news about a plumbing bill or about something he'd done wrong at school or anything else that might set the man off. She dances around uncomfortable subjects, afraid to put a foot wrong because she knows what happens if she does.

She takes a deep breath. 'I've thought about this for days, Mike. And I never wanted to say anything.'

'Mum, please,' Mike pleads.

'Well, she said that she wanted me to talk to you because you were starting to behave like your father and she was worried that the kids were going to get hurt and I asked her... I mean I hardly knew what to say but I had to ask her so I did, I asked her if she ever got hurt and she told me that—'

'Mum... Mum.' Mike is not going to listen to this. 'Anything she said is a lie. You know me. I wouldn't hurt her or the kids, you know that.' He raises his voice as he picks up the half-full bottle of beer and paces around the kitchen, feeling its weight in his hand. He thinks he can actually see red, actually see the colour red in front of his eyes as rage fills him up, and he lifts the bottle to chuck it against the wall, only stopping because he knows the noise will bring the kids downstairs. *That lying, lying bitch.*

Why include his mother? Why upset his mother?

'Please don't be angry at me, Mike. I didn't want to say anything but I can't stop thinking about it and I had to know. But I do know you and I know you wouldn't hurt those babies, or her.' His mother's voice is filled with desperation. She cannot have a son who is abusing his family and Mike knows that.

Taking a deep breath, he speaks slowly and carefully so that he does not give in to the rage. It's rapidly being replaced with shame anyway, shame that anyone, especially his mother, could believe this about him. But she's not the only one, of course. Lana and probably the guy who treated Sandy before that and now the police believe the same thing and there is nothing Mike can do about it because even his picture evidence means nothing. 'I have never and would never hurt my family. I promise you that. Sandy is... I don't think she's right in the head at the moment. She's behaving very strangely and I am trying to get her help, but you can't believe anything she says.'

'Oh, darling,' says his mother and he can hear the relief in her voice, 'why didn't you tell me? I would have come to stay and help – you know you can call me. Shall I come? I could set off tomorrow.'

Mike finds his eyes filling with tears and his shame intensifies at his weakness. 'No... no, it's fine, really, everything is fine. Everything will be fine, don't worry.' Things would be easier with his mother here, but would he be able to tell her to leave his father at home? Would she agree to that? And does he want her to see what's going on here, to know that Sandy is actually missing, or that the police and her therapist think she's missing because he did something to her? No, he doesn't want that. He can't deal with having to explain this to anyone else right now. 'Things are all right, I promise,' he says.

'Okay... okay, you call me anytime, anytime at all, and tell Sandy she can do the same.'

'I will, but I need to go now, Felix is calling me.'

'Of course, of course, you kiss those babies for me and I'm here for whatever you need.'

'Thanks, Mum, love you.'

'Love you too.'

Mike ends the call and sits down in the silent kitchen in the silent house. Sandy must hate him very much. Her hatred is gorge-deep and filled with anger. Why would she have done that to his mother? How could she have done that? Sandy would have known how devastated his mother would be to hear that about her son. It was an incredibly callous and cruel thing to do. But it shouldn't surprise him.

He finishes the beer, opens another one, drinks half of that and then he listens to the message from the detective again.

Screw it, he thinks, tapping on his phone to return the call. The man won't be at work but it doesn't matter.

'You've reached the message bank of Detective Nathan Franks. If this is an emergency, please hang up and call triple zero, otherwise leave a message at the beep.'

'Yeah hi, I mean, hello, this is Mike Burkhart, my wife is... You called me about my wife, Sandy. I'm just returning your call.'

There are a thousand other things he could say but he hangs up and then he goes upstairs and checks on his sleeping children before he puts himself to sleep with beer. He dreams of his hands around his wife's neck, of strangling the breath out of her pretty body.

He thinks about her forgetting the insurance policies and about the lies she told her therapist and he wonders if, perhaps, Sandy is, as he told his mother, not right in the head, if something is actually going on with her. Has she had a breakdown and disappeared or has she disappeared on purpose to drive him crazy and to make his life miserable? If something is wrong with her, he would be able to find some sympathy for her, but if she is doing this with intent, if she knows what's going to happen to him because of it, then he needs to know why she has done it. And he also needs to know what else she has planned. What exactly is Sandy hoping to achieve by disappearing, and what does that mean for him?

TWENTY

TUESDAY NIGHT

Lana

It's after 4.30 p.m. and I find myself too wired to sit down. Dinner just needs to be warmed up and I've already put on a load of laundry, and I contemplate a glass of wine but I know that's a bad idea. I pace around my small kitchen, opening the fridge and searching in the pantry for something that will make me feel better. But there's nothing I want. My hand goes to the wrist where Mike grabbed me and I touch it, still feeling some sensation of his hand around it, of the strength the man has.

But Sandy is fine, that's what the detective said. So how come Mike didn't know that? How come Sandy hadn't contacted him to tell him she was fine? Why would he come to my office if she had? The questions keep coming up as I try to understand exactly what's going on here.

And suddenly I cannot stay in the house any longer.

'Iggy,' I call.

'Yeah,' my son replies from the living room, where he is watching television and eating his apple.

'Do you want to ride your bike next to me while I have a run?'

'Yes, yes, yes,' he shouts, bouncing into the kitchen with delight. 'We haven't done that for a million, billion years.'

I laugh at his joy, taking a moment of pleasure from the day.

Outside it's cold, the temperature dropping quickly, and I know that soon it will be dark. It's September and the beginning of spring but any warmth feels very far away. I pick streets where I know there will be fewer cars and some lights. Iggy and I have done this before and he knows the rules: he rides on the path and I run behind him.

It's hard at first, my knees complaining and my lungs burning with each breath, and I am momentarily upset at myself for not doing this more often, especially since Iggy enjoys it so much.

But soon I settle into a rhythm, my breathing evens out and I feel a rush of endorphins. Iggy zooms along in front of me and I'm pleased that very few people are out.

After half an hour we get to the end of the cycle paths and Iggy stops so we can turn around. His cheeks glow red with exhilaration and cold.

'Hold up a minute,' I say, 'I need to check my phone.' I want a minute to catch my breath before we go back and I know Iggy is not tired at all.

I glance down at my phone and see I have a new message. Shock ripples through me as I open it and see who it's from.

Sandy. I read it once and then again.

Lana, help me. He's going to kill me.

Where are you? I type back quickly, seeing that the message came through fifteen minutes ago. I stare down at the phone as sweat dries on my body and the cold wind seeps in through my layers.

But there's no reply. Now what? Now what the hell do I do? 'Okay, let's go,' I say to Iggy.

And we're off again. My feet pound the pavement as I struggle to keep my thoughts in order.

Finally, we are home and I tell Iggy I'm going for a shower. Standing under the hot water, I again turn over the idea that this is all some sort of sick game that Sandy and Mike play together, that they like the attention and the fear that this generates. Is that possible? They have two small children and Mike works, so where are they finding the time for this kind of thing? Unfortunately, this wouldn't be the strangest thing I've ever heard of in my time as a psychologist.

At conferences there are often whispered tales of odd patients. Ben's experience with Carla comes to mind. I know why he didn't want to work with Sandy. It must have been so hard for him but I wonder if he has considered that this is some sort of game between Sandy and Mike.

Sitting down on the edge of my bed, I call his number, wanting to leave a message saying that I hope everything is okay. But he answers the phone.

'Lana, hi.'

'Hey, Ben, I just wanted to check in and see that everything was okay... with your parents. I'm not sure what's happening but I just wanted to check in,' I finish lamely.

'Ah, thanks for calling.' He sighs. 'Honestly, it's nice to talk to someone who understands about this stuff. My dad has bipolar disorder and he was off his meds and my mother couldn't cope so I was up all of last night on the phone, speaking to his doctors and trying to be there for her. I know I can't see patients on so little sleep but I came in just to make sure no one needed to see me urgently. I got a nap in and I'll call my mother soon because I need to make sure that she knows she has my support. I feel so bad for being here when I should be there. I just want to make sure that it's all under control again.'

I feel a pang of sympathy. Everything going on with Sandy and Mike shouldn't be affecting Ben, not now when he has his own family stuff to deal with. 'If you want to go over there, I'm sure it'd be okay – I mean I'm sure Kirsty can reschedule all your patients.'

'No, no, it's fine. I won't have to take time off after all because I found him a place at a clinic and it's private so it's not cheap. Basically, I need to work.'

'I understand and I'm glad you got it sorted out. But if things change, do what you need to do. I'm sorry you're going through this.'

'Thanks, Lana. Anyway, that's life,' he says with a dry laugh. 'Is everything okay with you?

'Well...' I begin, unsure of how to explain things.

'I have been thinking about Sandy but I assumed you would tell me if there was anything to know. Have you heard from police?'

'Um...' I take a deep breath, relieved to be able to talk to him about this because I really need to talk to someone. I fill him in on today and then I explain about the message that I just received. I tell him about my theory that this is some sort of game between the two of them.

'That's bizarre. But do you think it's actually some kind of game? I mean what's the payoff?'

I know that this is an important question because it's the question we try to encourage our patients to ask of themselves when they are engaging in destructive behaviour. What's the payoff? What are you getting from binge-eating or gaming or dating emotionally unavailable men? Human beings are not that complicated and even terrible, damaging addictions have some sort of payoff, regardless of whether a person is able to acknowledge and understand it or not.

'I don't know. Maybe they get off on the idea that a stranger is thinking about them and worrying? But what if the police have it wrong and Sandy is actually in danger?'

'Maybe call them again, explain about the message.'

'I can't. Detective Franks seems to believe that I'm overly invested in Sandy and specifically warned me off. And Franks says that Sandy is actually bothered by my behaviour but I can't just ignore the message either.'

Ben says nothing for a bit . 'You're not thinking of going over there again, Lana, are you?'

I realise that this is exactly what I am thinking about. If I go over there and tell Mike I'm willing to listen to him, maybe I can figure out what's real and what's not.

'Lana,' says Ben, 'tell me what you're thinking.'

'The police think I'm the problem, Ben, and it may be that this is all some sort of game, but what if it's not? What are my options here?'

Ben sighs. 'Okay, listen. If you're going to go over there, I'll come with you, okay? We need there to be two people to make sure that whatever he tells us, we can corroborate it. And you need to... bring that gun in case he really has done something.'

I don't know what to say to that. Having the gun has made me feel safer. I couldn't physically stop Mike any other way. But it feels like a scary escalation to bring it when I go over to Mike and Sandy's house, as though I am inviting more violence into the situation than necessary.

'Do you really think we need it?'

'We're just going to talk and hopefully it'll all get cleared up.'

The gun is only a prop and he's offering to come with me. It will be different to last time, when I found myself in the house alone with Mike.

'Okay, okay good, so when do we go over there?'

'I mean... tonight if you can get someone to watch Iggy.'

Lana, help me. He's going to kill me. Sandy's message was clear but was it all for show or is she really in danger?

I can't go rushing over to that house again. I feel pulled in different directions with each passing moment. This is real and a woman could get hurt. This is a game and these two people are looking for an audience. This is just a misunderstanding and the message was a mistake.

Whatever this is, I need to consider that I am a mother with a child and I can't make any stupid decisions.

I need to take a step back from this, do some proper research on Sandy and Mike, consult some of my case studies, see if I can find anything on the internet like this.

'No, not tonight,' I tell him, 'tomorrow night, Wednesday night. Iggy sleeps over at Oliver's on Wednesday night.'

Ben breathes down the line. 'Okay. Whatever works for you.'

I feel a rush of guilt all over again. *But I tried to help. I called the police and they think I'm the problem.* 'I know we're both worried now but I feel like I need to look into this a bit more.'

'Of course. I'll see you tomorrow at work, I hope.'

'I hope so too,' I reply. 'Get some sleep.' I'm not rushing into this again. I'm going to take some time, google something like this and see if anything pops up and, that way, I will be ready for what happens tomorrow.

I end the call and go downstairs to have dinner with Iggy. I sit and listen to him read after dinner, feeling a warm glow of pride at how well he's doing.

Once he's in bed and I'm back in my room, I grab my laptop and scroll through different cases that I have studied, trying to find something similar to what I believe is happening here. But there's nothing that is even close to what I think this is. And then I google 'Couple gaslight therapist' and only find endless articles and posts from people complaining that their therapists are gaslighting them. I do find some information about cluster B antisocial personalities like narcissists, who may lead the therapist where they want them to go.

I don't know if I would call Mike a narcissist but it's probable that Sandy is. I have been picking up something strange about her in every session. Is Mike being used by Sandy?

The theories circle in my brain until the alarm I have on my phone buzzes. I have it set for eleven every night or I don't get enough sleep.

Exhausted, I close down my computer and look at my phone. I try Sandy again, just in case she answers, in case she is fine, in case this is all over and I simply don't know it.

But, once again, I am told the mailbox is full. I sink into sleep more confused than ever. Is Sandy missing? Framing me? Framing her husband? Playing a game?

Or is Sandy dead?

TWENTY-ONE
WEDNESDAY

Mike

He wakes at 5 a.m. on Wednesday on the sofa, the house dark and cold, his mouth filled with cotton wool. He knows he's going to have to get his shit together and stop drinking, start parenting. Sitting up on the sagging blue sofa, he drops his head into his hands, not sure how he will manage to face another day.

After a few minutes he looks up and takes in the chaos in the living room, where dirty plates are stacked on the coffee table and the kids' things are scattered everywhere. He didn't empty their bags last night so the lunchboxes are still in there.

'Get off your arse, loser,' he hears his father say and he lets a surge of anger motivate him to stand up. Grabbing as many plates as he can carry, he goes to the kitchen and stacks them in the dishwasher. It's still dark outside.

'Twenty minutes,' he says aloud, deciding that he will clean and tidy for twenty minutes and then he can make himself a cup of coffee before his shower.

It doesn't take as long as he assumed it would once he gets going and he even manages to cobble together a lunch of cheese sandwiches for the kids along with apples to go with the processed crap he adds to their lunchboxes.

His reward is to use the last capsule for the coffee machine, something else he needs to add to the ever-growing shopping list in his head.

While he waits for the coffee to drip into the cup, he cleans a bit more, wiping down the kitchen counter and throwing out some rotting bananas from the fruit bowl.

With his coffee sitting in front of him, he is hit by a wave of exhaustion at what the rest of the day holds. He will have to get the kids to school and then drag himself into the office to answer Kellie's questions all day long as Paul mopes around the office, occasionally touching one of the framed business awards he has hung on the wall.

And Mike knows that all day long he will be waiting for the detective to contact him or for Sandy to turn up or even for the police to come to the office to arrest him for accosting Lana yesterday. That idiotic move churned through his alcohol-fuelled dreams all night long.

It's now nearly 6 a.m. and he knows the kids will be up soon. He should make some eggs and toast for them using the last of the eggs and the bread, but he doesn't really have the energy to move.

Looking around the kitchen that Sandy hates, his gaze lands on a high cupboard in the corner and he gets up, opening it and reaching for the pale blue jar with the words '**Cookie Jar**' on the front in thick black letters. Sandy brought it home from some craft fair when she was pregnant with Felix.

'What's that for? You don't eat cookies and those things don't keep them fresh anyway,' he said.

She shrugged and smiled. 'I know but it's so cute – we can throw loose change in there.'

And that's what they have used it for, for years. Few people carry cash these days but Mike still finds himself with coins on the odd occasion he does use actual money.

The jar was filled with coins the last time he looked, gold one- and two-dollar coins as well as lots of silver. He wonders how much might be in there and feels himself flush with embarrassment that he thinks the money may help, but his lost job is on his mind all the time. How long until he can't pay the mortgage? Even fifty dollars extra would bring some comfort right now.

He reaches up with both hands because he knows the jar is heavy but when he lifts it with some force, he nearly smashes it into the top of the cupboard because it's so light.

Confused, he brings the cookie jar, which does not rattle with coins as it has always done, back to the table and then drains his coffee.

Opening it, he sees that it's stuffed full of pieces of paper. He reaches in and pulls out a handful.

And then he smooths the pieces of paper, some crumpled, some neatly folded, with his hands and stares down at them in horror. 'What the hell?' he mutters.

Each piece is an article, either from a newspaper or printed out from the internet.

Reading through the headlines, one after the other, he realises that Sandy is not suffering from some kind of mental breakdown. Sandy is planning something. And he is in trouble because he has no idea what she is going to do.

Every article is about an abused wife who kills her husband. Every single one.

And in each article, the wife has not gone to prison for her crime.

**WOMAN WHO BEAT ABUSIVE HUSBAND TO DEATH
CLEARED OF MURDER**

WOMAN ABUSED BY HUSBAND ACQUITTED OF FATAL STABBING

BATTERED WOMAN FOUND 'NOT GUILTY' OF HUSBAND'S DEATH

There are at least twenty articles, some going back decades. Mike reads snatches of the stories that come from all over the world.

A Minnesota woman was cleared of all charges in the stabbing murder of her husband, telling reporters outside court that, 'It was him or me. I knew that the next time he started hitting me, he would not stop until I was dead.'

Friends of the Sydney-based woman have expressed gratitude to the judge for finding her 'not guilty' of murder in the first degree after she hit her husband with a hammer, killing him in two blows. 'She suffered for years at his hands. She was always covered in bruises and every time she tried to leave, he found her and beat her again. No one seemed to be able to help. He had too many connections, too much money, and everyone she reached out to failed her,' a friend who did not want to be named is quoted as saying.

Today, a woman from Manchester has escaped a prison sentence for the poisoning murder of her abusive husband. After many years of emotional and physical abuse, the woman felt she had no choice but to end her husband's life. Council for the defence stated that she had acted in self-defence and this was accepted by the jury.

The ghoulish collection stuns him. Over the last few years of his marriage, he has seriously questioned the kind of woman he is married to, but looking down at the articles, he understands he has underestimated just how different a human being Sandy is. And now she's disappeared and the police want to question him.

Incandescent rage floods through his body and he stands, lifting the jar and chucking it across the kitchen, where it connects with a wall and shatters into pieces, blue shards of pottery flying everywhere.

'Dad, Dad,' he hears as he stands staring down at the wreckage. 'What was the noise, Daddy? There's a noise,' shouts Felix, and Mike wants to roar with frustration but he can't do that because now he's woken the kids and he has to clean up the mess. He hates his life, hates it.

Two hours later he's dropped the kids at school and he's parked outside work, giving himself a pep talk so that he can get through the next hour and the one after that. He will have to leave early again today to pick up the kids but Paul doesn't seem to mind – but then, why would he?

One comforting thought comes to him as he gets out of his car: he is here and Sandy is not, so whatever she had planned, whatever she was thinking, it hasn't quite worked out that way. Even with his heavy day weighing on him, he is able to smile at that thought.

Paul calls him in for a meeting as he walks through the door.

'I can give you one month's pay as severance. I know it's... a paltry sum for someone who's worked for a company for ten years but there's nothing I can do, Mike, just nothing I can do.' The older man shakes his head sadly and Mike wants to protest at the unfairness of it all but then the company going bankrupt will have to get in line behind all the other unfair things he has twisting through his mind.

He shrugs. 'Not much you can do, Paul. I understand.'

'I'm not the one making the decisions anymore. It's the worst feeling in the world, I swear, it's just the worst.'

'I hear that,' says Mike and he gets up to leave. *You have no idea how bad things can get, no idea at all.*

'Is your wife back from her... where did you say she's gone again?'

'She's taken herself on a little holiday,' says Mike, unable to conceal the bitterness in his tone.

Paul looks at him over his glasses. 'Not the best time for it.'

'No,' agrees Mike, 'no, it's not.'

He's grateful to leave at 3 p.m. so he can get the kids, grateful to not be watching the front door, waiting for the police. The detective has not called him either and he debates with himself over calling again but decides against it.

When he pulls up outside school, his phone rings and he sees that, as though he has conjured the man out of thin air, it's the detective. Lifting the phone to answer it, he watches his finger tremble as it goes to slide across the screen. And then he puts the phone down on the passenger seat, watches it ring until it stops. *I can't do it. I just can't do it.*

He takes the kids grocery shopping, letting them choose what they want as long as it's on sale. He doesn't have the energy for an argument. In his head he plans some meals that he knows he can cook while Lila and Felix debate a bar of chocolate over a packet of small chocolates, eventually deciding on the packet so they can share it equally. The total for all the groceries makes him sick and he contemplates putting some stuff back but the kids are ratty and tired and he just wants to get home.

For dinner, he manages a passable spaghetti and sauce for the kids although he assumes that part of the reason they don't complain is because they are allowed to watch television while they eat, and he gets through bath time and bedtime with the usual issues. He cannot imagine doing this alone for the rest of his life but the kids won't be little forever. There are plenty of single dads in the world, plenty. He has stuffed all of Sandy's hideous articles at the top of the cupboard, not wanting to look at them but also wanting to keep them for when she does turn up, if she does turn up.

Just after 8 p.m., he's in the kitchen, scrolling through job ads, despite having already looked today, hoping that something new pops up, when his phone vibrates with a text.

It's probably Paul with yet another request from the auditor which Mike has no interest in reading but he opens it anyway without looking at who it's from.

There's something you need to know about your wife. Please contact me.

Mike stares down at the words. Is this a joke? And if so, why? He doesn't recognise the number. It could be the detective again but why would he change numbers? And a detective wouldn't send a message like that. Maybe it's Sandy? But she wouldn't say 'your wife'. Who knows something more about his wife?

Screw it, he thinks and then he taps on the number.

TWENTY-TWO

WEDNESDAY

Lana

I wake on Wednesday morning more exhausted than I was before I went to sleep.

'I want Nutella toast for breakfast,' Iggy calls. 'I can make it myself.'

'And what are the rules?'

'Be careful and no metal near the toaster,' he shouts and then I hear him going downstairs.

I wish I didn't have to go into work but I have a full list of patients today so I get out of bed and into a shower, standing under the hot water for longer than I should and having to go without breakfast as a result.

By the time I get to work, I am in a horrible mood, with a lack-of-caffeine headache brewing.

'Morning,' chirps Kirsty and I dredge up a smile for her. Sandy's message from last night circles in my head.

'Is Ben in?' I ask.

She shakes her head. 'No, he called to say that he had to be on the phone all night again with doctors in the UK, but he did tell me to let you know that he will be meeting with you tonight.' Kirsty raises her eyebrows as she says the words and I know she wants to ask exactly why Ben and I are meeting tonight.

'Thanks.' I make myself a quick instant coffee before going to my office.

I have fifteen minutes before my first patient so I sit down at my desk and sip my coffee while I stare down at Sandy's message. *He's going to kill me.* Is it genuine? Should I have called the police last night, and what are Ben and I going to find out when we go over to her house tonight?

I could call Mike, I suppose, and ask him outright if this is some kind of game he and his wife are playing. But maybe it would be better to catch them at it. I can imagine going to the house tonight and having her open the door and everything between them being just fine. And I will be glad to have Ben along so that I have someone else to be a witness to their gaslighting.

I look up Mike's number on Sandy's patient records and add it to my phone, not giving the contact a name. I don't want his name in my phone, and the moment this, whatever this is, is over, I'll delete it.

I really hope Ben was telling the truth about meeting me tonight. I can't go over there alone although I know that if he doesn't make it, something is obviously very wrong with his father. I feel selfish for only thinking about my own needs right now when he is dealing with an ailing parent but I need him with me.

I pick up my bag to put it in the filing cabinet, taking the gun out to hide in the drawer in case Mike turns up again. He wouldn't do that, would he?

Holding the gun, I lift it up and down, feeling its weight. I have no idea how to use it. I don't even know how to check that there's a bullet in the chamber. They're only blanks but if I want the gun to make a noise, I need to know it will do that.

Glancing at the time, I take a quick picture of the gun and then google how to open it and check. I will never need to use it, I'm sure, but I want to know.

There are an amazing number of videos on using guns, cleaning guns, checking for bullets and everything else to do with guns. Most of them are from the US, and I click on one that looks like it will give me a good overview.

I'm clumsy as I try to manipulate the gun as the man on the screen is instructing me, but finally, I get it open and manage to get the bullets out, studying them one by one.

I take an image of the bullets and google them, staring at the screen on my phone.

And then I delete everything, wiping my search history and putting the gun away. My heart is racing and my hands are sweaty. I'm sure I have no idea what I've been looking at or what I'm doing.

I get through two patient sessions, paying only minimal attention but somehow managing to make each one think I am listening, before I have an hour-long break.

With my phone in my hand, I get up and stand by the window, feeling the sun that's coming through warm my body. The days will gradually get longer and brighter and summer will be here soon. But where will I be? Will this all be far in the past?

Everything I read about the gun only hours ago circles through my mind.

And then I open my phone and call the private detective who helped me catch Oliver cheating.

I have no idea if he's even still in business or what he will make of my request but I am tired of feeling like I am being dragged along by an out-of-control car. I need to be the one driving this now.

'William?' I ask when a man answers.

'Yes,' he replies and I take a deep, relieved breath.

'It's Lana Stanton. You did some work for me four years ago – you caught my husband, Oliver... well, you caught him and I'm not sure if you remember me...'

'Lana Stanton,' he says and I can hear the tapping of a keyboard as he looks up my name. 'Oh yes, yes, I remember. How can I help?'

'I need to explain and it's a bit complicated and I don't have long.'

'Is it your husband?'

'No, we got... divorced.'

'I am sorry,' he says and he does sound genuinely sorry. I can imagine that there must be some guilt when he thinks about what he does and I wonder how many marriages he has helped end.

'It's fine but now I have... a problem.' I speak quickly and I can hear him tapping at his computer as I do, taking notes. He listens and asks questions, and twenty minutes later I have explained as much of the situation as I understand.

'Leave this with me. I'll get back to you as soon as possible.'

'I know it's a lot to ask but as you heard, things are very complicated, and I'm sure you have other clients but if you could do this today, if you can figure out what's happening and get me some answers, I will be very appreciative. As I've said I can't go to the police without more information. They think I have too much of an interest in this client.'

'I understand and I'll do my best,' he says.

It's nearly time for my next patient, but when I get off the phone, I see I have a text from Ben.

So sorry I couldn't come in today. My dad had a reaction to the medication. I think I need to take some time and go and see them. I've told Kirsty to cancel my patients for the next two weeks.

You do what you need to do. I completely understand. I hope you manage to sort it out.

I'll still come with you tonight though, don't worry.

I allow myself a relieved sigh. I thought he was going to bail on me.

Just making sure we're on the same page – what exactly are we hoping to get from going over there? I think it's important to figure out our objective so we both know exactly what to do.

I think about what I hope to achieve, what I really want from this situation. I want to expose this couple for what they are doing, make sure that they are punished for playing with me. It's not a nice emotion but it's what I feel. I won't say that to Ben though.

I want to know that she's safe and that she is actually just taking a few days away.

I agree. And once we've established that, you suggest that she go and see someone else. She's not answering your calls so you can leave the message with Mike and then tell Kirsty. There's no way you should be treated like this, and if anything happens to her, it's not your fault.

That's the problem. I feel like it will be my fault

because I allowed her to bring him in to talk.
Maybe that's what triggered this situation.

You're a good person and I know you always try and do the right thing.

Thank you, I reply as Kirsty buzzes me to let me know that my next patient is here. *I'll see you tonight.*

See you then.

The rest of the day feels like it goes on forever but I know that by tomorrow this will all be over, one way or another.

I am incredibly grateful to get a late call from William. And he has more information for me than I would have dreamed possible. He seems to have access to websites I don't have access to or perhaps he is simply better at using the internet. In a short amount of time, he provides me with quite a lot of information. I feel like the game that is being played is becoming clearer. My fury grows with each new revelation from William.

I leave the office, thankful that Becky and Oliver have Iggy so I don't have to worry about him. At home, I allow myself a glass of wine and then I make a few calls of my own, checking on Iggy, who is eating homemade chicken tenders prepared for him by Becky, and my mother, who tells me about her book club meeting. I am really just passing the time until Ben gets here.

He arrives at my house exactly when he said he would.

'I'll drive,' I say because I've been once to the home once already and he nods.

In the car we are silent until he asks for my phone. 'I want to read the text she sent,' he says and I wonder if that's because he doesn't believe me. At a traffic light, I open my phone and hand it to him and he stares at the screen.

The light turns green and I pull off, and it's only when we're parked outside Mike and Sandy's house that I realise Ben is still holding my phone.

'You believe me, don't you?' I ask as he hands it back to me.

'Always,' he says and he touches me lightly on the shoulder.

'I'm here for you, Lana. Let's sort this out.'

I grab his hand and he squeezes his support and then we make our way to the front door and ring the bell. I take a deep breath and remind myself that this will all be over soon, very, very soon.

TWENTY-THREE
WEDNESDAY NIGHT

Mike

Mike hadn't been able to believe who answered the phone, who he was speaking to. When the call was done, he sat in stunned silence, but bubbling inside him was an undercurrent of absolute fury.

'You're a prize idiot,' he heard his father say and the man was right because that's exactly what Mike is.

All day long, the macabre headlines from the articles have run through his head, making him feel sick. Every article, no matter where it came from or who it was written by, was written so that the reader couldn't help understanding that the man, the abusive monster, the arsehole who was hurting his wife, got exactly what he deserved. Good riddance to bad rubbish.

No one ever thinks the abused wife is lying because she never is. Women don't do that.

But Sandy is not like any other woman he has ever known. In the beginning that made her interesting, exciting to be with, addicting. But now he understands she's dangerous. And he's the one in danger.

But he's not going to accept that. This is not how the story ends for him. The call that made him so angry is how this ends, how he makes sure that he is not 'the monster' in one of those articles.

When the bell rings just after 9 p.m., a time when the police come to call, Mike hopes the kids stay asleep. 'Here we go,' he mutters as he makes his way to the door.

Standing on his front step are Lana and a guy. He wants to push the door closed. He doesn't want to do this. He understood what he heard on the call and he knows he can't trust anyone. That's the only thing he knows for sure.

'Please don't shut the door,' says Lana quickly, as though she has heard his thoughts. 'I'm asking you to please let us in so we can talk. We just want to talk.'

Mike scrunches his eyes closed, a hangover headache beginning. He went to Lana's office to talk to her, to get her to listen to him, to understand what she had told the police, and she wouldn't talk to him then, but she's here now.

'This is Ben. He was originally Sandy's therapist,' says Lana before he can ask the question.

Both of these people believed everything Sandy told them. For a moment he's grateful for the four beers he's had, the alcohol dampening the rage he feels towards these two. Misplaced maybe, but he can't help it.

Part of him wants to shut the door and go back to his next beer. He has no desire to deal with this, especially after the phone call that he's now thinking may have actually been all lies and a way to trap him into admitting something. But he's not going to admit anything, not one single thing. That's the thing about living with someone who lies the way Sandy does: he is questioning everything now, even himself.

'Can we come in?' asks Lana. 'Please?'

Does he believe everything he was told on the phone only an hour ago? Maybe, maybe not, but the more he thinks about it, the more sense it makes. He has been back and forth over it with each sip of beer. Is he being lied to? Is he being told the truth?

He won't find out unless he speaks to these two people. They seem to know more than he does but then everyone seems to know more than he does.

He steps back and lets them in and then he turns and walks to the living room, putting his beer down on a console as he goes.

He turns to face the therapists, raising his hands, feeling a tiny streak of relief that it is not the police. He can handle two therapists. 'Look, before you say anything, I want to apologise for yesterday. I didn't mean to grab you and I hope I didn't hurt you. I really didn't mean to scare you,' he says to Lana, who has her handbag over her shoulder but one hand actually in the bag as though she's looking for something. Ben stands quietly next to her.

'It's okay,' says Lana, 'I know you didn't mean to.' Her voice is soft, her tone even. 'But we did want to ask you about Sandy because we are worried about her.'

Mike shrugs. 'I am too but… hopefully, she'll be back tomorrow.'

'She sent me a message,' says Lana, her chin lifting a little, and at the same time, Ben crosses his arms over his chest. The way he's just standing there is unnerving.

Mike isn't sure how to respond to this. Sandy's phone is under their mattress. He knows it is.

'Don't you want to know what she said?' asks Lana, her eyes narrowing.

'Sure,' he replies, wishing he had his beer in his hand, 'what did she say?' He makes sure to keep his arms hanging loosely by his sides.

Lana pulls her phone out of her bag and opens it to a screen, turns it around slowly and shows him the message.

Lana, help me. He's going to kill me.

'When did she send that?' he demands.

Lana looks down at her phone. 'Just before five last night.'

'I don't believe that's from her,' says Mike.

'We just want to know what's going on,' says Lana with a quick sideways glance at Ben. Mike has never seen Ben before. There's no picture of him on the clinic website. He's a good-looking man and he looks so confident, so sure of himself standing in Mike's home with his arms folded.

'That's not from her,' he says.

'How do you know?' asks Lana and her hand goes back into her bag. 'It's from her number. I have it saved in my phone.'

Mike's stomach churns from too much alcohol and too little food. This whole situation feels precarious, out of control.

He dredges up a part of himself with the ability to conceal his emotions, the part that never gets a chance because he usually, as the saying goes, wears his heart on his sleeve. His heart, his anger, his love, his hate. But he has to be a different Mike right now. Someone is playing with his life. Of that he's sure, but he's just not sure how exactly or why. For now, he will play along.

'You know, I'm not sure who you two think you are but you don't really know Sandy. My wife has taken herself off for a few days, leaving me to deal with everything, and I don't appreciate you getting involved in something that is essentially a private affair.'

'We're worried about Sandy.'

Mike chuckles at the words. They are worried about Sandy, who is collecting articles on how to get rid of her husband and get away with it. That's who they're worried about?

He's so sick of this shit, of having to do everything himself, of being screwed over by his boss in a crappy market, of having to take care of his kids when he needs time to figure out what to do next, of feeling like he's a failure as a husband and father. He's sick of all of it.

'Sandy,' he says, gritting his teeth, 'is a manipulative bitch who is probably really enjoying the fact that you're worried and I'm worried and that I have to take care of the kids and the house while I'm in the middle of everything else.' He looks at Ben. 'So you two can just get the hell out of my house, and when she gets back, I'm sure she'll be happy to know how much you both cared.'

'Now, just a minute, Mike,' says Lana and she glances at Ben again, who is staring at him like he knows something, like he really knows something and he's just waiting for Mike to confess. 'We just want to be sure that she's okay,' says Lana, holding up her hand.

Mike opens his mouth to ask them to leave again when a blood-curdling scream tears through the air from the back of the house.

TWENTY-FOUR

Lana

I stand frozen. The sound is everywhere at once as I look at Mike. His eyes widen and his face pales.

'Sandy,' says Ben. It's the first word he's uttered since we got here. The only word he's uttered. Sandy. We all heard it. It must be her. But is it?

No one moves. I can feel shock rippling through my body.

Only hours ago, I thought I understood everything that was going on. Only hours ago, I made a decision to end this whole charade.

But now I am unsure again.

No one moves and it feels like we are all holding a collective breath, waiting for the sound to come again.

TWENTY-FIVE

Mike

'What was that?' shouts Felix, his obvious concern floating down the stairs. Felix is a light sleeper.

'Nothing, just a neighbour,' shouts Mike. 'Stay in your bed, go back to sleep.' The last thing he needs is Felix and Lila getting out of bed.

Pinpricks of panic run up and down his skin at where the scream came from, at who it could be, at what this means now.

'That sounded like it came from your back garden, Mike,' says Lana, and Mike watches as her hand goes back into her bag.

'I don't... don't...' stutters Mike, looking around him. He has not anticipated this.

Part of him hopes that was it, that there will be no more screaming, but even as he thinks this, he knows it won't be the case.

'Help, help me!' a woman's voice screams and then she screams again and again, repeating her entreaty.

And in a split second, everyone moves.

Mike turns, running towards the kitchen and the back of the house. The screaming seems to be coming from outside, from the garden shed, from his garden shed where only he goes. It's filled with crap and spiderwebs and not somewhere that anyone but him, on a summer's day and in need of a lawnmower, has any interest in.

He can feel Lana and Ben following him.

He opens the kitchen door that leads to the back garden, a cold spring wind hitting him in the face, and hears again, 'Help, help me.' He runs out into the garden, towards the shed, where the door is padlocked from the outside.

'Help me!' she screams again, and Mike's whole body is suddenly covered in sweat despite the temperature. Where is she? Is it her? What the hell is going on?

He grabs the lock, struggling to open it; in his panic, he's forgotten the combination. The scream sounded so desperate, so real.

Lana is right behind him. 'Open it,' she yells, 'open it.'

Trust me, he was told on the phone, but he can't trust any of what is happening now. Why is Sandy screaming for help? Why? Whatever game is being played has turned on him again.

'I'm trying,' he yells back. 'I'm trying.' The whole situation is completely out of control.

Her hand emerges from her bag. 'Open it now,' she demands and he turns to look at her. She's holding a small hand-gun, something he's never actually seen in real life.

'Open it,' she says again, her voice filled with menace.

This is not happening, he thinks as he fumbles with the combination lock, searching his mind for the numbers that have, for the moment, completely disappeared.

TWENTY-SIX

Lana

My heart is racing. It's obviously Sandy in the shed; clearly she's been locked up here for the last few days and somehow been coerced into making a call to the police. Or is that what I'm supposed to think? The voice didn't sound like it was coming from inside the shed but rather somewhere in the garden. I have no idea what's going on and right now I am more confused than ever. What if I'm wrong about everything, and what I thought I understood only hours ago is wrong?

Mike is fumbling with the lock. Is he trying to open it or trying to stop us getting in there?

I hold the gun out towards Mike, my hand trembling even though I'm trying to hold it steady.

Glancing frantically around, I look for Ben because I want to give him the gun. He's the one who knows what to do with it. But he's not in the garden. He's probably gone to look after the kids. That's good – somebody should. But I wish I'd gone, I wish I had gone to them and Ben was here holding the gun.

'Are you mad?' whispers Mike as he twists the dial on the lock. 'Don't point that at me. It could go off.'

The sound of scraping metal makes me startle and turn and I look back at the house to see Ben standing by an upstairs window that looks out onto the garden. He's opened the window and he can hear and see everything that's going on. He doesn't look worried or even concerned. He's just standing there, statue-still, staring down at me and Mike.

'You need to get her out of there and let her go,' I say loudly.

'She's not... I don't know how she...' He keeps turning the dial. 'I can't remember.'

'You're lying,' I yell at him. He shakes his head.

Sandy is silent now. 'Sandy, Sandy,' I call, 'I'm here, it's Lana and I'm coming to help you. We're here to help you. Are you okay?' I bang on a cold tin wall, feeling its reverberation through my hand.

But there is no sound from inside the shed and only the sound of the rushing spring wind is in the garden.

'Sandy, Sandy, can you hear me?' I pound on the tin wall again. But all is silent. I step forward and push Mike slightly with one hand. I have to admit that having the gun makes me feel powerful, not as frightened of his height and his size. I make sure that Ben can hear me and see what I'm doing. He needs to be able to tell the police what happened here.

'What's the combination?' I demand and he shakes his head but then he seems to remember.

'It's the kids' birthdays, their dates um... um... twenty-third of the sixth and twenty-ninth of the ninth... two, three, six, two, nine, nine.'

I can't turn the wheel of the padlock and hold the gun so I step back. 'Do it,' I say and he does but the combination doesn't work.

'I'm calling the police.' I glance back to the house as I say it.

Ben is still watching me. I had no idea what would happen here tonight and I feel as if I'm making this up as I go along.

I can't wait anymore and this is not working the way I thought it should. I imagined Sandy would reveal herself, would reveal the game and I would have caught them in the act. I didn't expect the scream.

Using one hand, I take my phone out of my bag and press triple zero. The police need to be here no matter what happens. Hopefully they can sort out what's been going on.

'I'm calling the police, Ben,' I yell so he knows what I'm doing. I turn quickly and then I see what I've been waiting for on Ben's face.

I see a flicker of panic.

I turn back to Mike, lifting my phone a little so Ben can see me make the call. I look down at the screen.

'No, Mike, don't hurt her,' I hear Ben shout from the window, and I swing around to look at him. Out of the corner of my eye, I see Mike move towards me, and without thinking, I squeeze the trigger of the gun.

TWENTY-SEVEN

Sandy

I am filled with glee as I watch what's happening, watch what my screams, my schemes have produced.

He is filled with panic and I'm so excited to see it. He will get what's coming to him. He will pay for trapping me in a banal existence with someone incapable of giving me what I needed.

I watch from the back of the garden, standing behind the thick trunk of a gum tree, protected by the darkness and wrapped in the wind, my body shivering with cold or excitement.

This is better than I could have ever hoped and I know that tomorrow, when this is all over, I will want to remember everything. I will want to savour it so that I can go over it in my mind again and again.

Come on, come on, I think as I watch her slightly shaking hand holding the gun.

Do it. Do it now.

I glance up at the house, see him watching from the window.

And then she yells that she is calling the police and I can feel it all unravelling. It can't go wrong now. I have waited for this moment for too long, planned for it for too long.

'No, Mike, don't hurt her,' he shouts down into the garden, his voice carrying the threat to the woman with the gun and the man fumbling with the lock, to my therapist, Lana, and 'the husband', Mike.

The hand holding the gun trembles with panic and then she does it, just like that.

She shoots him.

I want to leap out and announce myself but I know I need to stay hidden, that I need to savour this alone. Joy runs through me as I look up at the window of a bedroom and see him there, watching me, watching it all and then – he's gone.

TWENTY-EIGHT

Mike

An explosion of sound fills the air, too loud to have come from such a small gun. Echoes bounce around the garden as the sound stretches and Mike's ears ring.

He feels like the physical force of the sound pushes him backwards and he stumbles as his foot hits something and twists. And then he goes down, his head banging against something hard and sharp.

Pain begins to spread through his body as his head spins.

He tries to get up, to make his body move because he needs to get to the kids, needs to protect them from whatever is going on.

White stars dance in front of his eyes and his limbs won't move.

Above him, the moon turns, a sliver of light in the darkness, and then he closes his eyes so he can concentrate.

And then everything is black.

TWENTY-NINE

Lana

I am frozen in place with the gun in my hand as I stare at the man I have fired at. I don't understand what just happened.

I look down at my hand in horror, my breath coming in white puffs. *The gun is just for show, Lana, for show. It's filled with blanks.*

'Daddy, Daddy,' I hear and I turn around, the gun still clutched in my hand. Two small children are standing barefoot on the cold grass of the garden. They are holding hands and both of them are carrying stuffed toys. Lila and Felix. Lila looks like her mother and she is holding a purple teddy bear, and Felix resembles his father, a stuffed koala clutched in his arms. I stare at them, horror surrounding the clashing thoughts in my head, the gun heavy in my hand. In my other hand, a voice on my phone is trying to get my attention.

'Police, fire, ambulance, hello, hello, police, fire, ambulance, hello, can you hear me?'

I called them. I didn't know I called them but I did.

'Is my daddy dead?' asks Felix, his voice loud enough to be heard by the man on the phone.

'Hello, hello, ma'am, can you talk to me? I'm trying to trace your phone. Can you talk to me? Is someone hurt?'

My hand is trembling as I lift the phone to my ear, my gaze on the children, who are frozen in place. It is too cold for them to be out here in the garden, especially since they are both barefoot.

'I... shot him, I didn't... please, you need to send help, you need to send help.' My voice rises as a panicked hysteria starts to take over my body. I am shaking and I can feel hot tears on my face. *Did I shoot him? Did I really shoot him or did he just trip over?*

'Okay, calm down, calm down, can you tell me if he's breathing? Can you give me your address, can you check if he's breathing?' The man is barking orders at me and I cannot seem to make sense of it but finally something sinks in and I say, 'Anderson Street, number twenty-one, it's... I came to find Sandy. She screamed. We thought she screamed. Ben is here; he was watching, he was...' I am not making sense and I know that.

'Okay, ma'am, I need you to check if he's breathing, can you do that for me? The ambulance and the police are on the way and I need you to stay right there because they will be there soon. But can you check if he's breathing for me?'

I turn away from the children and look at Mike, completely still on the ground. Why is he just lying there? I feel my body sway a little as I study him, noting that the grass around his head is darkening with what looks like blood. Is it blood? Oh God, is that blood? It must be blood. He hit his head on something. My stomach churns as I take deep breaths and then I drop the gun and my phone and crawl over to him and touch his head, feeling something slick and wet soaking into the sleeve of my white jumper. Blood. I gag as I push against the wound with my hand, trying to stop the bleeding. 'Mike, wake up,' I whisper. 'Wake up, please.'

The police are coming. The ambulance is coming.

'Daddy,' says his little girl, and I turn, keeping my hands on the wound. She takes a step towards me, towards the gun lying on the grass, glinting black in the dim light. I grab the gun quickly.

'Stay back, honey,' I say, my voice wobbly with tears, 'stay back.'

I can't put the gun down. The children are here and a gun is dangerous to have around children. Where did I get this gun? Why do I have it? Everything is mixed up.

Ben. Yes, Ben gave me the gun. Where is Ben?

'Ben,' I shout, turning towards the window again, 'Ben.' But there's no response, just me and two terrified children in the dark garden, backlit by the house, their eyes wide, pupils dilated with fear.

I can hear sirens now, a screaming noise. I can hear them and I know they are coming here. They will take the children inside, they will find Sandy, they will find Ben. Is Sandy in the shed?

Or is that just one more lie?

I want to move, to speak, but I can't seem to do anything. The man on the phone is still talking to me but I can't seem to hear him over the buzzing in my head. *This wasn't supposed to happen. Not like this.*

I sink onto the cold grass, still clutching the gun. White noise surrounds me. I can't keep up with my thoughts so I just... stop.

'Is my daddy dead?' I hear a small voice ask again, and I want to respond. I know I need to respond but I simply... can't. I don't know why he is lying on the ground. I don't know why there is blood. My jumper is wet with it now, the smell creeping inside my nose.

There wasn't supposed to be any blood. The gun was for show and it was all a show. There wasn't supposed to be any blood. A howl of despair builds inside me and I can't stop it. I hear myself screaming, making a noise that should not come from me. But it's me.

Suddenly there is movement everywhere, lights everywhere, people everywhere and so much shouting. I close my mouth and look around, taking in all the movement. Two men with a stretcher are shouting and a policewoman is with the children; she is guiding them back inside. The whole house is now lit up and someone shines a torch in my eyes. I squint against its brightness.

A man is yelling at me, 'Put the gun down, put the gun down now.' The torchlight disappears and I can see that it's a man in uniform, a policeman, holding a gun, pointing the gun at me.

'You need to look in the shed,' I tell him even as he shouts. Because what if she is in the shed?

'Look in the shed,' I say again.

'Put it down, put it down now,' he screams, his face screwed up with anger, and I look down at my hand that is still clutching the gun and then somehow, I manage to make my fingers release it, drop it, and it lands on the ground in front of me. 'I didn't mean for it to happen. I was only trying to help.' I wail the words into the air, hoping that he will somehow understand.

'Don't move, don't move,' he screams as he walks towards me and I want to cover my ears with my hands. There is so much noise. I can still hear sirens, and behind me another man is shouting, 'Can you hear me? Can you hear me, mate? Open your eyes, can you open your eyes, it's okay, we've got you, we've got you.'

'Sandy is in the shed,' I say as the policeman with the gun leans down in front of me and picks up the gun I was holding, and then someone is behind me, pushing me forward onto the wet grass and grabbing my hands behind my back. Plastic goes around my wrists, pulled tight, and I wince as my shoulder muscles protest. Ben is not here. If he was, he would be explaining but he's not.

'Someone get me the bolt cutters,' I hear a woman call and I am hauled roughly to my feet. I stand in stunned silence as I watch Mike get wheeled away on a stretcher with an oxygen mask on his face. 'Is he okay?' I ask as the hand holding my arm clamps more tightly but no one replies.

There is a metallic clang as the bolt cutters slice through the lock on the shed door and then the door creaks open, and a policewoman steps inside with a torch.

'Nothing there,' she says quickly. It's only a small tin building, and if Sandy was in there, she would have instantly been seen.

But of course, she's not in there. She was never in there but she is here somewhere, hiding, watching this, enjoying it.

The wind whips around the garden, rustling the leaves on the trees, and I search each dark corner. Sandy is near. I know she is near. I know she was the one who screamed and I know what she's done.

But what have I done? Mike wasn't supposed to get hurt. That wasn't supposed to happen.

I feel myself sag, my knees collapsing underneath me, and I give into a moment of darkness.

What have I done?

THIRTY

Mike

He can't breathe, can't breathe. There is something covering his face and he wants it off.

'No, no, don't do that.' A woman's voice. 'We've got you, mate, stay calm, we've got you.'

'What happened?' he tries to say but the words are garbled, caught up in his throat. He was trying to open the shed because Sandy was in the shed, except she wasn't. And Lana shot him.

But she didn't shoot him because that's not where he's hurt. He would feel pain where a bullet entered his body – wouldn't he? – and he can't feel pain anywhere except on his head. The garden is a mess and he has been meaning to clean it up, to put away the scooters and the bicycles and other outdoor toys, but he didn't get around to it. And when he stepped back, he tripped over something, Felix's scooter maybe? And he went down. The pain he felt was sharp, hard, metal. He must have passed out.

Sandy wasn't in the shed. He knows that. Then who

screamed? Sandy screamed. Where was she? Somewhere in the garden.

That means it was true; everything he was told only hours ago, on the phone, was true. He didn't want to believe it but now he has no choice. His wife is not just unhappy and troubled but deeply disturbed and willing to hurt others for her own gain, but the articles in the cookie jar told him that, the terrible articles hidden in a treat jar for only his wife to enjoy.

'My kids,' he says.

'They're with the police. If you have family who can take them, the police will find them. But they're safe. Don't close your eyes, okay, keep talking to me. I need you to keep talking to me.'

Mike wants to close his eyes. He really wants to but he turns his head to look at the paramedic who is tending to his head wound. She has blue eyes and is wearing a mask.

'Am I okay?' he asks.

'You're going to be fine,' she says as his heavy eyelids drop closed.

He's certain she is lying. He will never be fine ever again.

Lana

The room is cold, small; the air smells of disinfectant and former occupants. I lay my head on the table, not caring about germs. I have been here for an hour, a day, a year. I have no idea. I want to sleep. My mind drifts to my bed at home with its rumpled white duvet. Every morning, I plan to make my bed but I'm always running late and I always leave it, returning to the mess at night. I would give anything to be there now, looking down at the crushed pillows and reminding myself to try and make the bed in the morning.

I don't know how I ended up here. I can't find the start of the thread so that I can pull the story apart. And yet, I have to. There will be lots of questions and I have some answers but not enough. I don't know enough.

How do you find the start of such a story? Was it when I first met Sandy? When I first met Mike? Or when I first met Ben? Does it go back even further? Did it begin with my divorce? With the birth of my child or even further than that? My school years perhaps?

How did I allow myself to get here?

I know what I am doing with these circular thoughts. I am avoiding thinking about the small room, the sticky table, the fact that my wrists hurt from the plastic ties that were around them.

I picture Iggy and I see the gap where two front teeth have recently fallen out. He brought me the first tooth covered in blood, tears in his eyes. 'Why is it bleeding?' he cried.

'Sometimes it does.' I smiled, consoling him. He was ready for the next one, was proud of the little bit of blood there was.

I can't stop the image of blood running through my head. Thick, red, spreading on the grass. Not Iggy's. Iggy is safe. Iggy is safely with his father.

And I am here, my head on a sticky table, trying not to think about blood. I have never seen so much blood. Heads bleed profusely and I knew that but I still wasn't expecting so much blood.

The door to the room opens and two men walk in and I sit up, blink. One of them is holding a cup. He places it down in front of me.

'Thought you might need this.' He has a moustache but no beard. It's not often you see a man with only a moustache these days. I don't like the way it looks. Wrapping my hands around the cup, I nod. It's lukewarm and black. I don't drink my coffee black but I gulp it anyway.

'Lana Stanton,' says the other one, no moustache or beard, only a light ginger stubble and very pale skin. 'You've been arrested on the charge of attempted murder. Anything you say in this room may be taken down into evidence and held against you...'

I watch his mouth as he speaks, letting the words wash over me.

I think about Iggy instead. Iggy's gap-toothed smile, Iggy's laugh, Iggy's endless questions about everything from dinosaurs to dinner drown out anything the detective is saying.

Last Monday, only two, no... three days ago, I arrived at work early because Iggy slept over at his father's house. I wanted to get some work done before I saw my first patient of the week, a patient I had been reluctant to take on.

But she never turned up.

And now I am here and a man is in the hospital and these two detectives are going to ask me to explain it to them but I can't.

I can't even explain it to myself.

I listen as the detective with the moustache finishes speaking, telling me my rights. I hear only the word 'lawyer'.

I have a right to a lawyer and I need one. But I need to ask some questions first and I need to tell these detectives about the scream, about Sandy, about all of it. I close my eyes and take a deep breath. 'Concentrate, Lana,' I whisper despite the detectives watching me.

'Is Mike okay? Will he be okay?' I ask. He hit his head and that's what I'm worried about.

'Hard to tell,' says the detective with the moustache. 'We're waiting for an update from the hospital.'

I send a silent prayer up to the heavens that he is okay.

People die from hitting their heads. Not often but it does happen.

'Do you want to explain what happened?' the detective with the ginger stubble asks, and I peer at his badge: Detective Grafton.

'I do,' I say although I feel that it would be better to ask for a lawyer and then stop speaking but then what happens to Sandy? Because Sandy needs to be found and the things she has done need to come to light.

I rub my forehead with my hands and then I explain as quickly as I can, starting with Ben asking me to take on Sandy as a patient. I want to make sure that they understand I would never have had anything to do with her if not for Ben. Ben, where is Ben? Did he leave the children alone? Did he just run after shouting at me through the window and startling me into firing the gun? I'm sure he did.

Both detectives are silent as I speak, only stopping me once or twice to get dates and times right. I cannot help but feel that I am metaphorically shooting myself in the foot here. I should have kept quiet.

'If you ask Ben, he can tell you the same story. Everything I've said is true,' I say. They won't be able to ask Ben because I don't think they will find him.

'And Ben was with you at the house, you say,' says Detective Grafton, some scepticism in his tone.

'He was. We just wanted to make sure she was okay after the text she sent me. Have you seen the text on my phone? The constables took my phone, have you seen the text? I mean, that's why I asked him to come with me...'

Detective Grafton pulls my phone out of his jacket pocket and hands it to me so I can find the text. They sit in silence for a minute as I scroll through my messages, struggling to find the right one, but it's gone. There's no record of the text. There's no record of any text from Sandy at all.

'I... It's gone,' I admit, 'but it said, "Lana, help me. He's going to kill me."'

Detective Grafton nods his head as though this is exactly what he has been expecting.

'Do you remember the number it came from?' he asks, knowing that there's no way I will.

'No, but she did send me a message, she did. Detective Franks told me that she called him and said she was fine. Why would she send me a message saying her husband was going to kill her?'

'And you're sure it was her who sent the text?'

'I had her number saved with her name. If you find her, she'll tell you, she'll tell you she sent the text.' I know that Sandy will do nothing of the sort. She will lie about the text. She's lied about so much; it's just one more thing.

'Here's the thing,' he says, 'we can't actually find her. Our constables searched the house, their house, and they found her phone. It was under the mattress in her and Mike's bedroom. We don't know how long it's been there but the battery was nearly dead. A call was made from it on Tuesday to the station where Detective Franks works. We can't unlock it yet so we have no record of anything else but the call was logged with our system.'

'That's weird, don't you think?' I sit back and fold my arms. I haven't told them everything, not yet. I suppose it's the therapist in me but I am leading them to where I want them to go. When I reveal all, I need them to trust that I have it right. Detective Grafton and his colleague exchange a look and I understand that while I believe I am leading them, they believe they are in the lead.

I push my hair behind my ears, wishing I had tied it up. I am starting to feel desperate and I still can't think how to explain things so they believe me. 'And have you spoken to Ben? What did he say?'

'We haven't been able to locate him. Do you have a number for him and maybe an address?

'He was with me. Right up until he shouted at me through the window, he was there,' I say, slapping my hand lightly against the sticky table for emphasis.

'He wasn't in the house when police and the ambulance arrived,' says Detective Grafton and then he stares at me, letting the words sink in.

And of course I understand it all because I was right. But now things have gotten a little more complicated. I didn't expect Ben to just leave and now I'm not sure what to do. But why would he have stayed? He knew the police were on the way.

'You can see the messages between us on my phone,' I say. 'You can see that we planned to go together and we did.'

Detective Grafton offers me a quick smile and picks up my phone, scrolls through it for a few minutes. 'What do you have his number saved under?'

'Ben Summers,' I reply, holding out my hand. He hands me the phone and I go to find the messages between me and Ben, but they're gone as well. Ben's name is no longer in my phone.

I can only shake my head in admiration at Ben's thoroughness.

I had one objective, but of course, Ben had another.

The objective was to find Sandy and to make sure that the truth was told.

Three days ago, I understood the world one way. I was a therapist who was worried about her patient, a single mother and a woman who was trying to do her best.

But today, many hours ago, everything shifted. And now it's shifted again.

'I know you've said you got the gun from Ben,' says Detective Grafton, scepticism at Ben's very existence in his voice.

'I did,' I reply.

'Right, but we can't find Ben right now and we've had our constables look through records of gun ownership, which is something police have access to, and we can't find a Ben Summers anywhere. Also, the rules at gun clubs are very strict in Australia. He is allowed to own a handgun but he would have had to go through quite a long process to obtain a licence, which as I have said, we have no record of, and once he has the licence, he is required to store the gun at his gun club.'

'I know that,' I say. 'I mean I didn't know that when he gave me the gun, but I know it now.'

'And when did you find out that information?'

'After I spoke to a private detective.' Both detectives sit back in their chairs. Detective Grafton gives his head a scratch.

'You're going to need to explain that,' he says as there is a knock at the door.

'Come,' he calls and a policewoman in uniform steps into the room and hands the detective a note.

His brown eyes widen as he reads the words and then looks at me and says, 'The gun was filled with blanks?'

'Not originally, not at first. Not when Ben gave it to me.'

'I don't understand.'

'Neither did I but I do now.'

The detective sighs. 'Okay,' he says. 'Just tell us everything.'

I lean sideways in my chair, try to stretch the muscles in my back. I feel like I have been here forever.

'I knew something was wrong when I looked at the bullets in the gun. I wanted to make sure there was one in the chamber so I took them out, just to see.'

'And they weren't blanks?'

'No,' I say, shaking my head. 'The gun Ben gave me was filled with real bullets. He wanted me to kill Mike.'

The detective folds his arms and I can see him thinking, *This is all bullshit.*

'Let me tell you the rest of it,' I say before he can end our interview.

'But remember,' he says, 'anything you say may be used against you in a court of law.'

'I understand,' I tell him, my heart thumping in my chest, and as I start to speak, I know that I am putting my entire existence – my job, my son, my freedom – on the line. I am putting it all on the line so that I can finally be the one in control of whatever has been going on.

THIRTY-TWO

Mike

He struggles to lie still while the doctor stitches his head. 'That's a nasty cut you've got there and you banged your head pretty hard so we would like to keep you overnight and monitor you and get a scan in the morning,' says the young woman.

'Who are my kids with?' he asks. He is lying on his side, facing a wall while she works on him.

'They're with social services for the night.'

'They'll be scared – can't they come and sleep here? Their mother is...' He stops speaking because he doesn't want to say 'missing'. Besides he has a feeling she won't be missing for much longer.

'I don't think that's a good idea. You may have a concussion and you need to rest. Do you have anyone else who can take them?'

Mike gives this some thought. He could call his mother or Sandy's mother. His mother would love to help. But if his mother takes them, then they will be in the house with his father and he doesn't want that. He has made very sure to protect his kids from his father, making sure that they usually see his mother alone. And they can't go to Sandy's mother. He wouldn't want the kids to be somewhere Sandy could get at them. Who knows what else she would do?

'I don't,' he says.

'What about your wife?' enquires the doctor as she snips the thread she is working with and drops scissors back into a metal dish. Nobody has told her what's been happening. The police haven't briefed her.

'No, their mother is not... capable.' Because that's the truth. She is incapable of being a mother, of being a wife, of being a person. But he didn't know how incapable until a few hours ago.

And now he's not entirely sure how this is going to play out. He rolls onto his back, letting his head rest gingerly on the pillow.

'Oh, your sister called asking about you,' says the doctor. 'Maybe she can take the kids?'

'No,' says Mike, 'she can't.'

'Okay...' The doctor sounds like she would like to ask many more questions but then Mike would have to tell her that he doesn't have a sister, just a wife, a missing wife now found and clearly asking about him. And why is she asking about him? *She wants to know if the deed is done.*

'If you have your phone, you can call her and tell her that you're staying overnight. If she can pick you up and stay with you after that, just for the next day or so, that would be good.'

'I actually...' he begins as he tries to figure out how to explain to the doctor that he doesn't have a sister, that the call obviously came from his wife, who has been planning to kill him.

The door swings open and a nurse pokes her head in. 'Are you done here? Mr Winston has bled through his bandages.'

'Yes, right,' says the doctor and Mike never gets to finish his sentence. He doesn't know if she would have believed him anyway. It sounds insane.

When the doctor leaves, he closes his eyes, his head throbbing. Will they give him some pain relief soon? He hopes so but at the same time he thinks that he needs to be alert. Because Sandy wanted him dead – he is sure of that. And he's not dead. So what is Sandy going to do now? What is she going to do about that?

THIRTY-THREE

Lana

Detective Grafton stares at me, a frown on his face.

'That's ridiculous,' he says and I shrug.

'Maybe but... we just needed to know the truth, Mike and I, we needed to know.' What I don't say is how humiliated I felt. My intelligence is the one thing that I have been able to hold onto throughout my life, especially in high school, and now it had proved lacking, because I had been fooled. And I had been made a fool of by those I considered to be less intelligent than I am. It infuriated me and I wanted to be the one to solve the problem. I didn't want the police to do it for me so that I remained the victim.

'Explain it again,' he says.

I finish the last of my cold, bitter coffee, grateful that Oliver has Iggy and even grateful to Oliver for his one lapse that signalled the end of our marriage, the lapse that led me to find William.

'I once used a private detective named William Owens a few years ago when I believed my husband was cheating on me, which he was. When Ben gave me the gun recently, his explanation sounded right but I'm not an idiot. He told me the gun was filled with blanks, that it was only to scare Mike. But when I opened it...'

I see myself now, just yesterday, googling how to check the bullets in the gun Ben had given me.

Once I had worked out how to check the bullets, I poured them onto my desk, taking a picture and googling that.

I think what I felt most was profound shock. I toyed with the idea that Ben had made a mistake, that he had somehow mixed up the bullets, but I dismissed that quickly. Ben would not have made a mistake. Blank bullets look very different to real bullets. I looked at as many pictures as I could find.

'He put real bullets in the gun,' I say.

'Yes,' agrees the detective, nodding his head so I will go on.

I wanted it to not be true. I wanted it to be a mistake but then I began to go over everything that had happened since Ben asked me to take on Sandy as a patient. And I began to get a shadow of an understanding, but I didn't know what the whole picture was, not yet.

'I didn't know who to talk to or who to ask. Detective Franks thought I was the problem because Sandy had called him, saying that I was bothering her. So I called the only person who I knew could help me. William.'

I swallow after I have said the words because I remember the feeling of humiliation that washed over me as I asked him to look into Ben and into Sandy and Mike. I sent him images of the gun and the bullets, and the picture I had taken of Ben talking to Kirsty – something that I did without understanding why I was doing it. I had no other pictures of Ben, and when I googled him, as I should have done when he started working for me, his image didn't come up anywhere at all. My own stupidity had amazed me. Why hadn't I googled him the first time I met him? I had taken his résumé and simply accepted it as the truth.

'I asked him to look into Ben. I showed him the gun and the bullets and he did some research and then he was able to confirm what I was beginning to suspect.'

'And that was...?' says Detective Grafton.

'May I?' I hold out my hand so he can give me back my phone, and when he does, I search out the article that William sent me after only a few hours of searching, and hand it to the detective to read. I think I must have read it ten times that evening as I waited for Ben to arrive. I was unable to believe what I was reading and embarrassed for myself because I had believed everything Ben had told me. It made me question every single instinct I thought I had as a therapist and as a woman.

UK police are searching for a man named Simon Black for fraud. Mr Black masqueraded as a therapist for over a year, befriending a woman named Carla Swan. Ms Swan was a widow and was encouraged by Mr Black to lend him money, support his practice and invest in shares with him.

'I'm a complete idiot,' Ms Swan told this reporter. 'I thought he loved me and all along he was simply using me for my money. Once he had access to my accounts, he emptied them almost overnight and I have been left with nothing.

'I have tried to contact him and I currently have a private detective looking for him. I will not let him get away with this.'

Mr Black, pictured below, is thought to have left the country. Police have been unable to trace him.

'And this is Ben?' asks the detective.

I take my phone back and pull up the image of Ben and Kirsty together. Ben didn't delete it because he didn't know it was there. 'It's Ben,' I say, showing the detectives.

'Sandy told me about the insurance policy that Mike took

out on her but William found out about a second one she took
out on Mike.'

'Second one?'

'For two million dollars,' I say.

'You have proof of this, of course,' says the detective.

I shake my head. 'I don't have proof of the policy but
William must have it. I can give you his number. I also asked
him if he had access to blank bullets and he did. He dropped
some off for me.'

'Just like that?'

'No,' I say with a shake of my head, 'not just like that.
William was pretty upset about my plan but I convinced him
that it was all under control.' I don't know if I did manage to
convince William or not but while I was still at work, he did
leave three blank bullets in my mailbox in exchange for the six
real bullets I found in the gun. I felt like a spy collecting them
and then loading the gun, making sure that there was one in the
chamber so that it would fire if I needed it to.

I still thought I wasn't going to have to use it, that it was for
show, that when Ben and I went to the house, Mike and I would
somehow get a confession out of Ben after we confronted him
with all our evidence. That was the plan.

Ben thought he could frame me and Mike. But we were
going to tell Ben that we knew everything and get him to call
Sandy. We were going to record everything for the police. It
seemed simple enough.

But we never got to that part because Sandy screamed and
everything was derailed.

'We're going to have to verify this story with Mike,' says
Detective Grafton.

'You can also speak to William. Hopefully, he's connected
with the private detective in the UK by now. The woman that
Ben— I mean Simon stole from hired her own detective to find
him.' I remember the message sent by Carla to Ben, sent by a

woman who had been conned and abandoned: *You don't get to abandon me and survive it. You just don't. I've found your number now and soon, I'll know where you work and then I'll know where you live.* Ben led me to believe she was a crazed stalker who had ruined his life and relationship but instead, she was a woman struggling to find the man who had destroyed her life. I feel deeply sorry for her. I understand why she feels like an idiot for trusting Ben; I feel like a complete idiot as well.

'Wait here,' says Detective Grafton and he stands.

'Is Mike okay?' I ask him because I need to know. 'There was something in the garden, maybe a kid's toy, and he hit his head against it, but that's all that happened.'

'I'll check,' he says. Both detectives leave me with my empty coffee cup and a phone that's on two per cent battery. I need to save the battery in case Oliver needs me.

I watch the clock on the wall as I wait and it ticks towards 3 a.m. I am wired and exhausted and I can't see a time when this will be over.

Twenty minutes later, Detective Grafton returns alone.

'We have spoken to Mr Owens and we will be interviewing Mr Burkhart tomorrow. He's in a stable condition and being kept in for observation overnight.'

'Thank God.' I sigh, unable to conceal a yawn.

'It's fine for you to go but please be available to speak to us and do not, under any circumstance, leave town.'

I stand up, everything aching. 'Can I get a lift home?' I ask.

'A constable will help you with that. They have your bag at the front.'

I am grateful to leave, grateful to be able to go home to my own bed. I think about Mike's children, who have an awful mother and a father in the hospital. I hope they are being taken care of.

Detective Grafton walks with me to the counter where a policewoman is waiting with my bag.

I am about to leave when a thought occurs to me.

'Detective,' I say because he has walked away from me. He stops and turns around.

'I think that Sandy is not going to take it lightly that Mike isn't dead. That was the plan. I think she was going to make sure it happened and then appear again to mourn her husband and collect the money.'

'We'll check in on him,' he says.

'Tonight, or now,' I say, because it's the next day. 'Don't leave it, check in on him now.'

Detective Grafton must be able to feel my sense of urgency because he bites down on his lip and his phone goes to his ear.

'Yeah, mate,' I hear him say to someone. 'We need to get to the hospital.'

Relief warms my blood as I follow the constable out to a police car. They believe me and they will check on Mike. I've done everything I can.

I hope they're not too late.

THIRTY-FOUR

WEDNESDAY NIGHT/THURSDAY MORNING

Sandy

The cold air hits my cheeks as I run, my breath white in the wind. The first week of spring has brought with it more chilled air, more rain.

Dawn is many hours away and the streets are empty of people; only silent, parked cars glistening with frost under the streetlights take up space.

I stop, just to catch my breath, panting as saliva fills my mouth.

And then I hear him. The heavy thud of his running feet echo through the air. He is getting closer, much closer. I turn and start to run again, my heart pounding and my lungs burning.

I'm tired and I can't run any faster. My legs are filled with acid and my eyes are streaming, blurring my vision. But I can hear him. I round a corner, seeking shelter, looking for somewhere to hide, but as I turn my head, I feel his hands on me, feel him grab my hair, pull me to him.

His long arms wrap tightly around me, pulling me to his chest, where I can feel his heart beating.

'You can't run from me,' he hisses. 'I'll always catch you. Always.'

A cry escapes my throat because I know it's the truth.

'You won't run again,' he states. And I know that's the truth as well.

This will be the last time. The very last time.

One last little game, before we have to be apart.

I run, he chases me and then when he catches me, it is sweeter than anything.

He holds me tight and I can't help laughing as I turn to kiss him because I know that after tonight, our new life begins. After tonight it will be me and him. The children exist but there are places children can go, places they can be sent so they don't interfere.

Money fixes everything. And very soon, I will have a lot of money.

'They wouldn't really tell me anything when I called the hospital,' I say, panting as I catch my breath. We like games, the two of us, playing with each other and with others. 'But I don't think he's dead. I don't think she killed him.'

'And that's why we need to go there and make sure it's over. I only heard the shot and she was standing so close to him. He may die in the night but we need to make very, very sure. I saw him fall but then I needed to run. So, we go and we make certain and then it's just a matter of waiting. I catch a plane to the US tomorrow night, but as soon as you have the money, you call me and our life begins.'

'Okay,' I agree.

It will take some time, I know that. We will have to be physically apart and I know that too but we are together in this and we will be forever.

I had a plan, my own special plan. I was always going to end his life. But I wasn't going to go to prison for it. I did my research, collecting every story I could find. So many women find themselves in terrible situations, trapped in abusive marriages where they are pushed and pushed until they snap and they push back. And then an abusive man is dead. And everyone is sorry for her.

The two life insurance policies were my ticket out of the banal and the ordinary. I had to get creative to pay for them, buying clothes and then taking them back, asking for cash and putting it into a secret account. I had to find stores that would do that for me as I stood at the counter with my sob story. 'My wallet has been stolen with all my cards. Please give me the cash for the return.' People are easy to fool, especially if you shed a few tears.

That was my plan. I found the therapist who would be witness to my abuse, who would one day be able to tell the police that I was a battered woman who had finally, after years of being hurt, had enough. And then I would be the recipient of an outpouring of sympathy, and 'the husband' would be gone so he would never be able to tell his side of the story. His side of the story wouldn't exist. But then I walked into *his* office and everything changed, absolutely everything, because I sensed, even in the moment I met him, that I had found someone just like me.

We drive to the hospital together. I call again, telling them I am his sister, asking how he is, but I get another unsatisfactory reply. 'We will know more in twenty-four hours.'

I ask for his room number and they give that to me. Why wouldn't they? I'm his sister.

It's nearly 3.30 a.m. and the hospital car park has emptied out. Hopefully this will be easy and he will be weak.

'Are you sure this will work?' I ask him and he smiles.

'I'll be with you,' he says.

My heart is racing, adrenalin flowing through my body. It's not fear. It's excitement, an excitement that was unlocked the moment we met, the moment we recognised each other. There is nothing more glorious than this.

He never gave me any therapy, not the way my husband thought he would. Instead, we spent the hour we were together indulging ourselves. And when I told him my plan, he thought I was brilliant because I am. But he had a better idea, one that involved Lana, sweet, gullible Lana. I could see her jealousy of me, of my beauty, written across her face whenever she looked at me. I wouldn't need to kill 'the husband'. Lana would do it for me. It was perfect. She would do it to save a battered woman. I knew she would. She likes to rescue lost souls.

The corridors are empty, nurses in other rooms speaking with hushed voices.

I push open a door and there he is, still in a bed, the man I'm here to kill.

I should never have married, never had children but I didn't know there was an option. I didn't know that someone else like me existed.

And tomorrow, I will return from my break and I will be shocked at what my therapist has done, heartbroken over the loss of my husband who I tried so hard to help become a better person. Poor Mike. He was never going to change.

'Ready?' Ben asks me.

'Ready,' I say.

THIRTY-FIVE

Mike

He wants to sleep but he can't seem to let go. He can't allow himself to fully relax. His children are with a stranger. They must be so scared. Have they let them share a room, a bed even? They're so little.

With some effort, he grabs his phone from the side table, opens it and checks for messages.

He and Lana had a plan but he wasn't supposed to fall over and hit his head. The sound the gun made shocked him, causing him to stumble back. It sounds different up close and he can't help thinking it was a stupid idea to go through with the whole thing. He should have made sure the garden was clean, everything cleared up. But he hadn't expected to have to go into the garden.

He hasn't been thinking straight since his call with Lana, since the call he made after he got the message: *There's something you need to know about your wife. Please contact me.* He couldn't believe it was Lana who answered the phone, and he was going to hang up but she said, 'You need to listen, listen to what I have to say.' And then there were a lot of things he couldn't believe but that actually made perfect sense. The cookie jar was on his mind the whole time. Sandy had planned it all so carefully.

In the many hours since then, he has spent the time going over every moment of his relationship with Sandy. How long had she been planning on using him for life insurance money? What kind of a human being had he married? How had he not seen through to the core of who she was from the beginning? And more importantly, how can he ever trust himself again?

In truth, he and Lana had no idea how it would unfold. They suspected but they didn't know what was going to happen. The scream from the garden was clever and it turned the whole thing on its head.

'Ben has given me the gun for a reason,' Lana told him on the phone. 'He wants me to hurt you. They want you out of the way. But if I can get Ben to your house, maybe we can get him to confess.'

The phone call comes back to him in snatches because he was in shock, because it was so hard to take it all in.

It had all been a set-up.

'How long have they been together?' he asked Lana.

'How long ago did she have her first therapy appointment?'

'Months,' he replied and shock was replaced by other emotions – humiliation and anger, fury actually – and he knew that if Sandy had been standing in front of him, he would have lashed out, would have finally given back what he had been getting for years.

'I need you to focus here, Mike,' she said, dragging him back into what felt like the worst conversation he had ever had in his life as she explained what the private detective she had spoken to had found out.

The idea of a two-million-dollar life insurance policy was

almost laughable. How had she been paying for it without him knowing?

'We need to tell the police,' he said. 'I'll call them now.'

'Maybe, but Detective Franks said he heard from Sandy so they are unlikely to believe you or me.'

'They couldn't have heard from her. She left her phone here.'

'Oh... oh,' she said and he could feel her mind turning.

'I haven't hurt her, you know that, you know that's the truth.'

'I do,' she replied quickly, 'I do, yes, and so we need to find a way to make sure they get caught.' Relief rippled through him. She knew he wasn't the liar.

'Call Ben,' he said, 'and then let me know what he suggests. Tell him you're coming over to talk to me. But I need you to know that my kids have to be safe. I can go along with a little ruse but I can't put my kids in danger.'

'Of course not. I have a child and I wouldn't let that happen. I'll tell you what he says after I speak to him. If we confront him together, maybe we can get him to confess. I will be recording everything.'

Once they both had a vague understanding of what Ben and Sandy had planned, they were able to figure out what to do. The life insurance policy was nowhere in the house that he could see. Sandy must have it with her. Two million dollars, a huge amount and separate to the small policies they took out on both of them. When did she take it out? She is, essentially, in charge of all their finances and he knows that over the past few months he has signed papers to redo their mortgage so they get a lower rate, but is that what he signed?

And now he thinks about the parts of himself that he has suppressed, pushed down, shoved away. He never wanted to be his father, never wanted the anger to explode onto other people, certain that if he just didn't allow it out into the world, he would

244 NICOLE TROPE

be a better husband and father. He hadn't counted on Sandy as a wife. He hadn't counted on her assuming he was weak and stupid because he let her express her anger.

He's an idiot.

Round and round the thoughts go and that's the one that sticks in his head, that keeps repeating. He's an idiot.

When he hears the door swing open, he's relieved because maybe he can ask the nurse for a sleeping pill although they are unlikely to provide that to someone with a concussion. Maybe a cup of tea will help.

'Hey, do you have something to help me sleep?' he asks, blinking as she shines a small torch in his eyes.

Instead of the calm voice of a nurse, he hears a snigger, the sound of someone who is trying to cover up a laugh. And Sandy's scent fills the room, the scent he smelled in the bedroom. Because she had been back to call the police, to get her phone and speak to Detective Franks and get him to back off so she could go ahead with the plan. So brazen, so sure of herself. She just waltzed back in and called the detective and then waltzed back out again, not caring about her suffering children who missed her. She had also, somehow, sent Lana a text saying she was scared Mike was going to kill her. And she probably sent it while he was there with the kids.

Sandy and Ben hadn't wanted the police anywhere near this situation until it was over.

He starts to struggle to sit up but before he can even move, a pillow covers his face.

He kicks his legs and tries to scream, knowing that he should be able to push her off easily but he can't get the pillow to move away from his face. As his hand goes up to lash out, the pillow is pushed down harder and he realises that it's obviously not only Sandy holding the pillow but rather a man whose strength matches his, especially since he is hurt. He tries to scream, to hit, to move, anything, but he can't seem to shift the pillow.

'He shouldn't be this strong,' he hears a man's voice say. 'She didn't actually shoot him. Shit.'

It's harder to breathe, harder to think as adrenalin and panic swirl around his body. Deep gasping makes his chest hurt. His body feels weaker, less able to move, to fight but he keeps trying.

The pillow is pressed down harder; his ability to take a breath diminishes to almost nothing.

Who will take care of the kids? Will she take care of them? Does she love them at all? What will children raised by such a woman be like?

He can't fight at all anymore.

Lying still to conserve the last seconds of his own life, he sees his mother's hand, stroking his head, sees Lila's defiant chin, Felix's blue eyes. His heart pounds, his head vibrating with pain.

'Someone's coming,' he thinks he hears the man say.

And then he hears Sandy. 'Wait, where are you going? Don't leave me here, don't leave me,' she whispers, even as her hands struggle to push the pillow down.

Sandy is not as strong by herself and the force of the pillow releases slightly so he starts to fight again, but he's been deprived of oxygen for too long and he can't seem to find the strength to fight her off.

'Come back, come back,' she whimpers as she struggles to hold the pillow, and Mike feels a surge of adrenalin run through him as he tries one last time to get the pillow off his face.

But he's still so weak. Now there is light everywhere and his last thoughts are of Felix and Lila.

EPILOGUE

TWO MONTHS LATER

Lana

'I brought coffee,' says Gemma when she sees me talking to Kirsty at the front counter. Kirsty is different now, a little quieter, less sure of herself. She has also been bruised by what happened. She thought that Ben was in love with her.

They were seeing each other outside of work and she had fallen for him, fallen for his lies and his stories, just like I had.

It was hard explaining it all to her but she's young and she will be fine.

'I feel so stupid,' she told me when I told her what had happened.

'You aren't, you weren't. Don't think like that. We were all taken in,' I said.

I'm grateful she's still with me because we can talk to each other if we need to.

Gemma puts the cup of takeaway coffee down in front of me and then hands one to Kirsty.

'You're so sweet – my turn tomorrow,' I say and Gemma smiles.

Gemma is a child psychologist, specialising in children up to the age of sixteen. She did her thesis on depression in children after the terrible loss of a friend when she was a child. Life can drive a person into becoming a therapist. I understand that.

I know that Gemma is thirty, that she is engaged to her boyfriend of two years, that she wants two children. She lives in a unit on the beach and her parents are from a leafy North Shore suburb. I follow her on Instagram, where she posts pictures of the beach and her cats and inspirational quotes.

At one point during our first meeting, I stopped myself asking what I could see were almost intrusive questions to explain, 'I need to know that I can trust the person I'm working next door to.'

'I completely understand,' said Gemma, and her willingness to talk made me aware that she had probably read the few articles on the internet that had been written about my situation. I have no idea how a journalist even found out about what had happened but I chose not to worry about that and the story disappeared quickly enough anyway.

I'm still processing what happened. Ben was using a different name but then of course he was. He is a professional conman and the therapist in the UK who goes by the name of Ben Summers was horrified to learn that his credentials had been stolen. When I found a Ben Summers on the internet, his picture didn't match the Ben I knew so I moved on.

'Ben' is actually Simon and he has pulled off this particular scam once before, but in a different way. I knew that from the article William found but I think he's done it many more times, and those times have simply not found their way into the light. Simon may not even be his real name.

Ben's 'stalker' was actually a woman, Carla, he had an affair with after she fell for him as a patient. She was single and wealthy and he left her with nothing.

Her messages to him were an attempt to find him and get

her money back, something that will probably never happen. A detective in the UK tracked Ben down and gave Carla the number, and if she'd had the money, she would have come out here to confront him. She was in the process of trying to get the police in the UK to take action against Simon.

Simon is a conman but things were taken a step further when he and Sandy met. Two narcissists who didn't care who got hurt.

Sandy started attending therapy in order to provide herself with a cover story as an abused wife. But then she fell in love with Ben and made him her accomplice. Or he made her his.

Ben/Simon is a psychopath and all he wanted to do was hurt as many people as possible. And he wanted money.

Sandy is in prison awaiting trial. When the police arrived at the hospital, it was to find her holding down a pillow over Mike's face.

Ben/Simon was nowhere to be seen. He left only moments before the police arrived. And Sandy has told them that she acted alone, a strange decision that I don't really understand.

The police haven't been able to find Ben.

Obviously, Ben was involved. I think they planned it together but I think that whatever game they were playing, it was being played on another level by Ben. I don't know if he even needed the money or if it's just a game to him, and Sandy didn't realise she was being played as well.

Leaving reception, I go to my office, where Gemma has left my coffee on my desk.

I dream of that night in the garden sometimes, hear the sound the gun made and see Mike stumble back and fall and then lie still.

Iggy is, thankfully, completely unscathed because he had no idea of anything that was going on. All he knows is that he got to spend an extra night with his father. I needed time to sleep, to process, and I'm grateful to have Oliver and Becky as part of Iggy's life.

The police have been critical of our plan, as they should be. But they haven't charged me with anything although they did mention 'obstruction' in the first week after the two detectives opened the door to Mike's hospital room and found his wife holding a pillow over his face.

I've spoken to a lawyer just in case and I will be prepared if I need to be but I'm hoping that won't be necessary.

I know they are looking for Ben/Simon but they are not looking very hard. They believe they have the only culprit of this scheme in custody. Sandy has refused to talk about his involvement and is still insisting that Mike was abusive and that her actions were that of a battered women who could no longer take the abuse. She can be very convincing. I was certainly convinced and that's part of why I'm struggling right now.

Sandy is protecting Ben. Even after everything he did, she's still protecting him and sometimes I have to admit that I do feel sad for her as she sits in a small prison cell, wrapped in her delusion of his love. Love makes people do crazy things. Have the police told her about Kirsty? Have they explained that while he was sleeping with her, he was also sleeping with another woman? And if they have, does she believe them? Sometimes the facts don't matter at all.

Anyway, my sadness for Sandy only lasts seconds before it is replaced with another feeling, one that I can't admit to anyone.

It's a kind of smug joy, schadenfreude, at the downfall of this beautiful woman who was a beautiful teenager, a beautiful cruel teenager.

That first day in my office she looked straight at me and didn't recognise me. I may have changed but no one changes that much. She had simply forgotten me. I was nothing to her.

Janine and I were her targets at school, played with for

laughs. I have hated her every day of my life since Janine decided that she couldn't take Sandy's bullying anymore. To have her look at me like she didn't know me was galling. I liked hearing that she was unhappy, that all her beauty had not provided the life she thought she deserved. She deserved nothing as far as I was concerned. But she is smarter than I thought she was. She had me questioning myself, wondering if the way I was responding to her was because of our history, a history she didn't even remember.

She is smarter than I thought she was but not as smart as I am, and I figured it out so now she is in prison, where her beauty will not be an asset. She is in prison and I am living my life. As a sixteen-year-old, I vowed revenge for my friend, but after I left school, the years slipped away and I knew I wouldn't get it. I always imagined that Sandy had married a wealthy man and was living a beautiful life. To have her walk into my office, troubled and suffering, felt like a gift. Until I realised that she was using me like she used everyone at school, for laughs, for a game, to satisfy her own needs.

But now it's over, and as I take a sip of my coffee, I send a message to Janine, as I do every day, closing my eyes and imagining her laughing because she and I did laugh together. *We got her*, I silently tell my friend. *We got her*.

For now, I'm concentrating on my patients and my son, embracing the mundanity of the everyday and being thankful for it.

'Vanessa is here for you,' says Kirsty over the intercom.

'Send her in,' I reply, and I stand and open the door to my office.

I'm good at this. I can help, I reassure myself as I do before every session now.

I can help.

Sandy

I won't be here forever.

He's not dead after all. I failed to kill him. So, no harm done really. Pity.

And now, all I need to do is to get Mike to use the house as surety so I can get bail. He refused the first time but I'm hoping that he will see that I'm ready to be a mother and wife and that I'm sorry. I'm working really hard to show him that.

It's the only reason I keep seeing the children, the small alien beings that came from inside me. I make sure to be the best mother I can be when the social worker is here and she's so stupid, she believes I love them with all my heart. I tell her that every time. I cry when they leave, struggling to produce the tears that are needed sometimes but I've had a lot of practice at tears.

I tell her that I need to be near my children, that they are suffering without me. I'm getting there. I can feel it. Mike will have no choice. He loves the children in the weird way that I never could. He would do anything for them.

And the moment they let me go, the moment I can leave this terrible place and walk out into the sunshine, I will run.

And I will find Ben. I can't live without my soulmate. And I know he can't live without me. He didn't mean to leave me, I'm sure of it. He just got scared and he wants me to find him, to be with him. When he hears I am free he will contact me. Of course he will. He hasn't contacted me in here because he needs to keep himself safe.

Every day, I wait for a message from him, but he's being quiet for now, lying low until we can be together. That's the smart thing to do, obviously.

We didn't get the two million but the money I took from the mortgage will get us started. We can go anywhere and be together. He's taking care of it for me.

It was the perfect plan. Lana would kill Mike for us and then I would turn up and claim the insurance money and Lana would go to jail. That was just a bonus, an added extra that I never thought of.

I knew who she was the moment I saw her, recognised her instantly despite the fact that she's not Lardy Lana anymore. I remember her ugly little friend and how the idiot couldn't take my little jibes. I was sad when she killed herself because then I only had Lana to play with and she hid out in the library. It was such a delight to see her and know that she was going to be part of the game Ben and I were playing.

I didn't quite anticipate her figuring things out but I couldn't control everything.

It doesn't matter. I don't care about her. I want to be with the man who understands me, who has managed to touch a part of my soul that I never thought I had.

They are making me speak to a therapist in here and she keeps telling me that I've made a mistake about Ben, that he doesn't really love me, that it was all a game and I was being played. She's wrong, she's absolutely wrong.

We were playing together. We are meant to be together. He's my soulmate and he can't live without me. He told me that over and again.

All that keeps me going is thinking of seeing him again. Knowing that he is out there waiting for me helps me sleep at night despite the noise and the light and the crazy women who are in here. I don't belong here with the mad people, the criminals and degenerates.

Each morning, I wake up, knowing that I am a day closer to being free of everyone and running to the man I love. I see us on a beach together, cocktails in our hands, laughing about what we've managed to do.

'Burkhart,' the guard says as she unlocks my cell door.

I stand, wait patiently.

'Your children are in the family room,' she says and I plaster a smile on my face, make sure that tears shine in my eyes.

'Thank you,' I say as I follow her. 'I can't wait to see them,' I tell her, even as my skin crawls at the idea of them touching me. I haven't seen Mike since everything happened. He has some stupid little restraining order against me but I wouldn't want to go near him anyway.

'You're a good mum,' she says. 'Even in here it's possible to be a good mum and I know that you're trying.'

I sniffle a little, my acting very practised now.

The door to the family room opens and there they are. My tickets out of here.

'Mummy,' shouts Lila and she launches herself into me, wrapping her arms around me, but Felix doesn't even look at me. I will have to work harder with him. It's important that when they leave, they go home and tell their darling daddy that they miss me and want me to come home.

'I've missed you both so much,' I say, letting a few tears fall as the social worker watches me. Stupid woman.

And then I settle down to play with my children, willing the hour to pass quickly so that I can be alone again, alone with my thoughts of Ben and the life we will one day have together. It's going to happen soon. I can feel it. I can absolutely feel it.

Mike

'Beer, Mike?' asks Liam, and Mike nods, taking an ice-cold can from Liam's hand.

On Friday Liam holds a BBQ for their small staff of five. 'Just a way to say thanks for all the hard work every week,' Liam has explained. It's a warm spring day, the sun bright in a perfect blue sky, and as Mike opens the beer – non-alcoholic, for now – he lifts his face, feeling the heat.

He's happy in the new job so far. They're very busy and

making sales seems easy because everyone loves the high-end furniture and Mike loves feeling like he's selling something someone actually wants. He's also earning a lot more than he was with Paul, which is good because he really needs the money.

He's still trying to work out exactly how to move forward with Sandy. Right now, there is a social worker who comes and takes the kids for a visit with her once a week. But he's not sure what's going to happen once she's sentenced.

According to Elise, the social worker, 'She seems disinterested in seeing them after a minute or two and sometimes it feels as though she is performing for me. As if it's more important that I see her as a good mother than that she connects with the children.'

Perhaps Elise shouldn't have told Mike this but he's glad he knows that the social worker is seeing the same things he has seen for years. Lila is too little to register it but Felix has noticed something. He's reluctant to go, whines about it and has to be cajoled into the car with the social worker with promises of pizza and ice cream for dinner afterwards.

Mike never wants them to accuse him of keeping them away from their mother so he will keep encouraging the visits. Right now, the only thing he has been able to tell them is that Sandy 'did something bad'. Felix is asking more and more questions but he's trying to figure out how to explain it.

Next week, he'll see a therapist that Lana recommended for the first time so hopefully she can help him figure out how to talk to the kids.

The truth is that Sandy will always be in their lives because she is their mother, and only when they are old enough to make a decision on whether or not they want to see her will he be able to leave it to them. He hates to think of how much damage she can do as they grow up but he knows that there's no way he will be able to stop the children seeing her without going to court.

And there is always the possibility that she simply turns her back on them. That's not something he likes to think about because it will cause his children pain and suffering and they've been through enough. He's having divorce papers drawn up now and he's hopeful she'll sign them without a fuss. Although that seems unlikely.

He's also hopeful that the therapist can help him figure out how to get this anger, this ever-churning anger against his soon-to-be-ex-wife, under control as well. Especially since the call from the bank.

At some point in the last few months, Sandy remortgaged their house, taking an extra two hundred and fifty thousand dollars, setting him back years in his mortgage payments. The giant life insurance policy wasn't enough for her, it seems. Any expectation he had of getting the money back disappeared with Ben, and even if Ben is found, the money has probably been secreted away.

He couldn't quite believe that Sandy had the audacity to ask him to put up the house for bail. He almost laughed. Almost.

'You done with that beer?' Mike hears and he turns to see Emily, who's in charge of all the administration in the company. They have bonded over being single parents and plan to get their kids together next week. Emily's son is Felix's age, and from what she's said, it sounds like the two of them might hit it off.

'I am, thanks,' says Mike, chucking the bottle into the bucket she is holding. 'Why don't you let me take that?' he says, reaching out for it, and she giggles.

'Ever the gentleman,' she says, her green eyes sparkling with good humour.

'I try.' Mike laughs, the warmth of the compliment running through him.

He walks around picking up anything that can be recycled as the BBQ ends.

Mike climbs into his car, looking forward to seeing the kids. He's a lot better at running things now and the house is mostly orderly, mostly clean, and the kids are good with suggestions on what he should cook for dinner every week.

He stops outside the school with a few minutes to spare before after-school care is done and he takes out his phone, opens it to the picture he has of Ben or Simon or whatever his real name is.

He was in the hospital room the night Mike nearly died. But he left just before the police arrived, and from what Mike understands from talking to the public prosecutor, Sandy is devastated about this and only this.

The fact that she nearly murdered her husband and the father of her children, that she will miss her kids growing up, that she will be in prison for a long time, means nothing compared to the loss of the man she thought was her soulmate.

The police have been unable to find him, although they probably haven't looked very hard.

But Mike knows where he is. The private detective Lana asked to look into him was very helpful when Mike called him after he got out of the hospital. He is, as Lana told him, very good at his job.

Ben/Simon is afraid to leave the country but he's left the state.

And next week, Mike has some sales calls in Queensland, which is where Ben or Simon is hiding.

A babysitter has been organised and Mike will have a lot of time to do what needs to be done.

Maybe he can get his money back but he's already kissed that goodbye. That's not why he's going to find him and speak to him.

On Tuesday he will surprise Ben or whatever his name is in

the cheap motel where he is holed up. On Tuesday he will allow the dark rage inside him out, just for a short time and only against one person. And then, on Friday, he will see the therapist and begin putting all this behind him.

He's not a perfect man but he is going to try and be a better man so he can be a better father to his children.

But first he needs to see the man who nearly took everything from him, including his life. It's what he needs to do. It's the only way he can let this all go.

He's not his father, and he knows that. But sometimes a man can be pushed too far.

Perhaps a better man would let it go, would be grateful to have survived and would move on, but Mike isn't quite ready to be that man. Not yet.

And next week can't come soon enough.

A LETTER FROM NICOLE

Hello,

I would like to thank you for taking the time to read *The Therapist*. If you enjoyed this novel and want to keep up to date with all my latest releases, just sign up at the following link. Your email address will never be shared and you can unsubscribe at any time.

www.bookouture.com/nicole-trope

This was an interesting novel to write. I particularly enjoyed getting into Sandy's mind. I know that it is, as Mike said, 'always the husband', but sometimes, it's the wife.

Lana's character developed over time. She was quite angry with the world when I first started writing her and I couldn't really figure out why until the bullying aspect of the novel crept in. I know that she will take some time before she can truly trust again. The idea of someone putting in the work Ben/Simon did for the long con was intriguing to me because he's obviously a clever man and what a way to waste that gift.

I see happiness ahead for both Lana and Mike but they will be forever scarred by their experience. And I know that when Sandy realises Mike will make sure she's not getting bail, she will lose interest in seeing her children, which is perhaps for the best. She never wanted to take care of anyone but herself so she doesn't deserve them in her life. I do feel a little, only a little, sorry for her because she will never see Ben again and she will always believe that he is waiting for her even though he never was.

As always, I will be so grateful if you leave a review for the novel, especially if you loved the book and can avoid those pesky spoilers.

I love hearing from my readers – you can get in touch on social media. I try to reply to each message I receive.

Thanks again for reading,

Nicole x

facebook.com/NicoleTrope

x.com/nicoletrope

instagram.com/nicoletropeauthor

ACKNOWLEDGEMENTS

My first thank you goes to Ellen Gleeson. Your input made this a much better novel and I'm so glad to be working with you.

I would also like to thank Jess Readett for all her help with publicity.

Thanks to DeAndra Lupu for the brilliant copyedit and for always knowing exactly what day it's supposed to be. Liz Hatherell for the very thorough proofread and Mandy Kullar for making sure everything is shipshape.

Thanks to the whole team at Bookouture, including Jenny Geras, Peta Nightingale, Richard King, Alba Proko, Ruth Tross and everyone else involved in producing my audio books and selling rights, and spreading the word on my novels.

Thanks to my mother, Hilary, spotter of the mistakes everyone else misses.

Thanks also to David, Mikhayla, Isabella, Jacob and Jax.

And once again thank you to those who read, review and blog about my work and contact me on social media to let me know you loved the book. I love hearing your stories and reasons why you have connected with a novel.

Every review is appreciated and I do read them all.

PUBLISHING TEAM

Turning a manuscript into a book requires the
efforts of many people. The publishing team at
Bookouture would like to acknowledge everyone
who contributed to this publication.

Audio
Alba Proko
Sinead O'Connor
Melissa Tran

Commercial
Lauren Morrissette
Hannah Richmond
Imogen Allport

Cover design
Tim Barber

Data and analysis
Mark Alder
Mohamed Bussuri

Editorial
Ellen Gleeson
Nadia Michael

Copyeditor
DeAndra Lupu

Proofreader
Liz Hatherell

Marketing
Alex Crow
Melanie Price
Occy Carr
Cíara Rosney
Martyna Młynarska

Operations and distribution
Marina Valles
Stephanie Straub
Joe Morris

Production
Hannah Snetsinger
Mandy Kullar
Ria Clare
Nadia Michael

Publicity
Kim Nash
Noelle Holten
Jess Readett
Sarah Hardy

Rights and contracts
Peta Nightingale
Richard King
Saidah Graham

RAISING READERS
Books Build Bright Futures

Dear Reader,

We'd love your attention for one more page to tell you about the crisis in children's reading, and what we can all do.

Studies have shown that reading for fun is the **single biggest predictor of a child's future life chances** – more than family circumstance, parents' educational background or income. It improves academic results, mental health, wealth, communication skills, ambition and happiness.

The number of children reading for fun is in rapid decline. Young people have a lot of competition for their time, and a worryingly high number do not have a single book at home.

Hachette works extensively with schools, libraries and literacy charities, but here are some ways we can all raise more readers:

- Reading to children for just 10 minutes a day makes a difference
- Don't give up if children aren't regular readers – there will be books for them!

- Visit bookshops and libraries to get recommendations
- Encourage them to listen to audiobooks
- Support school libraries
- Give books as gifts

There's a lot more information about how to encourage children to read on our websites: **www.RaisingReaders.co.uk** and **www.JoinRaisingReaders.com**.

Thank you for reading.

hachette
UK

Printed in Dunstable, United Kingdom